ARANA

Jennifer R. Povey

To all veterans who have found it hard to return to "Civvie Street."

Prologue

"Incoming!" Slava Koroskeya's voice sounded across the small yet somehow echoing space of the *EFS Atlantis'* bridge, a hint of an Eastern European accent in the way she clipped the vowels.

Half of the screens were down. She saw the fire on the remainder, and the planet "below" them: An ice world, far colder than Earth, under a harsh sun that gave little warmth.

She looked at the pilot. No. They could not jump. Not accurately, not this close to a gravity well.

How had that ship got ahead of them?

The pilot screeched. There was no other word for the sound that burst from him, his hands hovering above the jump switch, about ready to try something which might save all of their lives or put them in the ragged heart of a star.

One of their lookouts had already fallen silent, the *Atlantis* taking a pummeling from the aliens. Never meant to be a warship. Never meant to deal with this.

Pummeled, yeah, that was the word. Slava hated them with a passion with which she had not thought she could hate anything.

"We're never going to get away from them." A weak, thin voice, the pilot's voice, giving up on his desperate plan. The glint of the web on the back of his hands became more visible for a moment as his fists clenched.

The planet below them was, technically, survivable. If you didn't mind it being in the full throws of a near snowball Ice Age. It was cold, it was colder than cold, colder than any place on Earth had been since the warming.

Earth was cooling back down, but it would take time.

1

Slava knew the decision the captain was going to make before he made it. "Take us onto the planet."

"Sir, we'll…never take off again." Again, the pilot's voice, sounding far younger than he was, sounding like a fresh Ensign. But then, they all were.

"If we continue to fight, we're dead. Take us *down*, Lieutenant." He didn't add the clichéd 'that's an order,' for which Slava was grateful. It was an order. It was the one that might lead to their deaths.

The pilot did, the web seeming to glow on the back of his hands as he angled the ship towards the planet.

The *Atlantis* was not designed to land. She was designed to survive a crash. Those were two different things.

Slava flipped a couple of switches, triggering a litany she had hoped never to use. The recorded voice sounded through the ship. "Take hold. Brace for atmospheric entry. Take hold."

The *Atlantis* hit the atmosphere, Bounced a little, then angled more firmly downwards. Slava could almost see, almost feel, the flames that would be coming off of her hull, only making the damage worse. They screamed into the atmosphere.

There was no sound in space. There was sound now, the sound of a dying ship as she fell like a shot bird, fell into the ice and snow.

"Brace for impact!" She took her own advice, curling her body inward so she would not break a limb. She would get to live.

But for how long?

The *Atlantis* hit the snow and ice, burrowed into it, pieces of the ship flying off. Antennae broken, cracks forming in the hull. The cold air of the world rushing in, steam-like effects curling as it met the ship's warm interior.

It came to rest and snow fell on top of it, burying it. The ship would never move again.

On the bridge, the captain let his head sink into his hands. This was the worst failure he could imagine.

No, the worst failure he could imagine surviving.

In orbit above, the two alien ships scanned the planet's surface. Seeing no sign of the now-buried ship, they eventually left, leaving the system empty except for the surviving crew on the planet.

A distress call had been sent.

Rescue was not impossible.

Rescue was their only hope.

1

"Filthy Araña!" The words, Spanish and English alike, echoed across the Caribbean street. Ugly words, darkening the entire scene. Rendering the slightly crooked balconies on some of the houses uncertain, dulling the whitewashing further. No jewel-like tones here, those were reserved for the cruise port and the space port, for the places where tourists came.

José Ricardo Marin Lopez studiously ignored the insult, wishing he had worn a shirt with longer sleeves, sleeves that would cover the tell-tale glint. The reflection of the sun against the induction points. He would be hot, but that wouldn't matter.

Spider.

From hero to spider. The war was over, years over, and Earth had lost, and they had broken their promise. Their promise to remove it, to leave him just as he was when he was a starry-eyed volunteer.

They couldn't.

They couldn't remove it without killing him. He had to believe them, because the alternative was cruelty he could not imagine.

"I'm talking to you, war criminal."

He kept walking, feeling his heart rate rise, feeling the tingle of the web through his system. It wanted to fight that man. It wanted to kill that man.

He was a fool to provoke a webbed veteran, wired and conditioned to kill.

Conditioned to kill anyone not in Earthforce uniform because that was what Mars had done to them, had done for them. When even the kids might have guns. Red dust crossed his vision.

The man released a string of Spanglish invectives after him. They bored through José's self-restraint. He gave the verbal assailant the finger as he hurried on. He broke into a jog as he moved along the boardwalk.

The man was alone. He would not continue to go after José.

But the words still hurt.

Araña.

Spider.

Webhead.

And, of course, war criminal. He couldn't swear to not being one, the thought of what had happened, of things he had done, was as much what quickened his pace as…

He was not afraid of the man. He was afraid of what he, himself, might do to the man. Afraid he would hurt him.

He could already feel the web preparing, the shot of adrenalin. Imagined or remembered was the feeling of human flesh under his knuckles.

The desert training, the sparring under the Chilean sun, the thin air of altitude, all of that welled up within him.

He had to get away before he punched the guy, possibly killed him. No civilian could take on webbed reflexes, and his conditioning was telling him this man was a threat. Making his fingers itch for a gun.

It was a mistake to come back here.

It was a mistake to come home, to the land where he had been born. The island sun beat down on him, not as thin, not as cold. The sky arced overhead, deep blue, human space after the confinement of ships and domes.

José closed his eyes for a moment. He almost tripped over something, some irregularity in a sidewalk that had been washed over by hurricane after hurricane.

He was in the eye of the hurricane of his life.

Turn right. Keep moving. The cries of "Araña" were left in his wake. Left where he couldn't hear them, and his heart rate began to return to normal.

The web began to settle into quiescence, but it was still what it was. A serpent wrapped around his spinal cord. Venomous to him, and even more so to others.

A mistake to come back. Three houses down, inside. Into his father's house, into what had once been his safe space.

Breathing hard, feeling the adrenalin flow finally fade away.

Only once he was inside did he pull out his phone. No email. Only one message, from his father, saying he'd be late home.

Good. He didn't want his old man to see him like this, he didn't want anyone to see him like this, including himself.

He navigated to email. He sent a message.

"I'm interested," was all it said.

Araña.

Spider.

Could he ever be anything else?

Diego Luis Marin Centeno stepped into the room to find his son sitting at the computer.

José turned, looking towards his father. Heavier than him, a little darker-skinned, but otherwise the two men looked much alike. The same short-cropped black hair, albeit streaked with gray in the case of the older. The same very dark eyes, shining like the copper pennies his abuela used to hoard in big cracker tins.

"Your mom sends her love." Those were Diego's first words, spoken with a father's affection.

José managed a weak smile. "I can't stay."

Diego sat down opposite him. "I suspected that. Are you sure?"

"Araña," José said, softly.

"Not to me." Diego reached over and put his hand over José's, intentionally touching the silver mark, then released it.

"To too many people. It's not about me. It's not about the web." He glanced down at his hands, where the hint of silver was visible at his wrists. Necessary, that access point, but it marked him, made him always a spider. "It's about losing the war."

"You suffered more from that than they did." Diego paused. "It's been years."

José closed his eyes. He regretted it, a memory swimming to the surface. A woman pushing her child behind her.

He'd let them live, but it had taken everything that was in him. They were all combatants. All except the babies.

"Doesn't matter, does it? We lost. We shouldn't have ever fought." José felt a shake develop, felt the web respond, knew it sounded in his voice. "We thought it was right to fight, didn't we? But it wasn't. We haven't learnt a thing. We killed *children* on Mars, Papa." Not that he needed to remind his father. Months had turned into years. An eye of a hurricane yes, a calm time. But not a restful calm, the fierceness of the wall always and eternity in view. Confining. Threatening.

"José." That one word, that one name, delivered far too calmly.

"They call me Araña, but they should call me what I really am. Colonizador." He took a deep breath. "I'm sorry, Papa."

Diego nodded. "I know you are. I know you aren't angry with me. But the job isn't working out?"

"The job is fine. As long as I keep my hands covered, as long as nobody threatens me." Which meant...most of the time it wasn't fine. He bore the mark of Cain.

"Still the flashbacks, then."

"It's not flashbacks," José insisted, perhaps a bit too quickly. "It's the web. I can't get rid of it and it whispers to me." Maybe it was flashbacks, maybe part of it was. "I can't go back, Papa."

Diego put his hand over his again. This time, he did not let go, the slight contrast between their skin visible. "Then you know what you have to do."

"Go forward." An exchange, but the same exchange they had had when José had enlisted, bright-eyed and eighteen years old.

Believing the army would fix things for him. Believing it would give him vital skills. Not understanding that there would be a war. There had been signs, but not for them, not for ordinary people on Puerto Rico.

Not understanding what the war would do. What it would mean. What it would bring. Only that would be a war, and he would be part of it.

"Go forward," Diego echoed. "But for right now, I have arroz con pollo prepped. With habichuelas and tostones."

José laughed. "Clichéd. But you remembered the tostones." He'd heard far too many lines about that being all they ate, and the fact that it was one of his favorite meals had just made the teasing worse.

He missed the teasing. He did miss the camaraderie. If he'd been able to do his time, learn his skills, and get out. And not been so wide-eyed about it. So naive. Thinking that even after they did this to him, he could still learn his skills and get out.

"But delicious."

He couldn't argue with that. But he still had to leave.

The insults echoed in his mind. Including the one he knew, in his heart of hearts, fit.

"Welcome, Mr. Marin." The woman speaking was very light skinned with slightly curly red hair and the overall "red" impression of certain redheads. She wore a simple skirt suit. A nod to Reclaiming, that skirt.

José shouldered his old military duffle. It felt odd to be carrying it again, but it was the best piece of luggage for this. At least they used the right surname. Too many anglophones misunderstood and called him José Lopez.

"Please, step this way."

He followed the woman and found himself in an interview room. He sat down. Set down the bag.

"You're confident." There was a man on the other side of the desk, also white. His hair might have been gray, had he had any.

"I passed the pre-tests and I have one of the skillsets you need." English seemed a little rough on his voice after three months speaking almost entirely Spanish. But José hoped that his confidence did show through.

The white man flipped through his file. "Ah yes. Robot and small vehicle repair. That we can use. Now, you do understand that if you are chosen this will be a long-term, off planet assignment."

"And a dangerous one," José said, meeting the man's gaze. "I'm a veteran. I know the score."

He'd almost called himself a spider right there. Had he internalized it so badly? His eyes flicked to the room's small window. Outside was New Mexico. Spaceport America. More desert. A saguaro cactus was the only vegetation within easy view.

All of his journeys started in deserts and one had almost ended there, more than once.

"I have to say it." The man flicked through José's file again. "Impressive on the zero-G aptitude. And yes, they will have artgrav, but who knows...."

"Artgrav fails," José said, simply. "Usually at the worst moment." There was a running joke in the navy that when, not if, the artificial gravity failed, somebody was *always* in the head.

The man laughed. José finally had the presence of mind to read the name on the desk. *Derek Pritchard.* "That old joke."

José nodded. "So...what's the next step?"

"I like the confident ones." Pritchard stood. "But the next step is training, and not everyone's going to get a slot."

"And if I don't? Are there any robot repair jobs around here?"

Maybe here he wouldn't be noticed as much, maybe he wouldn't be just a spider.

Pritchard laughed again. "We'll have to see."

José nodded. He shook the man's hand, carefully, and then left. Pritchard was ex military himself, he thought. That confidence and, above all, the brief glimpse he had got of the man's shoes said it. Navy, most likely.

Maybe that was why the web hadn't so much as whispered. How much of it was the web and how much boot camp, how much the cold Chilean desert?

How much the small child smiling and then raising a gun towards him? What else could he have done? Laser pistols don't have recoil.

They also don't hole domes.

They do hole small children. He had to leave. He was breathing hard, stepping outside. Part of him wanted to talk about it, but to whom? His therapist? There was a laugh. He'd had several. The first two had helped.

The others, not so much.

No, he had to talk to somebody who had been there. To somebody whose judgment wouldn't show in their eyes. The judgment that was all the more painful for the way it echoed his own. It was not just that others wouldn't forgive him.

He wasn't forgivable, how could he be? He stepped outside, looked up. Breathed the chill desert air. Spaceport America. But he wouldn't be going into space yet.

Perhaps not ever. Confidence had brought him this far, confidence would move him forward. The fact that it was no more real than the memories that echoed along the web didn't make a difference.

It would move him forward, but could it be enough?

He shouldered the old military duffle again and walked towards the barracks.

2

"She's beautiful," José breathed. He didn't mean a woman, although there might be a few on the station. It was international, so there were fewer restrictions on the so-called fairer sex.

He meant the ship. The *EFS Endeavour*. In her cradle, ready for launch. Launchpad had no artgrav. He floated in space, feeling the odd sensation of free fall. Thankfully, he had never been prone to spacesickness. Seasickness, now, that was another matter.

The ship seemed huge, but much of it was the paired drive vanes. Faster than light. The old pipe dream, now achieved. They would send the energy of the artificial singularity outwards to punch a hole in space, translate the ship to another layer of reality where the speed limit was oh, so much higher.

The first ship had already gone out there. This one...this one would take him out there. The military were putting stardrives on their own ships now, because of course they were. Because, perhaps, they had to to do what they needed to do.

Or perhaps they didn't need them anymore. José shook his head. There would be a turf war in the Belt, in the outer system, sooner or later. Sooner or later Earth and Mars would fight a war again.

Hence the starships. Hence the finding of another system. Another place humanity could survive, just in case.

Plus science, but José was no scientist and he was a soldier, a cynic. Still. She was beautiful.

"She is, isn't she."

That voice, cutting into his mind. Familiar. A voice he had once heard in another place, another time, another life. Deep, rich, on the edge between tenor and baritone. A voice that could have been a lover's voice, if things had been different.

For a second he was buried in a foxhole, Martian gravity barely seeming to weigh him down. "...Obadiah?"

"In the flesh."

José turned to see the dark-skinned man right there, his short hair tightly curled.

They hadn't even been part of the same unit, Obadiah being a British man of African descent, but that thirty minutes in the foxhole had changed something. There are no atheists in foxholes. There are also very fast friends. A bond forms, in seconds, sometimes. They had strengthened it since. "You..."

"Chief of Security, *EFS Endeavour*. You aren't on my roster." He was almost accusing.

"That's because they put me in technical. Robot and shuttle repair."

"Oh, there's going to be plenty of need for that. Heck, if we go out for long enough, you'll be *building* robots."

José didn't tell Obadiah he was wrong, because he wasn't. Instead he looked over the darker face. The man, a few years older and an officer. They weren't close to being equals.

But foxholes made for friends fast and lasting. "I'm looking forward to it."

"Assuming the drive test works."

"They seem to have it down." José ran his eyes across the drive vanes and uncomfortably realized he was treating them much like a woman's skirt or, for that matter, a man's butt.

He tried not to objectify.

He did try.

But the ship brought out oddly similar feelings in him. Which said unpleasant things about his tendency to do just that.

"Oh, I don't really think we're going to end up inside Jupiter."

"You had to say that. Although I think this ship could *take* being inside Jupiter."

"To a point," Obadiah mused. "To a certain depth, yeah."

They were building the ships tough because they had to be. "Slow, though. She's not exactly built for atmosphere."

"Come on. Let's get a drink before we're both on duty."

José laughed. He wasn't going to turn down that offer, shifting position so he could kick off. A drink in microgravity wasn't as good as a drink on Earth, but it was better than no drink at all.

He did notice a female face watching them, an East Asian face, but he paid her little attention as they sailed past.

Obadiah "sat down." On Launchpad that meant you clipped yourself to a point with the belt harness they all wore.

There was a slight breeze through the bar to make sure nobody suffocated in their own exhalations. The space was decorated with a nautical theme that was at distinct odds with the lack of gravity, but which made use of it. José was pretty sure those cables would not hold that anchor if anything went wrong...but it would likely stay put anyway. José clipped on. "Have you met the Captain yet?"

"No. Chang. Chinese. Chinese Captain, American XO."

Politics, José thought. "And a British security chief."

The dark brown man laughed. "And that. Politics. Trying to represent Earth as a whole."

At least, José thought, the politics were keeping Earth's representatives from being just a bunch of gringos. "Maybe we've finally grown past the point of white men colonizing everything into humans colonizing everything."

Obadiah laughed. "Oh, no, I think we've achieved that." He pointed in a direction that might indicate Mars.

José flinched. "Were we really so wrong to fight?"

"Well, yes. But we would have been court-martialed."

"It might have been worth it." The child floated in his vision again for a moment. He blinked, forcing the memory away.

"It might have been. Certainly..." Obadiah tapped at his left wrist, finger touching against the silver of the web, even more visible against his darker skin.

"Certainly we'd both be better off without it, even if..." José shrugged. "We should spar sometime."

He still enjoyed a fist fight, a controlled one, and spiders could not exactly spar with the unenhanced.

"We should. Besides, I want to make sure everyone on the ship can handle basic self-defense. Especially the scientists."

José laughed. "The eggheads? They probably don't know which end of a gun you point at the enemy."

"Not that xenobiologist. She hunts."

"Hunters are conservationists?" José quipped. Not that he really saw the conflict, but some people certainly did.

"Just because she enjoys venison, from what I hear."

Women who hunted were rarer in the U.S. than they had been, since Reclaiming. But then, so were women scientists. José's respect for her went up a notch. Without even having met her he knew she was likely to be tough and resilient, just what was needed for this.

"So, the Captain?" José asked, finally.

"Chang Yi Hui."

"That's…" José blinked. "That's a female name."

"Sure is."

He laughed. "Well, that should set the Reclaiming types on their ear." José had little patience with those who had tried their best to force women back into the kitchen and the bedroom.

"The Chinese sent their best, most qualified candidate, and I'm sure they had no intention of doing so." Obadiah's British tones were so dry that José started to get a little thirsty.

"Of course they did," José agreed.

A robot waiter hovered next to them. José tapped the table to make his order. Beer. So cheap it was probably orbital synthetic crap, but… He wondered who on the *Endeavour* would be the home brewer and who would run the still?

The robot repair workshop was, thinking about it, quite a decent place for the latter. He wasn't good at it himself, but maybe he could cut a deal. If the officers thought the ship was going to be dry, they'd never met veterans.

Of course, he didn't say any of this, given Obadiah was an officer.

"Anyway. There's going to be a crew-wide briefing tomorrow. We'll all get to see her then. I hear she's pretty," Obadiah added wryly.

"Ugh." Not at the Captain being pretty, but at the fact that people cared. Obadiah was one of the few people José had confided in. In that foxhole. When he had thought he was going to die. It was a sin, of course, what he felt for Obadiah and other men, especially if you listened to the leaders of Reclaiming. But so were many other things. "If I can work with people without judging them like that, then what the heck is with straight people?"

"Less practice working with people without judging them like that. You know those Reclaiming types. Never be alone with a woman not your wife, never work closely with a woman not your wife…"

José thought Obadiah was probably right. But for now, he sipped his beer and glanced towards the windows. There was the frame of another ship being built. He didn't know its name or purpose.

He did know they were building rather a lot of ships…

* * *

Chang Yi Hui was, indeed, a woman. A small, neat woman in Earthforce dress uniform. Short, but there was nothing fragile or delicate about her. She had far too much presence to ever be overlooked.

A new dress uniform. They'd given the new Exploratory Division their own design. It was no more comfortable than any other dress uniform José had ever worn and worked no better in microgravity. He adjusted his jacket.

It looked good on her trim form. She wore trousers, as did every single woman in microgravity. Experiments had been tried with weighted skirts.

Those experiments were generally not considered a success. So, dress uniform for all was loose blue-grey trousers and a wrap-around jacket that, in a concession to the needs of space, fastened with hidden velcro rather than buttons. Otherwise, it looked like an old style naval blazer. There was no hat. A red stripe ran down pants and sleeves.

"With the launch of the *EFS Endeavour* we prove that the first ship, now exploring Epsilon Eridani, is not a fluke. We set aside the traditions of our military past." Her voice was light and clear, but carried so well José was almost hearing it twice.

There was a slight delay on her mic, it seemed.

"Instead, we take on the traditions of the *Endeavour*. The *HMS Endeavour*, after which this ship is named, journeyed to Australia and New Zealand at a time when we thought those vast seas empty of land and man. We were wrong."

So was she, José thought. Cook had already known Australia existed. But it sounded good.

She took one step forward. "And the first lesson we have to learn, the one we have to remember, is the lesson of Possession Island."

Okay, maybe she did know her history.

"Cook claimed Australia for England. But Australia already had owners. And that is the lesson we should carry with us. Any beautiful world we find may already have owners."

She looked around the crew. "We should learn the lessons of Possession Island, the lessons of Botany Bay, the lessons of Manifest Destiny. As we travel out among the stars, we should stay humble, and remember that man is not the master of the universe."

It was a good dedication speech, José decided finally, despite her factual error in thinking Cook had discovered Australia when it was actually some Dutch guy.

It was a reminder they needed. They were to find beautiful worlds, but they had to find ones that had no sentient inhabitants.

Or they had to negotiate, not colonize.

Colonizador.

José thought that the lesson that also had to be learned was that of Mars.

If they found a world, out there among the stars, and if men walked on it, then those men would have to be free. Earth could not hold them.

"Unfortunately, we won't be getting to look for new worlds right away."

Laughter, perhaps triggered in part by the change in her tone from philosophical to practical.

"Our first mission, gentlemen and ladies, is a shakedown cruise out to Ganymede. We'll be testing the drive, checking the spaceframe and, most of all, making sure the computers are cooperating."

This time the laughter came primarily from a lean man of rather uncertain heritage. Probably the computers were his job. There was no true AI on the *Endeavour*, given they were both extremely rare and had enough legal rights to say no. And enough value not to be desperate.

José would get everyone straight sooner or later., But not immediately. The thirty or so crew were all, except Obadiah, new to him.

He did know the lean white guy behind the captain. That was C.T. Wilson, the XO. American, from some place on the west coast. The part of the west coast that tended to be only truly welcoming to, well, white men. José decided not to hold that against him. It wasn't like he was openly waving a Pacific Republic flag, and he couldn't help his stork drop.

Obadiah was with the other officers. He glanced over at the scientists. They were easy to distinguish. Civilian clothing, but also a mix of genders and ethnicities. More women than he expected.

Of course, any woman to be a scientist these days would be good, by the very definition of still being a scientist. Reclaiming had forced that.

He did wonder how many papers had the names of a male friend or husband on just to get them published.

A Launchpad worker pushed through the crowd. No, it was a young Ensign, an officer. A late addition to the crew.

He pushed through the crowd and approached the captain and XO. José did not hear the words that were exchanged, but the three abruptly left the room.

Some message from the admiralty no doubt. A message that mere peons like him were not privy to.

Letting out a breath, he waited.

After a moment, she came back out. The brightness in her eyes had dimmed. "It seems our milk run has been canceled. I need everyone on board by 0800 hours."

3

Milk run canceled.

They had to be confident in the drive. But there would be no easy cruise to Ganymede. No brief shore leave at the scientific outpost there, which had to disappoint the scientists.

No chance to send a message back to his father while they were still in the solar system.

And he did not know why.

They were building an awful lot of ships.

As he left the room, dismissed, to get his stuff from his quarters on Launchpad, he revised that. Likely they would still swing by Ganymede, if only to take the outpost its mail. Or something. Maybe pick up some data, collect information the scientists could use.

But it would not be the out and back, the drive tests. They were needed.

"We're the nearest starship," came an entirely-too-cheerful British voice from behind him. Obadiah.

"We're the only starship until *Discovery* is finished," José pointed out. "I mean, *Atlantis* is already out there, but I'll lay bets…"

"Don't bother laying bets. It's already in the station scuttlebutt. *Atlantis* didn't send their routine check in, only an automated distress call."

They had to go rescue them. José hoped it wasn't anything serious. Some kind of technical failure. A drive failure and them not having the parts to fix it. Maybe the *Endeavour* was going to be a glorified tow truck.

Worst case scenario, *Atlantis* had poked a hornets' nest out there, had run into something that would and could be nothing but trouble.

The very worst case scenario was that they'd bumped into advanced aliens and started a war.

Because that, José thought, would be just humanity's luck. "Of course they didn't. Any bets it's little green men?"

"I'm not taking that." Obadiah's north-of-England accent, toned down by years of working with people who didn't speak Mancunian, was still as broad as that city's famous ship canal.

"Good, because it's not a real bet. I need to get my stuff...sir." He should get into the habit of calling Obadiah sir again.

Sirs and ma'ams were good. Ma'ams he was at least somewhat used to. The U.S.A. had not recruited women, but other countries had.

Especially China.

So, he could do ma'am. Or Captain. And he could sir Obadiah.

"I'd say drop the sirs, but I guess we're back on a war footing."

José glanced away. Obadiah, jumping straight to the worst case scenario. "I'll...see you on the ship."

That was all he could do, to push off and float away. It would be so nice to have gravity again, even if it was the oddly disconcerting feel of artgrav.

So nice not to be floating everywhere. He found his temporary quarters. His roommate was apparently ahead of him, his stuff already gone.

José shoved everything into the duffle that wasn't in it already in no particular order. Normally he would have bothered folding everything, but nobody was riding herd on him.

This would be his last chance to be civilian sloppy for months, and he was taking it. Then he headed for the ship.

The *Atlantis* had dropped out of communications.

He didn't know what that meant. He didn't know what it meant for the ship. He did know it meant he had to call his dad.

But on ship by 0800 hours to him meant on ship now, no waiting.

No risking anything getting in the way.

No, and he swallowed, waiting for somebody to tell him it was all a huge mistake and he wasn't going after all.

The ship was still in micro gravity. Yet, it smelled different from the station, a smell at once clean and oddly metallic. Clean corridors that would be kept as close to that as the crew could manage.

He made it to the bunk that would be his.

He called his dad.

* * *

The *Endeavour* shuddered her way out of dock. Dropping out of the "dry dock," as it was still called, and then sliding away from it.

Under tow. She wasn't under her own power yet. Like everyone else who was not directly involved in the launch, José stood in the observation bubble, watching Launchpad slide away from them. Earth was "below" the ship and not clearly visible. The moon was also behind them. Launchpad "led" the moon as it hung at L4. José shook his head. His field of vision contained only unblinking stars.

He wanted a last view of Earth. He was about to go further than Mars, further than Ganymede and the other Jovian outposts.

But not further than the *Atlantis*.

Maybe it wasn't better to be first, after all. Maybe it was better to be second and learn from the mistakes of those who went first.

Gliding away. Another shudder as they switched to their own ion drive.

José was uncomfortably reminded of what powered an FTL drive, but he set it to the side. At least for now.

Maybe the *Atlantis* had imploded. No. If so, they would not have had time to send a distress call. Their ansible had stayed functioning long enough.

But for now, just reaction. Just the same ion drive that had taken him to Mars. That would take them to Ganymede in a couple of months.

Or, they could get there all but instantly.

The solar system had suddenly got a lot, well, smaller.

"Take hold," came the PA. "Artgrav initiation in sixty seconds. Take hold." It sounded like a recording.

José made sure his feet were pointed at the floor and grabbed the railing at the side. One of the scientists was far too close to the ceiling and another was trying to pull him down.

Oh dear. That was a disaster about to happen, and he measured the distance with his eyes. It was more space than a normal person could cover.

It was not more space than he could. He counted the seconds in his mind. And at just the right moment, he launched, somersaulting through space to grab both individuals...and pull them gently to what was suddenly the floor.

Both of them seemed shocked. One of them was a woman, of such mixed ancestry she could only truly be called human. She blinked.

Maybe she'd never seen what a web...and training...could do.

The other, "He's a spider, Nevaeh."

From his tone, he almost meant it neutrally. Which was probably a sign of appreciation of the rescue. The sudden acquisition of gravity would have faceplanted him into the deck otherwise.

The thus-named Nevaeh looked at his hands. Then quickly shifted her gaze to his eyes.

She had, he thought, very nice eyes.

"Spider," she said, then glanced at her companion. "Isn't that a slur, Luke?" she said so mildly that it was a stronger rebuke than if she had yelled it.

"I'm sure he's used to it. Excuse me." Luke turned and walked away.

"Next time let him hit the bulkhead," Nevaeh suggested. "I sure will."

She'd probably been on the receiving end of a slur or two in her life. Curly black hair, medium-brown skin, vaguely Asian-looking eyes. That wasn't an appearance that earned privilege.

"Tempting, but I think we need him." He offered his hand. "José Marin," he introduced, using the shorter form of his name gringos preferred. "Robot repair."

"Dr Nevaeh Jordan," she responded, taking his hand. "Xenobiology. I'll be needing your services, I suspect."

José managed a smile. So, this was the one who hunted. He could tell from the specific callouses on her hand that she regularly handled a gun. "I suspect so."

"In fact, I will probably be swinging by your workshop. Shuttle bay level, right?"

"Right."

He'd be working on the shuttles too. This wasn't, Obadiah's nearest starship joke aside, anything like the giant ships seen on TV.

Maybe they'd build those. One day. Or maybe not.

He watched Nevaeh go. He wasn't sure if he wanted to be friends with her or something else, but there was definitely something about her that drew him in, at least a little.

Friends, he decided. It would make things too complicated to let anything else happen. No doubt such things would on this ship, but he would not be part of them any more than he would try to kindle what had almost sparked with Obadiah.

But friends were always better. Safer.

"Take hold. Drive test in five minutes. Take hold."

Plenty of warning, because you apparently did not want to be moving when a ship bent space and jumped through hyperspace, when the singularity they were carrying along with them was twisted to expand.

The drive worked by pulling on one's own bootstraps, science José did not understand.

But you really did not want to be moving during that brief transit. Most especially, he had been told, your *stomach* did not want to be moving.

He stepped into his office. He checked everything was secured. The drawers latched. The tie-down mesh over the work desk. Tied down a robot, then sat down and strapped himself in. They'd done the static tests. One more static test.

Then to Ganymede.

Then to where *Atlantis* should have been. The stars within reach for the first time, of man's joy and man's hubris. José was not sure it was the best idea, not sure at all, but he knew one thing.

He couldn't go…

…and energy flowed through the web, a tingle through him. Nothing he had ever felt before, but he was falling, falling and the stars were rising up to meet him.

He gave a short, sharp yelp, and then everything was normal again. He swallowed. He could tell he had passed out, he was drooping in the harness.

Web interaction with hyperspace? Nobody had warned him about anything like that. Nobody had said anything like that could or would happen. He should go to sickbay, he should tell them. But that sensation, that feeling of falling.

For the first time in a long time he hadn't been thinking about the war. He had only been in that moment, that bizarre sensation.

He wanted it again.

He should go to sickbay.

"Drive test successful. We will jump to Ganymede in two hours." A different voice. The XO's. Not a recording, this time.

Two hours.

He should definitely go to sickbay. Or call Obadiah and ask if he had experienced anything like that.

They weren't the only spiders on board. Maybe all of the spiders needed to get together, to compare notes. To find out whether it was just him. If it was, then something was wrong.

If it was not, then…maybe something was wrong with the *drive*.

That horrible thought had him out of his chair and out of the door. But where did he go? Sickbay or engineering?

Sickbay, he decided after a moment. It had to be sickbay. It was far more likely just him.

Just him, and what if it was a problem that would get him taken off the ship. Put back on Earth, where no matter what he did he would be "spider."

Mars would not take him.

The moon? Not likely.

Was there a job for a robot mechanic in the belt, where the scruffy prospectors ignored everything that was going on? He thought about it. Ceres could maybe use him. Quickly, before the stardrive became more mundane.

No.

He had to stay the course, he had to stay on the ship. This was the only place he was a man, not an araña.

That word had never bothered him as a child. He was not afraid of spiders.

He was afraid of the people who used that word, who let it fall from their lips with a black widow's venom attached to it.

"He's a spider."

He's a war criminal.

He was running away. He knew it, but he would do it with his head held high. And there was the whispering seduction of that feeling, as if the ship was one with him and the ship was one with the universe.

He could not give that up.

4

Epsilon Eridani.

It was not to have been their destination. It was the *Atlantis'*. It was likely not where they had been lost.

It was where they had been last heard from. Except for that echoing hint of a distress call, which they could not quite locate. The last vestiges of oddness flowed out of José as they fully settled into normal space.

There was nothing he could do directly in the search, nothing he could do but finish the probe modifications Dr. Jordan had asked for. She was their primary specialist on alien life.

Hopefully there would be work for her to do.

But it meant he was in his workshop, not seeing what was going on outside, not even feeling it any more. He was nothing more than part of the web, not even its center right now. Fly, not spider.

The ship shuddered.

"Take hold." No litany, just those two words.

What was going on? He thought he heard running feet as he took hold, and then he felt the ship lurch. He reached to grab the wrench on the bench before the artificial gravity failed.

It did. Spectacularly. The far wall became the floor, then they were in microgravity, then the floor was the floor again. Bile rose into José's mouth. He was not prone to spacesickness, but that...

That was an evasive action. He'd been on a ship which had zigged like that before, and one perhaps better designed for it than the *Endeavour*.

It wasn't an asteroid.

He wanted to be on the bridge. Or at least somewhere he could see something, not the bowels of the ship.

He had external view cameras for monitoring hull repair. He turned them on.

Space.

Stars.

And a dark shape amongst the stars, unmistakably a ship.

Unmistakably.

The enemy was here. No, that thought was the web, the web telling him everything not a friend was an enemy.

Everything not in uniform, the right uniform. That wasn't an Earth ship.

That wasn't a human ship.

He envisioned, imagined, the *Atlantis* coming under fire. They would have taken evasive action. They would have run. This wasn't a warship, by design, although he did feel the shudder that was them returning fire.

Or had that first shudder been them starting the fight? Why would they do that? Maybe it had been a near collision.

Torpedoes had been launched. He saw them streak towards the enemy ship, saw it evade with the speed that spoke of a skilled, webbed pilot at the helm.

Saw the spread that started to return.

The *Endeavour* lurched again.

And fell into hyperspace. Fell away from him, the entire universe before him again, laid out like a tapestry and panoply of stars.

Tumbling.

He felt the ship tumble, the shifts in the artgrav, the fact that this wasn't an instant transfer. There had been no warning.

Madre de Dios, he thought, despite not being a religious man. *We're trapped in hyperspace!*

He felt it.

He felt the world flow around him, the tumble, time looping around him. Knew he was going to die.

No atheists in foxholes.

The panoply of stars. He felt them, and he was tumbling, he was falling through space. He was reaching out, desperate, for any handhold. He was a man falling from a tree, the forest floor below.

He was an ape.

He grabbed one of them.

Grabbed.

Pulled.

And then fell into darkness.

Blackness faded out into light. Too much light, right in his face.

He was lying on his back, on a surface rather softer than...where had he been? That was right. In the workshop chair.

This was more comfortable.

He was strapped down.

He was, he slowly realized, in sickbay, secured to a bed.

"Uh..."

"Oh, you're awake."

"What happened?" he asked, rather lamely.

"We're not sure. Your web overloaded, but it was minor and it seems to be back to normal now."

Falling. Tumbling. "No. What happened *to the ship*?" He realized right away that he had no right to be asking that question. No right to be knowing or feeling...he could still feel that tumble.

The starlight was inside him.

"We got shot at. By aliens. Jumped out too fast and...we're not even sure at that point."

José tried to sit up, and was reminded he was strapped down. "Can I..."

The medic, a white man in his forties, unfastened the straps. "Sorry, but we weren't sure there wouldn't be any more sudden maneuvers."

That was better than them thinking he needed to be restrained. And likely accurate. He wouldn't have wanted to be thrown from the bed. He sat up slowly and felt a bit of dizziness.

Good job he'd been strapped in.

And then the door opened. Captain Chang strode in with a younger woman behind her. One of the bridge crew.

She looked right at him, her eyes narrowed into something close to a glare. But there was no anger in her tone, only concern.

"Dr. Warren," she said to the medical officer. "What happened to this man?"

"Some kind of web malfunction during the jump. I'm running tests, but I haven't seen anything like this."

The younger woman abruptly stepped forward. Before José could react, she reached to put her hand on his. She was webbed, he could see the glint even on her fair skin. She was lighter skinned, with dark brown hair and brown eyes. The kind of appearance that was often called conventionally attractive, but she fell short of that to him.

"Some kind of web thing?" she asked José, looking right at him.

Static jumped between them, not sexual, not biological. A resonance.

"I…" A pause.

"Captain, may I?" the woman asked. She was in her twenties, her accent spoke of French…no, French Canadian.

To José's surprise, Captain Chang shepherded the doctor out of the room.

His heart beat slowed down a little. He hadn't realized how nervous the CO was making him.

"Better?"

He nodded, swinging his legs off the side of the bed. Still a little dizzy.

"The starlight is in the web," she said to him.

The exact thought he had had, like telepathy. "What the…"

"You," she said, finally. "You managed to grab control of the ship after I lost it. Without being hooked in physically. You saved the ship, Mr. Marin."

"I don't understand."

She released his hand. "You were briefed on the fact that the starship pilots are webbed, right?"

"Yes. But most pilots are. For reflexes."

Spiders.

Different varieties. Maybe the pilots were more like spiders, the ship an extension of the web.

The stars an extension of the web.

"Right. Exactly. It was only after we started testing the drive that we realized that hyperspace has an electromagnetic resonance."

"That means anyone who is webbed is going to pick up on it." He should have asked Obadiah.

"Anyone who is webbed will feel the jump a little. You should have been told that."

"I think it was in the briefing packet somewhere." José had read it. He had…okay. He had skimmed it.

"But you…somehow you felt all of it." She looked, for a moment, like she wanted to kiss him.

It wasn't sexual. It was something else, a peculiar need for intimacy and understanding. A shared experience. "I don't get it." He didn't. He had felt…there was something wrong with his web.

"Neither do I, but…the captain wants me to run you through some simulations, when you're up to it. See what you can do."

"Are you suggesting..." He tailed off. "I failed the pilot aptitude tests."

"I know." She smiled. "Lieutenant Cecilie Lauxon," she introduced. "Chief pilot."

"So, what makes you think..."

"Like I said. You saved the ship. Think about it." Then she added, "And hyperspace is *not* normal space."

He knew he would have no choice. He watched her as she left the room, knowing the sexual fantasy he had felt the edge of was part of the starlight, not any real connection between them.

Did they really understand hyperspace?

He thought not.

The *Endeavour* had a fairly large mess, aft above the shuttle bay. Right next to his workshop, in fact.

This mess was for the crew, not the officers, but Obadiah had deigned to come down from "upstairs."

On a ship this small there wasn't so much of a divide. "So, what happened?"

"I don't know," José admitted. "You feel the jumps."

"Just a bit of a twist."

"I feel all of it. And I don't think anyone knows why. It's like it's some kind of magic. Or ESP."

"Ever been tested?" Obadiah asked.

José shook his head. "No. I always thought it was crap."

"Some people do have some sensitivity, although I dunno. It's about..."

"Hyperspace has electromagnetic resonance. The theory is that if you could jump into an atmosphere, you would make an electrical storm when you came out." José half-smiled. "I read up on that." The ship's library was comprehensive, if all digital. The entire knowledge of mankind, easily copied and stored.

"Right. So, either something weird is with your web, or *you* are the one with the electromagnetic sensitivity."

José thought back. He remembered Mars. He remembered the emptiness of the desert. Then he thought back further, to the beach. "Hrm. But...I don't know. I think it has to be the web. But now they want me to learn to fly this thing, and I *told* them I failed all the aptitude tests."

"But the scuttlebutt is that you got us out. Even if we still haven't worked out quite where we are."

It was going to be hard to find the *Atlantis* if they didn't know where they were. Hard to find home too. José swallowed. It hadn't occurred to him until now that they might be hopelessly lost.

And what if it had been an alien weapon that did this and the *Atlantis* was still in hyperspace? A distress call sent before they jumped.

"Which means you have the aptitude for this," Obadiah continued.

"People do unexpected things under stress. You know that. You remember that embedded journalist?"

"Oh boy. The Canadian chick who was trapped with us."

"She swore up and down she couldn't shoot the broad side of a barn, you pushed a gun into her hand anyway..."

"And she did what she needed to do. Poor woman must have needed even more therapy afterwards than we did."

"Must have." José let out a breath. "Point is that it has to have been a fluke. Has to have been."

"Don't you want to know where we are?"

It was a blatant attempt to change the subject. "We don't know."

"Oh, we don't know our coordinates, but we're in a rather interesting binary system."

José nodded. "Anyone living here?"

"That's what we're going to find out. Might as well do science while the navigators work out where we are."

José laughed weakly. "The scientists can do science. I..."

Can fly the ship.

But no. He'd failed the aptitude tests. He had the wrong type of web, made for strength.

Made to turn him into a fighting monster, not a pilot.

He couldn't fly the ship. He couldn't navigate the dive through hyperspace. It had been a fluke.

"Come on. We're both off duty. Let's go to the bubble and look."

José let Obadiah lead him upstairs. The lieutenant was right. This was the first alien system they were getting a proper look at. The one they had to flee barely counted. While he couldn't do science, he could at least look at it.

Could at least see the light of an alien sun.

5

The light of an alien sun. José had not seen much of it. Enough to believe that this was real. Not just one sun. Two, circling each other in an eternal dance He wondered what kind of beliefs would evolve on such a world. What relationship would they see between the suns.

Then he had been dragged to a simulator. "So, you say you failed the aptitudes."

José nodded. "It was a fluke."

"And a fluke we still don't understand. You shouldn't have been able to remotely connect into the system like that." Lieutenant Lauxon shook her head. "But I think your brain is going off into extra dimensions. You ran the hyperspace simulation fine." A pause. "And you ran the real space simulation acceptably. I don't understand why you failed.

José refused to address that. He seized on the remote connection part. "Maybe we should be looking into that." And how to keep it from happening again, except that he wanted it to happen again. And the idea of being a pilot? He had done the aptitudes in the first place for a reason. They'd told him it could never work, that he just didn't think well enough in three dimensions.

Except it could. His marks this time were a lot better. He was older. He was wiser. The hated infantry web might even be helping. But... He couldn't afford to worry about that.

He wanted to know who was at Epsilon Eridani.

"Maybe we should." She ran a hand across her braid, a gesture that made it clear that she would have run her fingers through her hair if it had been loose.

Loose hair on a starship was a bad idea. "I don't know. All I know is

I can't do this."

"Or you can't do it without…" She tailed off. "José, you did it once. That means you can do it again. I think you need to get out of your own way."

"Maybe somebody on board can hypnotize me?" he joked. Or maybe it wasn't a joke.

"I don't think we have anyone who can. It's not even a terrible idea, but…"

Get out of his own way.

Was he sabotaging himself? He had taken it as wisdom that he could never be a pilot, that he belonged in the army. Boots on the ground. He had believed them when they said he was no good, and Lauxon was saying the same thing. Or was she? She was saying they had missed something. Something which might make it worth him learning how to do this.

Then he had discovered he had more technical skill than he thought, almost too late. After being boots on the ground, on the red dust.

Children with guns.

He shook his head. "Or, we could try something else. Like…I don't know. A different approach."

"Let's take a break. We can go listen to Doctor Jordan talk about what they found on one of the planets."

José perked up. "Is it life?"

"Life, Jim, but not as we know it," Cecilie intoned.

José almost wished she was a reasonable romantic pursuit in that moment. "Is everyone on this ship a *Star Trek* fan?"

"Not the captain, but we're working on fixing that."

José laughed. "You brought *Star Trek*?"

"There's enough room in the ship's databanks for every work of science fiction television. Of *course* we brought *Star Trek*. All series. Including the bad ones."

José wondered what his chances were of being in on the watch parties. Probably marginally above zero.

After all, nothing changed the fact that he was not an officer or a scientist.

Even if they did put him on the bridge.

He wasn't sure he want to be on the bridge, in truth. He was an army man, not navy, and there was something about crossing that divide that was bizarrely unappealing. Loyalty instilled. Except that he did. It tore at him, as if one web was breaking even as another formed around him.

Conditioning.

The conditioning didn't spark with Cecilie, wouldn't spark with her. "Come on."

She was right. He needed to think about something else, he didn't have any robots to repair right now, and Dr. Jordan was an interesting woman.

And life in another star system. That had to be worth something.

"So," Doctor Jordan said. "The bad news, is there's nobody here to talk to."

After what happened, José thought that was the good news.

"The extra bad news is there's nothing we can claim or colonize. But...the ecosystem on the second planet."

He listened for a while, but although it was fascinating it didn't connect, somehow. Or perhaps it just wasn't enough to distract him from more practical terms.

Like how they would find the *Atlantis*. They had called the other ship, of course they had, but she was no more responding to them than she was to attempts to contact her from Earth.

José shook his head, trying to get the female pronoun out of his brain. But there it was. They couldn't find the *Atlantis* without, perhaps, jumping back to Epsilon Eridani and finding her backwash.

Which they couldn't do. That alien ship was probably still there.

That alien ship hadn't followed their trail. He hoped that didn't mean it was completely impossible. He hoped that didn't mean there was no way to find the *Atlantis*.

They had called back to Earth. They couldn't send data; ansible communication wasn't good enough for that, but they could send summaries.

They were in contact. They were lost, but there was a chance they could at least go home.

In the meantime, they were doing science. The trip would certainly not be wasted if they did plenty of that.

Plenty of science, José thought wryly. And he had at least contributed. But he had come here to get away. Listening to Jordan, he realized that he had not yet worked out what, exactly, he was running to.

He knew only what he was running from. He slipped out of the mess hall before she finished her presentation. Went up to the observation bubble.

It was empty, everyone was listening to the scientist. The odd mixed light from the two suns seemed to strike through the bubble, giving everything stark shadows.

Shadows.

There had been shadows amongst the stars. He remembered how it felt, and the memory flowed along the web, the thing which was now as much part of him as anything else, could not be removed.

Stars.

Shadows.

Lines.

Was it possible to...

They knew where they were now. A catalogue number. A system without a name. It would have one now. No natives to argue with about it.

No natives, so they could name it, but there would still be a war of names. Arguments amongst the scientists. Twin suns. Twin gods, he thought, wryly. But if they kept that tradition, they would eventually run out of gods. Keep that for Sol system.

He closed his eyes.

He couldn't feel the stars right now, he couldn't feel anything outside his own body, just the shiver of energy through the web.

Just the memories. He didn't want to go through those memories, not the more recent ones, not the ones from the war.

Somebody stepped up behind him. "Hey, José."

"Obadiah. You got bored too."

"I'd rather read the paper later," the security chief admitted.

José laughed. "I'm more concerned with getting out of here, surviving, getting home. Maybe finding the *Atlantis*."

"Maybe."

Obadiah was part of those memories he wanted to forget, but he was also a solid presence in the here and now.

With him so close he realized he was shaking slightly. "I'm sorry, I need to be alone. Sir."

Obadiah lowered a hand he had raised, turned and walked away, to the other side of the bubble.

Respecting him despite the difference in their ranks.

Streaks. Lines. He thought he saw something.

No, what did the *ship* see.

That was what he needed. What the ship saw. But would Lieutenant

Lauxon show him? Would she trust him?

Shadows.

Lines.

The patterns of a web.

"So, you want to…" Cecilie Lauxon had her head tilted to one side, but she was clearly listening. Respecting his idea, out of the box as it was.

"I have an idea, based on what I sensed. Do you see shadows and lines when you fly?"

"Yes. But we don't know what all of them mean." Honesty. She leaned back in her chair. "Go on."

"Contrails," José said. "When you're on Earth, you look up at the sky and you see lines where a plane goes. What if starships leave contrails in hyperspace?"

"It's possible. But the only way to be sure…"

"Would be to look behind us, which is not the way you want to be looking when you jump. But if you had a second person to do that, and could map it across to the ship's sensors."

"Then we could confirm their existence." Her eyes actually lit up, although there was also a faint flush to her cheeks. Embarrassment that she hadn't thought of it?

"And use them to track another ship in hyperspace," José said. "Eventually, anyway. We'd have to build something that could distinguish between ships." Some kind of hyperspace IFF indicator, at the very least.

Cecilie nodded. "Rather than hoping the *Atlantis* left a message for us, or that we could guess where she went from jump ripples."

"Which we can't do without going back to Epsilon Eridani to get shot at," José added wryly.

"Those people…"

José closed his eyes. "That's for the diplomats to deal with."

"Or worse. If we can track the *Atlantis*, they can track us."

"To Earth," José said. "They didn't back track the *Atlantis*, though."

"Yet," she pointed out. "They could have called for backup first. I would have."

José knew she was right. A single ship, even if it was reasonably well armed, wasn't something a spacefaring civilization would send unless, of course, they only *had* two or three ships. Who knew how many the aliens had, how advanced they were.

"If they had backup available." He knew that was a very faint hope.

"I'd say they do, just from the fact that they were waiting there." She pushed her braid back over her shoulder.

They might have an entire fleet. They might have an empire. They might…annex…Earth. Colonizador, José thought again.

No. The stronger word was appropriate for that. Conquistador. Conqueror. But he was not part of that.

It was not, in many ways, his problem.

"We could do a test jump and try it. I'll talk to the captain."

Doing a test jump would use fuel, but fuel for an artificial singularity was essentially *anything*. Including interstellar dust. They'd already be refueling. José nodded. "Thanks. It might be nothing."

"It wouldn't spend much fuel, and it might say something if we can *eliminate* the idea. I need you on my team, José." She sounded urgent, at this point.

"I still can't do it." He couldn't. He looked away from her. "But I can be your observer."

"Especially as you don't technically…I think the design improvement we most need is a proper co-pilot station."

"It is. Can we build one with what we have?"

"Maybe." She seemed skeptical.

José resolved to talk to engineering. If they could build a second pilot's station…they had built with the assumption that nobody *could* take over during a jump. That there simply wasn't time.

Apparently that was wrong.

"I wish we could get those aliens to talk to us. We might be able to learn from them."

"I'm more concerned about why they fired on us in the first place." Cecilie turned light brown eyes towards him, then shook her head and left. No doubt to talk to the captain.

But he didn't want to think about that question. He didn't want to think about that question at all.

6

"Take hold, take hold."

José glanced around the bridge as the final jump warning sounded through the PA. A small space. Pilot, himself at a sensor station that had been jury rigged. The captain in the command chair. Weps, a young woman, a gunner. Just in case. Cecilie and Weps were in the front two seats. He was behind Cecilie, flanking the captain. It made him even more self-conscious.

The idea made his heart beat faster and his breathing alter. If this electromagnetic resonance gave him such...feelings...when he wasn't connected to the ship, what would happen when he was?

He almost felt as if it was...he chased those thoughts away. Sensual, sure. Definitely sensual, of the senses. A shiver down his spine. The ship as lover.

He saw Cecilie's hand move to a switch. And then they jumped and he *was* the *Endeavour*. He *was* Cecilie Lauxon, her mind focused entirely on her task, her hands on the controls. Hints and shadows of what might have been a memory. Of something strong and powerful supporting him.

And there was, yes, definitely a shadow behind them, a string of shadows that faded out into a line. Afterimages.

"It's not a contrail," he said out loud.

"What is it then?"

Blue skies. Beaches. "It's a wake. Except instead of spreading out, it narrows."

And then they were back in normal space, the echoes of that connection. He could not look at Cecilie. He wondered if she could look at him.

Two pilots connected at once might be a bad idea, even in normal space. Where they were now. She was steering them back to their parking orbit, the same controls, the same techniques. Hyperspace was just a place, another layer to space where everything began to narrow to a point.

If you could get to that point you could…and José shivered.

No. You could get to anywhere in the universe instantly, but would you *become* the universe? A being that got there might find God.

Or become Him.

José pushed those feelings, the religion of his childhood, his mother with her rosary, out of his mind. Science said there was no God. Or rather, if there was a God, He was not the province of science.

Some Christians disagreed, said that understanding Creation was how you understood the Creator. Jesuits, for example.

Their astrophysicist, Dr Francis Marlowe, *was* a Jesuit. Somehow it would have been wrong to leave them out after all they had done for science.

"A wake?" the captain asked.

José frowned. "Somebody give me something to sketch on, please." He was self-conscious. On the bridge, being questioned by the captain.

He was handed a tablet and stylus. He quickly sketched what he had seen, trying to be accurate, not artistic. "So, like that. A reverse wake."

The captain waved it off. "Give it to operations. Let them compare it with the sensors."

Delegating, as a good commander always did. José still felt self-conscious. He didn't belong here, just wanted to.

He had never been a navy man.

Araña.

Spider.

What would have happened…no. Water under, his father would say. Water under. You never dwelled on the roads not taken, you only sought the best way ahead. Right now, he needed that wisdom.

He handed the tablet off. Took a deep breath.

"Mr. Marin, you are dismissed for now." But the captain had a slight smile on her normally mask-like features.

He took the opportunity to leave before she could change her mind. To flee to the comfortable safety of his workshop.

A wake. Of course. They could find *Atlantis*. They *could* find her.

But could they do it without being shot at?

* * *

He didn't quite make it to the workshop.

He made it to the mess hall, because he realized his stomach was still a little off kilter. Putting something in it was the smart thing to do.

Thankfully, the place was close to empty. The two people in there, one of them the cook, eyed him suspiciously.

Not just a spider now. Something else, something that might scare them more. He didn't know what to do about it, he didn't know if there was anything he even could do about it. All he did was collect a plate of food. He pushed it around, then forced himself to eat. Not enough sazon.

Not nearly enough sazon. He should have brought some in his personal allowance. You would think with the diversity on the ship there would be more flavor to the food than back in his military days.

But of course, they had to spice for the lowest common denominator, which was apparently Midwest American. Still. He had to eat. He had to fuel himself, even if that was all it was right now.

They could find the *Atlantis*. They could find her, they could leap through the stars, and he wanted that again. It was dangerous, he realized. It could be an addiction, something that he could not give up.

Or did not want to give up.

Or both.

Food helped. It brought him back into the world, back to real space.

Then Cecilie Lauxon walked in. "You okay?" she asked.

He looked down at his plate. "I think so."

"You'd rather stay in robot repair."

He smiled weakly. "Yes and no. I'm afraid that if I do learn to do this, I'll become an addict."

"Oh!" She sounded like she understood. "It's too much fun?"

"I think it's more than just too much fun," he said. "But maybe we can find them."

"Maybe. The issue is that we know they jumped out of Eridani, but I wouldn't take a bet against that ship still being there." Her lips quirked. "You were a soldier. You know tactics."

"That ship's still there," José said simply. "And apparently not willing to talk. I'm guessing either talks broke down with the *Atlantis* or they don't like aliens in their territory."

She shot him a look, then laughed. "To them, *we* are the aliens, aren't we?"

"The foreigners. And besides, would you want us poking around?"

He thought of the entire of human history. There was so much beauty, but also so many terrible things. So much that he wished humanity could forget, but which they needed to keep to learn from.

"No, but I doubt they know what we're like." Her lips twisted a bit. "Maybe they just assume all aliens are there to conquer them."

"They could have been burned in the past. I *hope* it's that the *Atlantis* crew messed up their diplomacy, though. 'Cause then there's a chance to fix things."

"Sure is." She frowned. "Maybe the reason they haven't gone to Earth is because they don't want a full-blown war. Maybe they just want us to stay out of their territory."

José considered that. "I don't want a full-blown war. I don't even want a little war." He'd known that coming out here could get him shot at again, of course. But he definitely didn't want a war of any size.

"I'm not surprised. I heard...things...about what happened on Mars. And I worry about what might happen when the Martians build starships."

He hadn't thought of that. "It might be a while. From what little I know they're more interested in arguing about whether terraforming is a good idea right now."

Cecilie nodded. "I suppose."

"But that's for the diplomats to sort out."

He meant that. That was one thing he wasn't. "And we won't know their motivation. But what about..." A pause. "What if we jump to points outside the system, right out in the oort cloud?"

"We'd be there for months doing micro-jumps to find their trail."

José nodded. "But it's...possible. Which means."

She smiled at him. "Let me think."

And then she stood and walked out. Perhaps he'd given her something to think about after all. He had certainly given himself something to think about.

He didn't get much time to think about it. Something in his subconscious was niggling at him. He wasn't sure what.

Until one of the men at another table said it, "It's getting warm in here."

José blinked. That was bad.

Then a moment later, the PA came on. "Damage control stations."

Something had gone wrong with the ship. Something was reminding them that it was not safe to be out here. That only human ingenuity gave them air to breathe, water to drink…

…and in this case, cooling. The slow increase in temperature hadn't been noticed right away, but José stood up. He unzipped his coveralls almost to the waist, revealing a white vest he wore underneath, as he moved.

His damage control station, until they changed it, was the shuttle bay. But he was ready to be stopped and grabbed.

Obadiah was right outside. "We have a damaged cooling vane."

"I noticed. Do you need me in the shuttle bay or…"

"We need you on the robots."

José nodded. "Okay."

He could control them from the workshop. He descended using the ladder rather than the lift, feet on either side to slide down like a fireman with a pole.

There was no more efficient way.

It was even hotter on the shuttle bay level, the temptation to just strip down to his skivvies growing by the moment.

It would only get worse if they didn't have this repaired soon. The increase in temperature was starting to snowball, to get worse exponentially.

How long before the ship became uninhabitable? The engineers would be rerouting to mitigate it. Trying to fix it.

But this was the kind of emergency repair you drilled for and hoped you never had to do.

In the workshop. He sat down, pulled out the console.

He had two robots already on the hull, and somebody had already redirected them to the vane. Looking at the damage, he could see what happened.

A small meteor hit in a bad spot. He directed robot #1 to start working on the patch, using the second as an observer. Sending a third one out there, just in case. Normally, engineering would have done this.

They were busy rerouting. The robot knew what to do, it was already in its repair subroutines.

José took a moment to, indeed, strip down to his boxers. If anyone saw him, well, he had worn far less in public on the beach.

It was already getting close to the temperature at which one did not want to go outside. Sweat poured off of him. Pooled in his eyes. They didn't have that much time.

The robot was patching the broken line. Some of their precious water leaked into vacuum, freezing. Could they get more in this system?

It didn't matter if they all got heat stroke.

He focused on controlling the robots, observing. Having the second one start to lay a patch weld over the part of the hull they didn't need to access. The temperature seemed to stabilize.

But the crisis wasn't over yet. They had things rerouted.

They did not yet have them fixed. His eyes went crossed from the work he was doing.

Three hours later, the ship was starting to return to normal.

Over the PA, "Ice cream in the main mess hall."

Somebody had brought ice cream? He would not have wasted his personal allowance on it, but...

Well, this was as good an occasion for it as any.

7

The stars glimmered, and they fell through them yet again.

There had been no better idea than to hide and try to find the *Atlantis'* wake.

José could do these small micro jumps. They'd given him new bars to indicate that he was a trainee pilot.

He still wasn't sure that he didn't hate it. He found it so hard when in normal space, when he couldn't think in three dimensions, when he couldn't always remember to look both up and down.

Then they jumped, and he was fine. It was like the laws were different in hyperspace, like they fit with who he was better. Sometimes he thought he could see the galaxy, the universe, the...

"Wake," he breathed. Was it the *Atlantis* or an alien.

"Follow it." Chang's voice, as if through a tunnel, from a distance. The *Endeavour* dived between the stars, dived like they were a shoal of fish. A narrow line, so narrow. Dotted, even, broken up.

Old.

Which was a good sign. It felt as if they had been hunting *Atlantis* for weeks, for months even, not a handful of days.

Could they be this lucky?

He followed it. The ship was like a suit he had put on. He'd tried to talk to Lieutenant Lauxon about that, but apparently she didn't feel the same way. To her it was still a ship, still a separate thing.

It scared him. What if he couldn't separate himself from the *Endeavour* one day? Part of him didn't want to, and that scared him even more. He felt alive. He felt *happy* in these moments, and that could be addiction. Or it could be a sense of purpose.

He followed, a scent trail, a wake, weaving amongst the stars and then they were *there*, dropping out of space, dropping away from it. In normal space and himself again and bereft.

If you went far enough into hyperspace you could see the universe. He wanted to, and he couldn't. Not now, not ever. He knew in his heart that would be beyond human understanding.

"Yellow sun. Nice system," the navigator said from behind him.

"Anything in the life zone?"

"Gas giant. It might have habitable moons. One planet on the very outer edge." An amused tone. "I think we just found Hoth."

José managed not to laugh. He handed the pilot chair over, breathing a little oddly. Was this harming him? Was it making him sick? No, he was just tired and oddly desiring real alcohol.

"Any sign of the Atlantis?"

The navigator, currently a young blonde man from somewhere in northern Europe, shook his head. Then he frowned. "There's a distress beacon, orbiting the third planet."

Which would probably end up being called Hoth, and José laid bets on the largest moon of the gas giant being Endor. Especially if it was habitable.

But the distress beacon was their target. If they had not found the *Atlantis*, then they had at least found where she had been.

Or where she was. José frowned, but it wasn't his place to bug the navigator. Just get his breath back.

They'd done it.

They'd actually done it.

But if the *Atlantis* was not in this system, then they would have to jump again, and soon.

If.

Her wake had led them here, and now they knew what it looked like. What it tasted like. He could find that trail again.

What was he becoming?

He stepped back off the bridge, leaned against the corridor wall, realizing he hadn't properly waited to be dismissed.

But he couldn't quite care. He was becoming something other than human.

He was becoming araña in truth, and the ship was now his web.

And that third planet? *Atlantis* had marked it.

Was there life?

Had there ever been life?

Or was it a cold wasteland, inhabited by microbes at best? He wanted to know, so badly it distracted him from his worries.

Soon, he suspected, he would.

The *Endeavour* glided into orbit around the ice planet. José watched from the observation bubble, which was challenging as the pilot tended to position them so the world was "below" them. It was, though, definitely kinda Hoth-like.

Larger than Earth. A couple of sizable moons. Breathable atmosphere, if you didn't mind that the tropics resembled a Minnesota winter. José definitely did. He wanted and didn't want to go down there.

Robots should go down there, he decided.

Then the PA. "We found *Atlantis*."

Found them. Where?

"Or rather...what's left of it."

Oh, that was not good.

"The ship apparently attempted an emergency landing on the planet."

The two ships were the same class. Neither was really designed to land. The *Atlantis* was never leaving this world, but if they were fortunate some at least of her crew might be. They could hope for that.

A list of people to report to the shuttle bay followed. The fact that his name was on it surprised him, but then he realized that they needed him as a tech.

They only had so many people qualified to repair shuttles, and it was possible one or more of the *Atlantis'* could be salvaged to retrieve survivors or, at least, supplies and the ship's black box.

And the shuttles had black boxes that might tell them something.

Crash landed. Why would they do that?

The obvious answer: To hide.

Which told José they didn't have much time. He used the shafts rather than the elevators to drop to the shuttle bay, doing the fireman's drop again.

He dropped down into the "belly" of the *Endeavour*. He wasn't sure what they would do if they did salvage a shuttle from down there. And he hoped they wouldn't ask him to land one. He had crashed every atmospheric sim he had run!

"Mr. Marin, shuttle two."

He nodded, then grabbed a repair kit before stepping inside. Lauxon was flying. The xenobiologist, Jordan, was also on the shuttle.

"We're going to do science?"

Lauxon laughed. "Dr Jordan has done four antarctic expeditions."

And Dr Jordan tossed him a literal, actual parka. "And you are going to wear this. There are gloves in the pockets."

Ah, so she was their survive-in-the-cold expert. José let out a breath. He didn't ask Lauxon how she felt about him being there.

Not happy, probably. Then the shuttle hatch closed. Them, and two of Obadiah's small security department. Hopefully everyone would survive.

This was a dangerous planet, hardly prime colonization material unless they could find a way to warm it up. Of course, if they did, it might be a nice place. Nicer than Mars, certainly.

And maybe there wouldn't be enough habitable planets that...and the shuttle was away.

He gripped his seat as they dropped towards the planet, felt the shudder as the shuttle hit the upper atmosphere. Red glow formed around them, reentry glow. Heat. Friction. He was about to be on a planet again. That shudder would last a while, though. He closed his eyes. He hated reentry, although at least on Mars the thin atmosphere made it less...unpleasant.

"Are you alright?" Jordan asked.

"I hate reentry." He saw no reason not to be honest with her. She might laugh at him. One of the security guys actually did.

Then pointed out, "At least we're in a ship, not a drop pod."

José screwed his eyes shut tighter at the mention of those two words. He didn't want to think about drop pods at all.

He didn't want to think about falling through Mars' thin atmosphere, the chute opening to slow them but there still being that thud, that horrible thud at the end. You came out shooting. You didn't care what or who you were shooting. You came out shooting because you were alive, and that was what soldiers did for as long as they were alive.

He took a breath. Another one. "Please," he finally managed. "Don't talk about drop pods."

"They're as bad as I heard, then?"

A shudder ran through him, one the parka could not keep out. "Worse."

The wind blew straight through José. The parka, the gloves, the scarf across his face, these things could not be enough.

They'd checked for microorganisms that could hurt them. Had come to the conclusion it was too cold and too dry to worry about that.

Not that it was completely dry, but the air had that particular aridity that came with a winter's day. José, subtropical in his origins, shivered inside his cold weather clothing. "We really do need a tauntaun."

Jordan laughed. "I honestly wouldn't recommend Luke's way of staying warm." She dropped down to take a sample of the kind of ice-snow mix under their feet.

"It would beat turning into an icicle!" He turned around slowly. "That's it, right?"

What was left of the *Atlantis* had plowed into the ice and then been partially buried by it. Twisted metal extended outward from the wreck.

Technically, this was a survivable world. There could be survivors. Maybe nobody but a Yeti would want to actually live here, but the crew of the *Atlantis* had a decent chance, José thought.

Assuming they survived the crash.

Assuming they had enough food. Water might be an issue too. The snow underfoot had fallen at some point, but José suspected that point was not recent. Would they have enough power to melt it?

Lauxon frowned, then pointed at him. "Take point."

He had a gun. He was better trained than them to use it. Point made sense. Even if he was sure there would be no real threats here. He certainly wasn't going to shoot at anyone or anything that might be *Atlantis* crew.

Which meant anything, really.

He thought he saw something blow through the air. It might have been some kind of avian. It might have been debris from the fallen ship. He ignored it, walking carefully towards the hull, using his gun to point to where there were tripping hazards half-buried in the snow.

Was that a bucket? Maybe.

It was something plastic, anyway. He nudged it with his toe, and it shattered. "Ugh."

Some plastics didn't do well in the cold. "What even is it anyway?"

"-40 with windchill," Jordan supplied. "Minnesota on a bad day."

José made a face, not that anyone could see it. "More like Siberia."

"Minnesota's worse," Jordan said with the firm note of experience. "I've hunted in temperatures almost this low."

He gave her a sidelong glance at that and shivered again.

If there were survivors they would be inside whatever part of the ship they had been able to shore up into something resembling intact.

He stepped over more debris and approached the hull. The base had buckled. He mentally went through the deck plan, the same as the *Endeavour*. The belly of the ship contained mostly cargo and shuttles. Supplies. It was entirely possible, as he looked up, that the rest of the *Atlantis* was intact.

"What about the drive?" Lauxon asked, abruptly, pulling out a pocket scanner.

"Gah." José hadn't even thought about the drive.

"Not scanning any unusual energies."

If the drive had broken containment on the planet, then José had to think. The singularity would have dropped into the planet, then dissipated. It would affect tectonic activity. It wouldn't eat the planet.

That only happened in particularly poorly-written disaster movies. Or ones where the writer didn't care about the science for the sake of the drama.

There was that one novel, where a controlled singularity had jump started the Earth to sentience, but José couldn't remember the title or author right now.

It was in the ship's library. He could find it.

"So it's…"

"Actually looking at the ship, I don't think the drive came here with them," Cecilie said, wryly.

She was right. It looked like the drive had been torn from the main body of the ship. But the singularity itself, the core.

They might have managed to eject it, too. Either way, there were no huge earthquakes going on right now and no unusual energies.

José put it out of his mind, walked over to the hull and pulled loose debris aside before stepping into the ship.

Such as it was.

8

There was a little bit of warmth as they stepped into the broken hull. Not enough. There was also a faint smell, distinctly rotten, but not strong.

José knew what decomposing bodies smelled like. This was not that smell. It was just…musty. Off.

He was most interested in any barriers between them and the rest of the ship. The cargo bay had been partially crushed, he had to stoop as he moved through it and he heard a slight, ominous creaking that made him ill-inclined to linger.

No, this ship had never been designed to land on a planet, and now it had done so, it was thoroughly broken and battered. There was, he thought, little that could be done to salvage it. The *Atlantis* was spare parts.

But *somebody* had been down here since the crash. He was sure of it, given there were no large animals that could have come here and removed… "The food stores."

"Those that are still accessible, anyway," Jordan said. "I can confirm there aren't any coyotes here."

José laughed, partly because that somehow led to a mental image of a roadrunner in this icy realm. Icicles, despite it being slightly warmer, hung from the roof of the bay.

"They took the food stores. Can we get up the tube?" Marcia asked.

José walked over to it, looked up. "No. How about the lift shaft?" Not that he liked the idea of climbing the shaft. The gravity on this planet was slightly above Earth normal, and the Doctor, not webbed, had to be feeling it already. Even he was feeling it a little, each motion a little sluggish, a little heavy. He wasn't sure about the air, either. Was it thinner or was that just the gravity and the cold.

No, he definitely didn't want to live here. He tried the lift shaft. "Lieutenant Lauxon, how's your strength?"

She shook her head. "Nothing like yours."

She "just" had a pilot web. "Could still use a hand here." At least if he forced the doors, there would be no pit to fall into. Not anymore. The decks were still closer together, even here. She came over to help him.

"One, two, three..." And they had it separated. He glanced at Jordan.

He didn't ask her how she was doing. But he turned to Lauxon. It was her plan. She outranked him, and he had to remember that.

Even if she treated him like an equal. The feelings they shared led to that. He wanted her, but he knew better. He knew that if he pursued any sexual feelings for her it would cause too many problems. Nobody on this crew, man, woman or other. Not unless he thought it would be something deep and lasting.

It wasn't what happened when you fraternized. It was what happened when you broke up. And this wasn't real, he was sure of it. It tied into so many other things.

Seeing the stars, all of them. He shook his head. Flashing back to that at least beat remembering the haunted eyes of that child. At least beat remembering...

It was slowly wiping it all away, putting it into a box. Just as his therapist had told him he should work towards being able to do. Just as he had lied to her that he was doing.

Because he hadn't wanted to end up in...what? An institution?

He was in one now. A madhouse, he thought with amusement. He shook his head and started to climb the shaft. It was dim, but not so dark that he could not see. It should have been well lit. The thought of the *Endeavour* ending up like this gave him a distinct pang. But, he had a rope, he could toss it down for the women. He wasn't worried about Lieutenant Lauxon.

He *was* worried about Doctor Jordan, hunter or not.

And then there was a flashlight above.

"Who the hell are you?" came a voice from the upper decks.

He was amazingly relieved to hear it.

The other group had not yet found their way onto the ship. Of course, they had the medic.

Doctor Jordan was doing scans of the survivors. There were ten *Atlantis* crewmembers left alive, including the bridge crew, proving that the design that placed the bridge in the center of the ship, with only camera views of the outside worked as designed.

And they were all a little on the thin side and a lot on the frustrated side.

But very, very glad to be rescued. José stood off to one side as Jordan cared for them and Lauxon talked to the sensor operator.

The captain, a lean man with dark red hair, was not saying much. Having lost his ship, he probably had little to say.

"So," the sensor operator said. "It was the aliens. They fired on us. We swear it was unprovoked. We swear..."

Jordan nodded. "How did you crash?"

"We jumped. They followed us. Somehow, they followed us."

José elected not to explain it for now.

"They had us cornered by this planet. We couldn't jump out. The best thing we could do was a landing we could walk away from. We hard-landed. We did *not* crash."

"The drive core?" Jordan asked.

"We ejected it while we could still get it clear of the atmosphere." He glanced at his captain for a moment. "So...you came to rescue us."

"We can take you back to Earth. Just not via Epsilon Eridani."

Or they could carry on. This wasn't so many extra people that the *Endeavour* couldn't continue her mission, José thought.

If they went back.

No, Earth would soon know what was going on. Would know the *Atlantis* had been found.

That they could be at war. And there was the chance that the aliens had already reached Sol.

José didn't think going back to Earth was a good idea, but surely nobody was going to ask his opinion.

He was a robot mechanic and junior pilot. Not even an officer, at least not yet. Pilots, by tradition were officers, and he swallowed nervously at the thought.

The man frowned. "If you could find us, they can find Earth. And they..."

"Who fired first?" Lauxon asked, abruptly, her higher voice cutting across the conversation like the bitter wind outside. Apparently not accepting his denial.

"The..." His Adam's apple bobbed, then he spoke slowly. "We did.

You'd understand if you saw them."

We did.

We fired first.

José swallowed himself, almost feeling his adam's apple bob. We fired first. A nightmare. A nightmare of diplomacy.

There were thirty people on *Endeavour*, ten survivors on *Atlantis*. At any point, this might become all that was left of the human race.

He shook his head. The aliens were probably too civilized to commit genocide.

Probably.

Jordan waved him over, had him help set a broken leg that had gone, perhaps, too long untreated, or not properly treated. Then, to his relief, the actual medics showed up.

To his relief, but he was not off the hook. They had to get these people back to the *Endeavour*. Even here, it was cold, cold as a freezer, and none of them had showered lately. Or eaten properly. Or, likely, slept.

They deserved better, after all they had gone through. "Mr. Marin?" came a voice.

"Can you help me see if I can get this lift working some?"

Glad to be asked to do something he felt he could help with, he went to assist the engineer.

He was alive. They were alive. And soon enough they would be off this ice ball, which would always be Hoth even if it was officially called something else.

Popular culture did that. It influenced, it called to people. It changed things.

This world would always be Hoth.

Back on the *Endeavour*, José wished that the showers were not timed to five minutes and, to be honest, lukewarm.

It still felt good. If that was exploring an alien world, he at least wanted better gear next time. Not just a parka, but long johns, and maybe something to cover his face better.

Or maybe to be able to explore, not just kind of wander around looking for survivors.

One third of the crew. That meant...and it finally hit him. Men and women had died on that world, the *Atlantis* was now their tomb. Or perhaps they would go back and...they'd have to use shaped charges to make graves on that.

Or they could…

José shook his head. They were dead. He had to think about the living. And how many shallow graves were on Mars?

How many of those were men and women who had never gone home?

How many of them were children? He leaned his head against the side of the shower stall until the water stopped, followed up by hot air to help him dry off quickly. He blinked a few times, chasing away the image of too short graves. Of headstones with dates so close together.

Shallow graves in red soil. A woman pushing his rifle upwards, screaming something in Cantonese.

Something, something, and his brain had finally found his third, uncertain language. Kids. Just kids.

All of them just kids, and he was just…

He closed his eyes again. He stepped out of the shower. The scientists wanted to survey the ice planet. To take notes. To get an expedition back here.

But to him, that planet was a tomb. A mass grave.

Yet, he…

He knew what he needed. No, not a religious man, but there had to be some kind of service. Some kind of memorial, even though he didn't think he knew any of them.

Didn't think so. Could he be sure some face that he knew from Mars would not show up on the screens? Answer was, he couldn't.

The stars could not wipe this out, not anymore. Twenty people had died on that world, either in the crash or from the bone numbing cold.

Twenty human beings, and could they ever go home again? He could not. Why not go outwards? Because sooner or later they would all die. Because they weren't equipped to be a colony.

They were scouts; that was what they had been built for and intended for. Not colonists, and this world would perhaps see domes, rising against the cold as those on Mars rose against the thin air and lack of a magnetosphere. Here, they would not need to worry about VLF shielding.

Or perhaps they would not be human domes.

He was tired, and sleep beckoned. So did warmth, even the shower not having reached his core. Or perhaps it was cold thoughts that had this effect.

Thoughts of death. Thoughts of war. Thoughts of the cold of the planet and the cold between the stars.

It had been very cold on Mars. A planet not meant for humanity, but claimed by them nonetheless. A place that had become home to those who had sought…something. Something they could not find on Earth.

How many of them had been, in their own way, spiders?

He found his bunk, tossed and turned for a while before he finally slept. Finally.

9

"Take hold. Take hold. General quarters. Take hold!" José all but dived onto the bridge for the nearest chair instead of walking on decorously.

The surrounding sensors, the screens that made it look like there was no ship around them showed not one of the alien ships, but three.

Take hold indeed. Lauxon touched her finger to her lips then pointed to the jury-rigged co-pilot's chair. Wary of there being a need for said take hold, José stepped across the bridge to take that position.

Lauxon was handling evasives, sending the *Endeavour* down towards the planet. Thinking of what had happened to the *Atlantis*, José grabbed the arms of the seat. It didn't entirely help that the bridge was literally the safest place on the ship, by design. Maybe surviving would be worse.

Then he realized what she was doing. He couldn't have done it himself, not yet, but she was grazing the atmosphere, bouncing off it and using it to send the *Endeavour* off faster at a different angle. The ship shuddered, weapons fire arcing through space. Small stars exploding around them. None on them yet.

Not a warship, the *Endeavour*, but smaller. Perhaps faster. Lauxon was certainly using everything they had. There was far more incoming fire than outgoing. The gunner was doing her best as Lauxon angled them back around, to bring the front tubes to bear. Torpedoes away, slight vibrations through the *Endeavour's* hull. José was glad he was on the bridge where he could see at least something of what was going on. Not down in the workshop, merely feeling it, and bracing himself, and wondering.

How were the *Atlantis* survivors doing? How could they be doing? Feeling the ship bounce off the atmosphere. Hearing that "take hold" and knowing only that something bad was happening.

They were fighting, not running. Why were they not running?

"They have us cornered," she said, finally.

Captain Chang wasn't on the bridge. From the command chair, CT Wilson frowned. "Another slingshot?"

"They'll be ready for it this time. There's no place we can go but down. Maybe we can fake crashing?"

José shuddered again. "Sir?" he ventured. "I mean, Lieutenant Lauxon."

"What?"

"It's not possible to jump this close to a planet, right?"

"No. We'd...we might end up in the heart of a star."

Wilson frowned. He wasn't the captain, and she wasn't up here yet. She might have been asleep, or in the shower.

"But we might not." José swallowed. He didn't want to end up in the heart of a star or so far in deep space they might take weeks to find their way home. Or never.

But he didn't want to be blown out of the sky either, and that last shot was close, so close. The *Atlantis* had made a different choice. The *Atlantis* was wreckage. He knew that they had an advantage, had that feel of the starlight to guide them.

The next one hit. The *Endeavour* shuddered, shifted sideways. The artgrav glitched, the ceiling being the floor for a moment, slamming everyone into their harness. His harness shifted, stretched, cold fear for a moment that it wasn't going to hold.

Then everything went left and then right side up again. "We're in the upper atmosphere."

He felt the vibration. He looked across to Lauxon.

"Jump," Wilson said, finally coming to a conclusion. José could hear it in his voice, the voice of a man who genuinely believed he was about to die.

Lauxon reached her hands out. Looked at José. Flipped the switch. He could all but smell the fear of the others on the bridge. Smell their sweat.

And the stars fell away from them, the world pulled them inward.

Graze the atmosphere.

Graze the atmosphere. He saw it; he saw what he would never have seen in real space. The path. The tunnel, and he reached out, and he was the ship for that moment. You didn't go away from the world.

You went towards it. A crackle of energy flowed through him and then they were away. Control it. Control the speed. It took all that was in him, he could feel sparks under his skin, sparks that were the stars. Keeping his hands on the controls. Eyes closed so the bridge would not distract him.

He threw the *Endeavour* across space like the ship was a dart he was riding along with.

Bullseye! Hitting the mark, dropping out into real space. He had no idea where, other than where it felt right to go.

Where the currents had swept them, he had let them do so, let the ship go where hyperspace wanted to push it. Hyperspace was not some kind of void, it had flow, it had currents eddying like the water through the Viesquez Strait, flowing like the Caribbean Current. A sailor would have understood more. It had *weather*.

No wonder the transition was so rough, no wonder it sometimes spit people out of their seats if they had not strapped in. No wonder some people got sick.

Maybe just going with the flow was a bad idea, but they were alive, and they had gotten unlost once. They could do it again.

The screens showed the distant light of a yellow sun.

"Is that Sol?" Wilson asked.

"No," the navigator said. "There's a gas giant far too close to the primary."

They had to find themselves again. Could they keep doing this? Would they end up somewhere unpleasant if they did?

"Any company?"

Sensors shook his head, looking at the screens, then at his console. "No other ships unless they're hiding behind something. No signals."

An empty system, then. Maybe that was why Earth had never been contacted. Maybe a buffer of empty systems had kept them safe. Protected. Protected until now.

Maybe Earth was a backwater.

Maybe it was just chance.

Or the aliens had seen them and flown right past. José could hardly blame them if that was the case. He would probably have done the same thing.

"Something weird happened here," sensors said, finally. José wished he could remember the man's name.

"Oh?" CT raised an eyebrow.

"That gas giant shouldn't be so close in. Look, it's practically crossing over with the second planet. Let me map the orbit."

So, something had happened to gravitationally disturb the system. José knew that much.

Sparks ran down his arms again.

"I..." He turned to Lieutenant Lauxon. "I think I need to go to medbay."

"Are you okay?"

"Web static." That was what it felt like anyway. A treatable problem. It just required a bit of a tune up. That was all.

"Go," she said, understanding exactly what he needed.

It helped that she was a spider. It really helped. He stood and left the bridge, knowing the scientists would have quite the discussion. Knowing it would already be starting up.

But he needed to know he was okay himself.

Static along his arms.

Stars along his arms.

"Web static," the medic agreed. "I'll give you a reset real quick."

He was a veteran himself. José knew his name now, Dr Tobias Schmit. He had not known him during the war.

He lay back. He didn't like resets. "How often do pilots..."

"A little more often than combat crew, I'm afraid. I might also be able to tweak your programming. I can't change the hardware, but..."

"I'll think about it." The web was part of him now, flowing along his bones, under his skin, replacing parts of his nervous system so much they had atrophied.

Sometimes they could take the web out. He'd had his too long. Araña, for now and forever.

"Where did you serve during the war? I've been meaning to ask?"

José could talk, but temporarily he could not move while the reset took place. "All..." A pause. "A number of places. Including Robinson Dome."

"Oh my..." He tailed off.

José wanted to talk about what had happened, what he was sure the Martians called the Robinson Dome Massacre. He was sure the dome had been rebuilt, of course it had.

He wanted to and he didn't, he couldn't. Then he had to. "Yes. I was there that day. They swarmed us."

He knew it was just an excuse. Yes, they had swarmed him, they had surrounded him. But they had been civilians, barely armed, just trying to protect their home. He remembered the sounds. The smell of blood, metallic and tangy and, worse, the smell of feces. "They swarmed us and somebody told me to open fire. I don't even know if it was my squad leader. And I got a promotion for it."

There, that was the admission. The reason he never wanted to call himself Corporal. Never would.

The promotion under fire, from blood. Earned, they had insisted. Completely earned. How would it not be?

It had not been earned. He hadn't realized it at the time, but it had been to keep him quiet. To silence him in the moment when they had panicked and opened fire on people who had not even been combatants in the Martian sense.

They hadn't known.

They hadn't known Robinson Dome was where the Martians had sent the disabled from the smaller domes, the ones which didn't have proper shelters.

The disabled. The elderly.

The ones who couldn't fight, and all he had seen was a mass of the enemy. Seen and fired.

The child. He'd seen her face, for a moment, light hair, light skin. He'd pushed her into the storage compartment. His one act that might make up for it all. That one act.

He couldn't judge himself. He wouldn't judge himself. But if God existed, he would be judged. Judged and face a long time in Purgatory for his actions.

His grandmother would have said that. His grandmother who had been buried with her rosary, who had died disappointed in him for his agnosticism.

He could not worship a God who called him a sinner for the way he was born. He could not do that.

"You okay?"

"No," he couldn't help but say. "But I will be."

"I'm not a counselor, but…"

"But you know. You know how messed up most of us are."

Doctor Schmidt laughed. "You can't help it. Look…if you want to talk about it I won't judge you."

"You will," José said, softly. "I can't judge myself. You can. You're on the outside, and you *will* judge me."

Araña.

War criminal.

"I know what I am."

"And you were…"

"Just following orders? Just following web conditioning? It wasn't an excuse in the past. Why is it now?" The guilt washed over him. He sometimes felt this, that he should be in prison.

Instead, they'd ruled he was a victim himself. Because of the web. Which he'd let them do to him, splayed out on the bed, unconscious and then, worse, conscious while they tested it, while they turned him into something no longer quite human. While pain and ecstasy mingled in ways he never wanted to think about. Those whisperings still there, still within him.

He'd volunteered for it. To get the better assignments. Not knowing what it meant.

Not knowing he would never again be a man, only an araña.

10

Cecilie Lauxon sat opposite him. "I saw what you did. I think I can do it now. But..."

"Your slingshot maneuver. It's the same technique. The problem is that if you pull away from the gravity well, you..." He lifted his hands.

"Bounce right back, and...let's just say that made a crater on the moon when they tried it."

Thankfully, the moon had lots of craters. Would have many more. One of the greatest challenges of moon colonies. "Hopefully a long way from anything."

"A good thousand klicks from Tianhe City. Nobody hurt but the test pilot...Yun Li-Min."

José flinched. Test pilots were, of course, crazy people who fully knew the risks they were taking. Still... "To test pilots," he said, finally.

"None of us would be out here without them." She grabbed a plastic cup of water, the nearest thing to a drink she had. "Vladimir Komarov," she said, somberly.

José opened his mouth to ask who, decided to look it up later. "Michael Alsbury," he countered, grabbing his own cup.

Sadly, she didn't look blank, but at least the next one was one he knew. "Arjun Khatri."

First man to die on Mars. "We could go on, couldn't we," he said, softly. Thinking of the Atlantis' dead, of course. Thinking of...

"We could, and we will into the future. You can't make progress without blowing up prototypes and, sometimes, you can't make progress without killing test pilots." Grim reality.

"Better making progress than in pointless war," he said, finally. "Are we making progress, Lieutenant?"

"We...I think we are. I need to go." There was something in her voice.

She finished her water, stood up and left. Were they making progress? They were further from Earth than any humans had ever been, they were alone.

Everyone on this ship was essentially a test pilot. Certainly everyone who had gone out with the *Atlantis*.

They were all part of the fraternity that included Komarov, and Alsbury, and Khatri, that went back to Leon Lemartin. And now he recalled who Komarov was. Russian cosmonaut. He was surprised Lauxon knew, or maybe she was an early space nut in a way he had never been. And he was proud of that. It felt like a belonging he had never attained before.

In the days when the moon had been as far away as they were now, almost, and when men on Mars was just a dream.

Men on Mars whom he had fought, women and children. He ran his finger along the glass, then got up and went to the robot workshop.

There was a cleaning bot which needed a software patch. It was something that wasn't flying the ship, that wasn't thinking about either the war or the feeling of the starwind, for want of a better word, on the *Endeavour*'s skin. It was thinking about numbers, and making sure they were correct.

It was a moment dangerously close to peace, and he was surprised when it was not immediately interrupted. Completing the task, he freed the little robot to go about its duties. It was like an animal, really. Not quite a pet, no, but it could almost be one. People cried for lost robot probes. The world had mourned Opportunity. Of course, the Martians had retrieved the rover, put it in a museum. Taken good care of it.

Empathy. He still had it. He still cared, for all that they had tried to condition it out of him. To turn him into a sociopath.

He knew men who had ended up that way. He didn't know where any of them were now. The ones who couldn't readjust.

Prison, he supposed, one way or another. The web twitched, somewhere between his shoulder blades at the thought. As if it wanted something from him, now. It had wanted to kill.

He had wanted to kill that day, he had had no other thought, and he should be in prison. Not here.

Or perhaps saving this ship had started him down the track of repaying that debt.

Perhaps.

The observation lounge showed only still stars and the distant orange orb of the gas giant that would eventually destroy this system's one habitable world.

What had happened here was a matter for the astrophysicists, not for him. They would talk and theorize. All José felt was sorrow. For a world he did not know and would probably never visit, a world that was going to die. Whatever was down there would be lost when the gravity tore it apart, and there was nothing he could do.

Nothing anyone could do. And maybe this would be what exploration would be about.

"I think I understand why Starfleet had a Prime Directive."

Obadiah, in his ear.

"Why?"

"Because if you aren't allowed to help, you don't come up against the fact that you can't."

José nodded. "Is it..." He tailed off. "There's not *people* down there." The world was habitable by the marginal definition of having oxygen, water, and life.

Rather like the one they were still calling Hoth. They hadn't found what anyone might call good real estate yet.

José wondered if they ever would. Perhaps earth-like worlds were rare, and perhaps any they did find would have people on them.

"There's life down there," Obadiah said softly, although from their current position, the planet was hardly down. Gravity wells were down. But outside the ship's gravity field, there was no true up, no true down.

It was how the language changed in space. "But that doesn't mean there are people."

"No, it doesn't. And I don't know if anything resembling civilization could have survived the climate damage."

José resolved to see if he could talk to Doctor Jordan about it. She would have an idea, if anyone here did, of what might be down there.

Without going and looking, and they weren't about to do that, not yet.

Her probes. "Doctor Jordan should use a couple of her probes."

Obadiah nodded. "She should. She's talking about going down there. I think she's crazy."

José laughed. "No, she's perfectly sane. And I doubt somebody like her can resist a living world right there."

Especially one with an expiration date. Of course, it might be thousands of years. Maybe. Maybe if there were people down there they would have time to find a way to survive.

"What if there are people and we *can* help? Should we?" he added.

Obadiah considered that. "Yes," he said, finally. "Not saying the Prime Directive is a bad idea. Saying that saving lives comes before following rules, no matter how good. But we can't."

"We don't know that. Yet," José said.

"We can't move their planet. We…"

"And what if they have time to build a space program. They could get at least some population off planet."

"To where?" Obadiah indicated the system with a sweep of his dark hand. "There's no Mars here to move them to."

José nodded. "They'd have to…build it," he said, finally. "Something to make Clarke City look small and unsophisticated. A station the size of a small world." He meant the habitat at the Lagrange point, Earth's largest.

That would be a dream for any civilization. To build such a place, to create a home for their people. And for one that was probably just trying to survive as tides and storms began to tear their world apart? Out of reach.

"Which *we* can't do."

José nodded. "But maybe somebody else can."

What if the aliens they had met had the technology, the skills these hypothetical people needed?

But for right now, the people were hypothetical. He hoped.

He hoped they did not exist.

"So," Captain Chang was saying. "There are sentient life forms on the planet. We didn't spot them right away because they appear to have responded to the storms by going underground."

Underground. Burrowing. Did they…no, José thought, they most likely did not know they needed to get off their planet.

"The kind of help they need is beyond our ability to give, so we're going to do the next best thing and record everything we can."

The ship was overcrowded. They should go back to Earth, and then somebody voiced that very thought.

"Shouldn't we take the *Atlantis* survivors back to Earth first?"

There was a rumble of agreement.

"We can't go back to Earth without disturbing the aliens. There's no route we can take that bypasses Eridani. None that we can find. We're still waiting for a response on a suggestion there. In the meantime, we do science."

She was right. They had to go back the way they had come, back to the system where the alien ships were still prowling. Not that José blamed the aliens.

"Is anyone going down there?"

She nodded. "Doctor Jordan is leading an expedition to the surface. We already sent probes, so we know where it will be safe to land for a while."

This wasn't all hands. José knew there was no chance he'd be able to go with them. He would be stuck here because if the aliens showed up, they needed him.

He wasn't sure he liked being needed. There was something very freeing about being expendable, he had found. Something about nobody caring whether you lived or died.

But they did. And there was something about that too, or would be if it was people caring about him. They only cared about his web, and whatever was going on with it that was letting him feel the electromagnetic energies through the ship. It was probably a malfunction. Yet he could feel the connections building, vibrating through not the web but his heart.

They didn't care about him. He was still the araña. Always would be now.

So, Doctor Jordan got to go set foot on another dangerous alien world. He should be glad he didn't have to go with her.

He glanced at Obadiah. Their eyes met for a moment, and the security officer nodded briefly.

Maybe he would go down with her. Maybe they would take volunteers. With the *Atlantis* crew, they had extra people.

Expendable people. José closed his eyes. He'd have to watch on the screens, then, like everyone else.

And hope they made it back. Dr. Jordan was certainly not expendable, but that was what the probes were for. To make things as safe as possible before the human explorers went down, to ready the site.

The captain vanished back in the direction of the bridge. Lieutenant Lauxon followed her.

José wasn't needed there. He wasn't needed until they jumped. So, likely, he should go back to the workshop, but he didn't want to.

He didn't know what he wanted to do. He was distracted, worried and, if he admitted it, bored. There was that point between utter terror and the next utter terror that a soldier hit, and he was stuck in that place.

So? He went to the workshop anyway, to finish out his shift there amongst robot and shuttle parts. In the familiar scents of metal and machine oil.

Ten minutes later, Doctor Jordan walked in. She was as attractive as the first time he had seen her, although there was nothing in her eyes that showed any interest.

"What do you need?" he asked.

"I'm a little concerned about the shuttle gyroscopes holding in those storms...not to mention sticking a landing. That's the pilot's concern, but..."

José nodded. "Give me the figures."

"I was surprised to find you down here. I thought you were bridge crew now."

He smiled. "The bridge doesn't need me right now."

"Let's hope you're right."

There was something under her smile he wasn't entirely sure how to read.

11

The shuttle descended through the turgid atmosphere. José held his breath, hoping the gyroscope updates and other work he had done held.

He wondered what it was like to live on a world where the weather had completely turned against you. Well, part of him knew. He was not old enough to remember the megastorms that had hit during Reclaiming, the ones which laid the island bare, forced them to rebuild over and over until the Earth reached a new equilibrium. Perhaps they were better off now. Not rich, no, but they had found their own stability. They had built an island that was proud to be what it was, proud to be that little bit separate. They had protected themselves from the worst of Reclaiming with politics and from the worst of the storms with the sea baffles that slowed the waves.

But this was different. This world was not going to reach a new equilibrium. It had been murdered, assassinated by whatever gravitational force had pulled the gas giant into its orbit.

The shuttle on the screens shook. Vibrated. He held his breath. This was something he was good at, something he knew he could do.

Then it vanished beneath the cloud layer.

"They…" Lauxon clamped her lips together. She'd called José up to the bridge.

Clearly she had been about to say one of those lines you never say when somebody is in real potential danger. Like 'We'll be safe here' or 'It was only the wind.'

Of course, down there, it was only the wind. "Don't say it," he couldn't resist.

"I didn't. Because if they do mess up, guess who has to go down there and get them."

José grinned. "Not me." He was still not managing more than a mediocre performance in the shuttle simulators.

"Unless I decide to take you with me."

"Aren't I too valuable now?"

"Both of the *Atlantis* pilots survived."

And they knew the logistics of how he had done what he had done. Not how it felt, no, but there were simulations. There were ways they could learn to do it.

Eventually, he supposed, it would be part of basic star pilot training. Routine. Well, except it made electromagnetic storms, so it would probably be illegal to do it in the atmosphere of an inhabited planet, barring a serious emergency. It wouldn't be fair on anyone under it.

Ensign Forester looked up from her station. "We have an incoming ansible message."

Chang nodded. "Let's hear it."

The voice that came over the speakers had an almost robotic nature, a side effect of the relatively limited bandwidth. It tended to even out one's tones and make one sound unnatural.

"Captain Chang, we are asking you not to return to the solar system. The aliens are here."

A pause, as if the speaker was collecting himself. A male voice, for sure. A slight Russian accent could be heard despite the ansible's effect. "Humanity is at war."

Not Earth. Humanity. Earth and Mars united against an external threat; likely the only thing which could unite them.

He thought of his father on Earth. He thought even more about more vulnerable locations. Launchpad. The outer system outposts. Domes on Mars.

He'd seen what happened when a dome blew. All they had to do was drop a rock with enough force.

All they had to do…and if they had a big enough rock, they could destroy Earth as a habitable planet.

"Send an acknowledgment only," Chang said.

José knew why they had to stay out here.

Because if Earth lost the war, they might be all there was of humanity. He'd had that fear before, now it sharpened within him.

If they were all there was, then what chance did they have?

Earth was at war. It was unreal to think about, José finally thought as he headed for the mess. Maybe somebody had some real alcohol. Some beer. Or heck, the rotgut that came from the inevitable still in engineering.

It was awful, but it was strong and it might, might make him feel better. Not to worry about his parents.

Not to worry, as ironic as it seemed, about his enemies. About those who had survived. Marsies were tough, they had to be. They made sure their kids were as tough as they could be. He'd heard things about how they treated the ones who couldn't keep up.

Things that made him glad he hadn't been born on Mars. But that was not the point. They would fight.

They would all fight and they had a chance of winning. Or did they? "We can't win," he grumbled as he sat down.

Obadiah turned his chair. "Probably not. But honestly, what would they gain from wiping out humanity?"

José considered that. "Not being threatened by us. I mean, look at what fear has driven in human history." If it wasn't fear, it was greed.

"Hrm. Maybe. But it would make more sense that we'd beat on each other for a bit, then sign some kind of treaty," Obadiah mused. "That's usually how war works."

José nodded. "It is, unless one side is completely insane and has to be beaten down to the point where they can't continue. 1940s Germany," he pointed out.

"That was a hot mess. Even Mars…"

"Mars didn't beat us down to where we couldn't continue. They just made it too expensive."

"White folks didn't learn anything from the American Revolution and, as usual, brown folks paid the price for it," Obadiah mused. "But this is a different situation."

It was. Would the… "They won't put boots on the ground. They don't need to. They're mad because we encroached on their territory…"

"They're mad," Obadiah said, "because the *Atlantis* shot at them. Which makes no sense. We're not warships."

"No, it doesn't. I have to wonder…I don't know." He hadn't talked to the *Atlantis* bridge crew. Nobody had. Chang appeared to have them all under some kind of gag order.

"None of us do. No, I haven't been told what happened either. Which probably means the brass are trying to work out what to do about it."

Obadiah was an officer. He meant the captain and the first officer. José's lips quirked. "You have something of a shine yourself."

"Apparently not enough for this. Chief of Security isn't good enough."

José nodded. "Hey. At least we aren't worrying about the doctor and her expedition."

Obadiah laughed. "I am. My assistant's down there. I should have gone myself, maybe, but they need the experience."

"Storms are going to be more of a problem than hostile natives, I'd imagine." The burrowers, as they'd been nicknamed, might not even come out onto their world's dangerous surface to find out what was going on.

José would, but you couldn't assume they thought like humans. Which went both ways. Maybe that's what the war was really about.

People not thinking the same way or about the same things. "But eh. As long as we can avoid getting shot at again."

"Amen to that," Obadiah said, then frowned at his pager. "Ugh."

"What?"

"Guess who's stuck on the planet."

Great. "So, while we weren't thinking about her…"

"…the shuttle she was on got buried. It's undamaged, they just can't get it out."

José made a face. "Oh well. We can tease her about it for the rest of the voyage?"

Obadiah laughed. "You might be able to get away with that. I think she likes you."

José considered that. And considered what particular meaning of 'like' Obadiah meant.

The shuttle bounced around like a giant had it in his hand and was demonstrating to his even larger parents how a plane flew. José was not prone to airsickness, and the web tended to reduce nausea, so the fact that he was queasy had to mean things were even worse for the others on board.

He kept his mouth closed in that tight manner one did when one was afraid one would barf. Lieutenant Lauxon was flying, and probably suffering the least, given how much being in control helped.

If she was still in control. The landscape below them seemed to ripple, seemed to be changing constantly as the wind tore at it.

This was worse than the ice planet. At least there, one knew what weather to expect. On a world like that, one knew that one would be cold.

Here? This was a dying world and its breath rattled in its lungs, following no predictable pattern.

Then they got below the weather and he realized it was also a beautiful world. A lovely one, even. The clouds hid the too-close orb of the displaced gas giant, hid the threat to this world. It would be easy to forget. Beneath him was a damaged, broken world, but struggling trees still showed patches of purplish green. Mud flowed between them, but there was a pattern to it. The wind tossed them again, but there was a world below them, a place where men and women could walk.

It would be easy, he realized, not to even know. Oh, surely, they knew something was wrong, but did they know what? Did they know their world was doomed?

He wished he could ask. Perhaps one day he would.

They landed with a thud that sent a vibration through both the shuttle and José's teeth. "Any landing we can walk away from?" Obadiah asked.

"Any landing is a good one," Lauxon grumbled. "If we'd bounced, we'd have flipped."

So, she'd done it on purpose. He pulled on his outer clothing, which would protect him from windburn. "Let's go help the other group dig out."

They'd brought the tools for it, including a robot that would be highly useful...it could literally dig into the mud around the shuttle without needing solid ground to stand on. If there was solid ground here.

If. That was far too big an if, he thought. Solid ground on a planet like this could be mythical.

They stepped out. They could see the other shuttle. It wasn't just stuck, it was at an angle. "Looks like the ground gave way under it *and* mud fell on it," Obadiah grumbled.

"Looks like," Lauxon agreed. She set out across the mud.

The robot followed. After a moment, so did José. The wind was not so bad here, or at least not so bad in this precise moment. He felt it blow around him, but it didn't threaten him with the cold, nor did he feel as if he was about to fall over.

The ground under him moved. Stirred. "Earthquake!" he called.

And then it opened up under his feet, swallowing him into the darkness below.

12

José came to in a dark tunnel. There was just enough light to tell him that he was awake and not blind, but not really enough to see anything, let alone to navigate by.

He struggled to sit up, felt the back of his head. He had hit his head on something, probably a rock. Other than that, he felt no injuries other than the inevitable bruising, but that bruising seemed to cover his entire body. He did not stand, not being clear on how high the ceiling was.

Under him was asphalt.

He blinked. Tapped it again. It was definitely asphalt or something similar. A road or path.

Technological civilization, under the surface of a dying world. As his eyes adapted, he saw that the path was lit. Just not that well. Or maybe it was more than bright enough for a people who might have lived underground for generations, whose world seldom saw the sun.

Maybe.

People.

The asphalt proved that somewhere here there were, or at least had been, people. People with large brains and manipulative appendages.

People worth saving, but there was…nothing he could do.

Surely, there was nothing he could do.

He slowly stood up. The ceiling did give enough space for him. He looked one way, then the other, then up. He had fallen at an angle, slid down into the tunnel. He wondered if repair crews would be along.

He thought about climbing out. He thought about standing here.

"José!" A frantic call from above. "Is your radio working?"

He examined it. "Not without a repair!" he yelled back. "But I'm working."

Laughter. The mood lightened a bit. "Can you climb back out?"

He looked up at the hole, assessed the distance.

"Not without a rope. I seem to be on a road or trail, not sure which without knowing how big they are. Asphalt surface."

"...dang. Let's get you out of there before..."

"...too late."

Something like a four-by-four rumbled up the road. On the front seat sat two fur-covered figures. They wore no clothing, but did have belts and one of them had a baldric like strap across their chest, rather like Chewbacca or Worf.

Neither had visible nipples or external genitalia. They had a faint musky scent, not at all unpleasant, but it made his nose itch. José flattened himself against the tunnel wall, hoping they had not seen him.

It was too late. They looked at each other, then both produced a rapid fire, high pitched chittering that was undoubtedly language. José had no gift for languages. He decided that one gesture had to be universal, lifting his hands so they could see them.

They also had hands, naked ones that kind of stuck out of the fur otherwise covering their bodies. Apparently dexterity trumped warmth. The fur wasn't that thick, either.

Come to think of it, it was quite warm in the tunnel, a pleasant temperature. They didn't exactly need winter coats.

One of them pulled a weapon, started to point it. The other pushed their hand down. He took a deep breath of relief at that gesture.

There was silence from above. José stepped out into the road, his hands still lifted, letting them get a good look at him. How would he look to them? Ugly at best, a threat at worst.

They were still chittering away. He wished he knew what they were saying.

He wished he could speak to them.

For a moment, all three of them were frozen still. Tension flowed through the air. A moment that was history, that was more than one history. Then he heard a voice from above. "José?"

He decided answering was safer than otherwise. "I'm good. There are two of the locals down here. I think they may be road crew."

Assuming the tools at their belts and in the back of the four-by-four were what they appeared to be. But they were armed, which said something.

Something about threats they had to worry about. "I'm more worried about whatever means they need a gun."

Could be bandits. Could be wildlife.

"I think…crap. I think we may just have met that."

He heard the sound of a gun going off. Wildlife, he assumed. "Are you sure it's wildlife?"

"It's a big cat. And it ran off when we put one in the air over its head. Well, cat-like thing." Something that lived in the tunnels, survived when the surface was uninhabitable.

The road crew stared. Then one of them pointed up the "slide" he had come down. Then pointed at him.

He nodded. "It's okay," he said, knowing they wouldn't understand. "We come in peace."

Chittering. He wished universal translators existed outside of fiction. He wished there was a rosetta stone for their language.

But they might have very different concepts. Some things were the same, though.

And then Doctor Jordan came sliding down into the tunnel. She must have joined the group while he was out.

The gun started to come out again, but vanished far more quickly this time, and without the assistance of the other alien.

Doctor Jordan also showed her hands, glancing at José, "I'm going to guess we haven't really started trying to communicate."

José nodded. "Well, they did manage to ask me if I fell down that hole." Of course, Jordan had made her way down in a more controlled matter.

It hadn't helped keep her from losing her hood and her hair being partially knocked out of her braids to frizz around her head. "That's a start. And they aren't shooting at us."

"They almost did. I can't blame them. They don't even know what we are."

One of the locals had dismounted from the four-by-four and cautiously approached them. From the way their nostrils were working, they were as focused on scent as sight. Perhaps more so, although they could see well enough to drive a vehicle down a road.

Jordan stood still. "Stand very still, like it's a dog sniffing you."

José had no intention of moving, although he thought it rude to compare them to dogs. They were people, and this was the most significant moment of his life. He felt happy for the first time in a long time. Like he belonged out here, and this was what he should be doing.

The local didn't just sniff at them. They tugged on José's sweater for a moment. José thought for a moment, then slowly moved to take it off. Clothes might well be an alien concept to a creature that was fur covered and, apparently, had no nudity taboo. He wasn't going to assume anything, of course.

The creature ran a hand over the cloth, then shook their head a little. "Take it to look at," José said. He'd be cold on the surface, but here in the tunnels his uniform was more than warm enough. He was glad that his sleeves still covered the telltale signs of the web, at least mostly. Would they see the glint at his wrists?

It probably didn't matter. They probably wouldn't know what it was.

Then the two creatures abruptly moved, herding José and Dr. Jordan towards the vehicle.

"I really hope they're taking us to their leader," he quipped.

Jordan frowned. "I don't even know where to start," she admitted, but she let them be herded into the back of the four-by-four amongst what were, yes, obviously road-mending tools.

The locals got back on and started to drive.

Take me to your leader was the classic line. And, perhaps, it was exactly what they were doing.

The four-by-four rumbled down the tunnel, which split into a fork. The driver took the left hand road, which led further down and into slightly brighter lighting. Then it opened up into a cavern.

No, José thought. This had been a valley, once. Somehow they had built a roof over it. This was far past an asphalt road.

This was a civilization that had adapted. Had built. Could easily build a space station. He glanced at the top, seeing something akin to a rock version of a Martian dome, then at Doctor Jordan. Her lips had narrowed. She said nothing.

The vehicle ducked under a road, emerged on the other side along a shallow trail which appeared to be restricted to official, or perhaps small, vehicles. It wasn't quite a city they were in. More like a small town.

Hopefully it wasn't all that was left of them.

Hopefully they could find a way to communicate.

The four-by-four stopped, and the locals indicated to them to get out. Keeping his hands as visible as possible, José did so, then turned to see if Doctor Jordan needed any help.

She gave him the look of a woman who preferred not to accept such, and hopped down on her own. Unlike him, she still had her sweater. His was still in the hands of the locals.

He followed them. He was not, he thought, exactly a prisoner. Not exactly a guest. Certainly he wasn't getting out of here, but he was taking his cues from the scientist.

After all, she was a lot smarter than he was. They went through a door into a building. It was slightly warmer inside, no doubt preferred room temperature for these people.

Whatever that meant when you lived underground. Whatever that meant when the surface of your world was lost to you.

If they had ever had it. He had to stoop slightly as he went through the corridor. Jordan was fine, except that her frizzed hair did brush the ceiling a little.

The locals were just that bit shorter. Into an elevator. It grumbled a little on the way up, rattling as if not properly maintained.

And then into what was obviously the executive suite. They had, indeed, taken them to their leader.

Their leader was a well-groomed individual wearing a gold or gilt chain around their neck. There was still no indication of sex or gender. Could these people be monoecious, like snails?

Maybe.

He glanced at Jordan again.

The local stood. There was a lot of chittering. He could hear patterns in it, but there was nothing to help him identify what any of them meant.

Then the local pointed at them, pointed up. Jordan repeated it in reverse, pointing up, and then at herself.

A storm of chittering.

The first two locals left. At least they didn't think José would be violent at all.

Then the leader of what he was starting to think of as the moles, perhaps rudely, turned to them. They pointed at themselves, chittered something.

He listened. Finally made it out. Jordan tried to repeat it. Failed. It was very like the old African click languages, and apparently she was no better at that than he was.

She tried another time, and came to a close approximation, then pointed to herself, said Elizabeth Jordan, to him, said José Marin.

Names. Then she pointed to both of them at once, as best she could. "Human."

It was a start.

It was, perhaps, more than a start.

13

The settlement seemed to be one of a small number, linked only by those narrow tunnels, tunnels which constantly collapsed and had to be rebuilt. Only a small amount of trade. The guns protected from wandering wildlife that might get in when the tunnel collapsed, often half-starved beasts, the remnants of a dying ecosystem. Or the other settlements.

They discovered this by maps and drawings, each learning a bit of the other's language. They discovered that they had found the right settlement. Or at least, they claimed that their enemies would have killed the offworlders.

That was a concept it was hard to get over. They, yes, were from another planet. From a planet that orbited another sun.

From a world where the skies were still clear. José wished he could tell them something to give them hope. But perhaps Earth's history was not the hope they needed.

If they could roof over an entire valley, then all they needed was the way to get off this rock. Away from it.

If they chose to stay and die, and some would, no matter what, that was not his fault, nor his responsibility.

It was he who drew the Lagrange colony. Pointed to bits of it. Instilled the idea. So much for the Prime Directive.

So much for protecting nascent civilizations from contact. They didn't seem to need it, though. They didn't seem to be scared or xenophobic at all.

He wondered about that. He waited for the other shoe to drop. But they were free to leave. That much was clear.

They had demonstrated they were not here to kill anyone, to steal children, or mutilate the livestock. That latter concept had also gone across, to much chittering laughter from the moles. José didn't believe Area 51 or any of that had happened.

It could have, though. They knew now that it could have happened, that aliens were real, that FTL was possible.

José just doubted it. He doubted that any aliens would come, mutilate cattle, leave. Mass hallucination. Hysteria. Or maybe some basic human fear, its true source long forgotten.

Now he stood looking at the city, from a balcony a few stories up. No, it was not New York or Los Angeles, but there was something familiar about it.

This was a city that had been rebuilt, he suddenly saw. He could see the scars. He could see the way houses were built on foundations that did not quite match them. He could see the empty foundations, where the people who would have rebuilt...

His grandparents had talked about the megastorms. Hugo. Maria. Leonidas. Had talked about what they had done to his home. To the island. He wished he could share it with them, could find the language and the words to say something as simple as "I know." Or "I understand."

Because he did, because he could envision how the storm had swept through this valley, ripping houses from foundations, lifting cars and people into the air. It didn't matter what shape the people were. He could envision the wind inverting, the gravity effects pulling atmosphere from the planet, not enough to render it uninhabitable, but enough for hideous updrafts.

Enough for death and destruction, and it would happen again, and it might be as soon as the next time when the atmosphere would become a whirlpool, pulled off into space, and this world would be a corpse.

"We have to help them," he said to himself.

"How would you propose we do that?"

"They have solid technology. They just have...probably the have the knowledge of rockets, but when your world is this messed up, you can't build that infrastructure. They need spaceplanes."

"And where will they go?" Jordan asked.

He held up his sketch of the station. "They build this. It's the only way. We can't get them out of this system."

"They'd need hydroponics. They'd need small livestock, which they don't have, they have nothing like rabbits. It's...I don't think we can do it, Mr. Marin."

He nodded. "But what would we be if we didn't try?"

She had no answer.

After the mud of the planet, the *Endeavour* seemed ridiculously clean. Pristine, even.

And isolated. José had nightmares often. Usually they were about the children. Now, they were about the storm hitting the valley. He'd drawn it.

He'd confirmed that he had envisioned it right. He knew about the storms, he was too young to remember them, but the scars flowed through from generation to generation. They called it generational trauma. Epigenetics. Something...

The storms had been nature, but they had been man's fault in so many ways. But these people, these people had done nothing wrong. Freak cosmic events would destroy them.

He closed his eyes, lying in his bunk. He almost felt the ship around him for all that they were in real space. Almost felt as if he could ask the cold steel for its own wisdom.

What did the *Endeavour* know? Nothing more than her crew, nothing more than those within her.

The aliens could help. That thought flickered through his mind.

The aliens were at war with Earth.

Which meant that the first step towards saving these people might be to bring peace, which he couldn't do. It would be down to diplomats and translators on Earth, on Mars. To people whose job this was, but who had never done it before.

Just as he had never done it before. So, what did it matter who did it? Who negotiated?

What mattered was Earth's survival. But what also mattered was this world's survival.

Verr was the word they used, as close as he could pronounce it, a clicking purr. What it truly meant, he didn't know. World? Earth? Home? All of those things, perhaps.

He pulled out of the bunk, tugged on his coveralls, secured his belt. The uniform of working ship crew, so far from anything resembling a dress uniform.

Even the captain wore coveralls most of the time now. In deep space, it was more like he'd been told submarines were like. You couldn't stand on ceremony.

He headed for the mess hall. Breakfast was needed, even if he couldn't face it.

"What are they like?" asked a voice.

It was one of the engineers, a redhead whose English carried a strong accent José could not quite recognize. Bulgaria? Romania? His eyes were bright.

"People," José said, finally. "I mean, they're not remotely like us, but they're people."

He hadn't been taken to their leader after all, only to a representative. Their leaders were biologically determined and too valuable to be allowed to meet with outsiders until they were absolutely sure they wouldn't shoot them.

Jordan had made notes and said something about moles, which had been what he was thinking.

Or had it been rats? He wasn't sure which it was. Some earth analog he didn't know enough about.

"Fuzzy, I hear."

"Fuzzy," José agreed. "Presumably they had no reason to evolve hairlessness and stayed all fuzzy."

He was assuming they were mammals. Or something mammal-like. Maybe none of the rules applied.

"And they live underground away from the storms."

"They're in kind of a domed colony on their own world." José didn't hide the sorrow in his voice. He wasn't going to hide his desire to help them.

"Which we can't fix. I mean…"

José's lips quirked. "Maybe there's a civilization out there that can move planets. We aren't it."

"Yet," the kid said, irrepressible. Kid, because he had to be in his early twenties. Years younger than José. Not old enough to have fought in the war, which made José feel even older. The war, the years since.

"Not in time for them. Unless time travel's possible too, in which case, wouldn't it already have been fixed?"

The math had once implied that FTL and time travel were the same thing. It hadn't worked out that way. You beat the light speed barrier by shifting to a layer of space where it was higher. The barrier itself remained intact.

"Maybe. Unless fixing it before we got here to make a note of it would break time." The young man grinned again.

José recalled his name. Piotr. He had just gotten everyone straight when they had added the *Atlantis* crew into the mix. Now he had more names to learn, but at least he'd remembered. If a little late…

The linguists were busy at work on the chittering Verran language. Well, languages, but one was enough to start with.

They definitely had different languages. Isolated colonies. Some of which refused to trade. One of which, the leaders of this one rather thought was dead.

Somebody had started using the word queens for those leaders. Biologically determined, somehow, and apparently all female.

Or maybe it meant something else. José was too busy to look it up - the *Endeavour* had all human knowledge in its databanks, but that didn't mean he could easily find what he needed, especially when he was being kept busy.

One watch on the bridge, in the pilot-navigator seat, just in case they had to run. One watch in the labs working on probes that could do a better job of triangulating the fate of Verr. What did it matter?

Would he want to know exactly how long he and his world had, if he was them? He was pretty sure not.

Their queens and kings, though, might need to. Might need to know what they could do to plan.

Spaceplanes were what they needed. The mythical space elevator was even less workable on their world's shifting surface.

But so were runways. The tides that swept over even their settlement domes, washing them momentarily clean.

The tides.

Could they take off from water?

Then he realized what the solution was. He pinged the XO, who was off watch.

"I know what they need to build to get off their planet."

"What?"

"A rail gun."

C.T. ran a hand through his trimmed beard. "Not feasible."

"Not feasible in a normal situation. But if you put it in the right place, you'd get a solid window each year when it's pointed *towards* Lucifer." The name for the gas giant had been inevitable. The Verrans had their own. "Lucifer's gravity would…"

"Pull the payload right up there. Yes…it could work. Making it man-rated…Verr-rated, I suppose…would be hard, but it could be done." A pause. "How the heck did you end up a gropo?"

"Couldn't afford college any other way," he said. An old story, that. And he'd wanted to go to college off island.

It hadn't happened.

"A natural pilot and you saw the engineering thing we were missing." C.T. looked mischievous. "I think your fate is sealed, Mr. Marin."

He stood and left without explaining what fate he meant, leaving José sitting there slightly stunned.

But he was right. José was more than just a gropo, but he was also that. He was still a spider and always would be.

Whatever had set that twinkle into the eye of a man normally known for being a hardass, he didn't know.

He decided he didn't want to know. Yet it added to that sense of content belonging. They were in a deep crisis, but for the first time he was where he wanted to be. He wanted to fly again…

14

The stars danced behind his eyelids. José knew something was wrong, but he didn't want to wake up.

Then he did, and their after images were still there, the web whispering along his limbs. He couldn't possibly need another reset. Not this quickly.

The medical technician had said there was no damage, but something felt wrong.

"Mr. Marin to the bridge, please."

He wondered how many times that had been said. Hopefully only the one. Sleeping through a bridge call would be embarrassing. He threw on his uniform and moved quickly, climbing through the shafts rather than using the lift. Hoping the exercise would make him feel better.

It did, a little, it quieted the whispers of the web to their normal level. He was never not aware of it. He tuned it out, learned to endure it.

It was always there, spiders running along inside him. Whispers of the stars, whispers of the ship. Mapping the connections that grew outside, the growing sense of home.

A rising sense of panic, as if he was for a moment a puppet of the web, just as he had been. If somebody showed up in front of him he would shoot them if he had a weapon, he could actually feel the weight of the rifle. Deep breath. He had been so much better. He could fly. He just had to hold it together.

Deep breath. He could not step onto the bridge like this. He took three more deep breaths, got his mind back in order again.

Stepped onto the bridge. They were still orbiting Verr. He still thought of them as burrowers. Would that become a slur.

No, if anyone used a slur, it would be moles, obviously. Or maybe they would embrace that word. If they could learn English. He wasn't sure. No, they could learn to understand it. Pronunciation might be another matter.

That world, the gas giant.

And a ship. A ship which hung in space in front of them, built to never enter an atmosphere. Built to travel between worlds.

He was in the pilot's seat before he thought about it. No Lauxon, maybe she was off duty and tired. If they had to jump, if they had to... they had people on the planet.

Lauxon was on the planet.

Jordan was on the planet. If they had to jump, they might not be able to come back.

Stall them, he thought, glancing at the short figure that was Captain Chang, seated in her chair, an odd air of calm around her. Practiced calm, no doubt. Maybe he would get that one day.

"We found their frequency. Making contact now."

The *Atlantis* had fired first. But humans could be trusted with aliens. The Verrans had not triggered the web at all, like they were animals.

Cute and fuzzy aliens, perhaps, were fine.

One of the screens flickered. A voice sounded that was wind chimes and bells.

Oh, for a universal translator.

"They're sending prime number dots combined with words, Captain," said the comms officer.

"Reciprocate."

No shooting. No weapons. Just the clear attempts to start to build a vocabulary to communicate. Prime numbers, then regular numbers, then you could move to concrete things. Ship. Man. Names.

But they weren't shooting. The shuttle should have time to get up here. José found himself breathing slightly hard. Tried to quell it.

The web was sensing a threat, or perhaps picking up on his levels of adrenalin, picking up on them and pushing him towards a state he did not want to be in, that was for sure.

He needed it checked, but he couldn't leave the bridge. Not when they might have to run, because they were not going to fight.

They could not fight. They could only run, from system to system, knowing they might carry within them the last hope of humanity.

More bell-like words, then there was video. The opposing ship's bridge.

An angel was at the controls.

As he blinked a couple of times, he realized the being was not an angel after all. It was a crystalline form, with multiple limbs and, possibly, multiple eyes. It should have triggered the arachnophobia of anyone on the bridge afflicted with such. But how could one be afraid of such a being. A rainbow shimmer crossed its form as the light shifted. Eight wings. Or the pattern of such.

Be not afraid. Had this being once walked the Earth, because if so there was a word for it: Seraph.

José wondered what humans looked like to it. Ugly, like they were going to teeter over. How could they be anything but. "Madre de Dios," he finally muttered. Hopefully too quietly to throw off any developing translation algorithms.

Whatever that thing was, whatever it appeared to be, it was nothing more than the creation of its specific evolution. What the heck was it made out of anyway? Diamond was a form of carbon, but surely they couldn't be under enough pressure?

Doctor Jordan wasn't there to theorize. Hopefully they did at least have a biologist on the crew. Or maybe they needed a geologist.

He let out a breath.

The creature was still singing. He caught things which might be words. "Kyrai." "Glyn." He didn't know what they meant.

They would find out, though. They'd made contact, peaceful contact, with a species that was at least as advanced as they were, a starfaring race.

Somebody so alien that he wondered what they could have in common. Would these people understand Shakespeare or a telenovela?

He pulled himself out of that reverie. At least they didn't trigger the flaring of the web, although it was still caressing him from the inside.

"I think," the comms officer ventured. "I think glyn is their species name, but I can't be sure."

It would work for now, José thought. If it turned out to be a kangaroo situation, they could fix it later.

Glyn. Angels. It was better not to think of them as such. But they had a beauty to them, they jingled and whispered as they moved.

Would they come to the ship?

Could they come to the ship? Could they and humans even exist in the same atmosphere? What if that crystal that formed their skin or exoskeleton or whatever required levels of heat or pressure or…

They could talk to the Verrans face to face. He was not sure they would ever manage that with the glyn. Did they…He closed his eyes. Not looking at them for that moment helped. It got his mind straight again. Well, as straight as it ever was.

Opened his eyes again. Now he could see their structure, the way the light refracted off the edge of them. The color changes.

The comms officer spoke up again. "I think there's a pattern to the color changes. Could be part of their communication."

Or just, José thought, something like body language.

"Never mind that," said Chang. "We can trade biological details later. Find out what they want."

Hopefully it was just a coincidence that they were here. Hopefully the answer to that question would not be "You."

The glyn was still talking. Was that word singular, plural, or both? For all he knew it… The ship seemed to shiver, he felt it.

And instinctively, he dodged. There was a torpedo, coming from the glyn ship. He heard their tones become dissonant, saw them turn to the side before turning off their screen.

The glyn had fired. Or had they? Had somebody fired without orders? He didn't know. But he had an idea.

"We can't abandon our people, Captain. Can we hide?"

She nodded. "I think we can. Run for the gas giant."

He did so…where was Lauxon? In real space, he stuttered, the ship tilted more than he intended. He couldn't let the computer take over, because the computer would not do what he knew Chang had in mind. Would throw up all kinds of safeties. Hyperspace was so much easier to fly in, when you had that flow. Realspace was just emptiness.

Charging for the planet. No further shots came after them. Charging for it…and into it.

Into the upper layers of the atmosphere. He could jump from here. Maybe they knew that. Maybe not.

Either way, it took them out of the glyn's view, out of sight and perhaps out of mind. The electromagnetic interference would render the *Endeavour* blind and deaf, that was the down side.

"Launch probes," Chang said.

Or maybe not. The captain probably had this in her array of things to do if they did encounter hostiles. He could feel the energy of the atmosphere against his skin.

No, against the ship's skin. Once the ship was still, he took his hands off the controls, let the computer hold the *Endeavour* in place. His palms were sweating, but he didn't care, he lowered his head into them anyway.

He could feel the planet, a living, breathing thing. Could there be life here? There could, and that life? He felt for a moment as if it was waiting to consume the Verrans, but he knew that was anthropomorphizing.

"We hold position. Wait and see what they do." Chang templed her hands, fingers touching together. "Opinions?"

The communications officer frowned. "My opinion is that they had an accidental discharge or a rogue crew member. One doesn't know with aliens, but I thought we were communicating fine."

"I agree," said Weps, brushing back her hair. "Did you see the color flash from the one talking to us? I mean, we can't tell, but were they pissed?"

They might be. José didn't say something not so much because he had no opinion, but because his thoughts had already been voiced by the others. It didn't seem like it could be deliberate. All they could do, though, was wait it out.

"They're looking for us," the comms officer added. "Not getting much from the probes, but they're definitely looking for us."

Were they looking for the *Endeavour* to destroy it or to apologize?

José wished he could possibly know.

15

Orange light crackled outside. The cameras showed it. The lookouts saw it. How long could the *Endeavour* hide here? José knew there was a limit to how much positive pressure the ship could take. All of the stories about using spaceships as submersibles were, well…it was a bad idea; that was all.

But for right now, the ship was fine. Crouched, somewhere between predator and prey. They could easily leave.

They had people on Verr, on the surface. Would the glyn work that out? Detect their shuttle? Destroy it? All they had to do was strand the women there.

They could not leave them, not unless the alternative was destruction. Lucifer's light flickered around them.

José could feel it.

"We have about five hours before we have to come out."

Or jump.

"Are they still looking for us?"

"They released a probe."

Which might or might not find them. The question was, was it safe to come out? Without knowing what was happening on the glyn ship?

José couldn't make that judgment. Those who could were, as the old saying went, above his pay grade.

He could wait for orders. He could possibly take a nap.

He waited for orders. The idea of sleeping through this, even if he wasn't needed right now, was alien. He was rested.

He waited for orders and he thought about the other times he had waited for orders. Sitting in the drop ships, waiting for the order to go down to the surface of Mars.

He knew now that he had been used for terror, that they had never planned on taking and holding ground, just...

It was all about intimidating the Martians into giving in, and nothing would make them do that. The antics had probably made their determination stronger.

They were human.

The glyn were not. He began to mentally calculate, the way Lieutenant Lauxon had been teaching him. He liked her.

He might almost say he loved her, but he couldn't let that happen, not out here.

Liked, then. Or maybe the word he needed was the old Greek. Philos. He wanted to be her friend, not just her student.

The glyn were not human. What if...what if the torpedo they had dodged had not even been a weapon? What if...the kid. The kid with the grenade. The kid smiling as she threw it at him.

She'd died, of course.

That one he had to argue was a combatant or he would go insane, or he would go far past sanity and into the state so many had come back in. When the thousand-yard stare he knew he had some days became glass-eyed catatonia.

They'd used web malfunction as an excuse, but everyone knew the truth. It wasn't the web; it was the effect of the war on a man's soul.

José had come out with his damaged, but whole. He just had to make up for what he did.

By saving Verr. Well, no. He did not owe that much, but he still had to try. Yet he did owe, and doing what he was doing paid those debts. Being part of this.

He closed his eyes again. Waiting was the worst thing for him right now. It made his thoughts circle around those he could not save. An entire planet at stake, in ways he could not comprehend. He tried to imagine moving a planet.

He could not.

But he could imagine that space station, could imagine the Verrans living on it, having children, loving in whatever ways they did.

Building a starship to find a new world where they could walk on the surface without fear.

"Probe approaching. They found us."

José tensed. His hands went to the controls. Could he actually jump from here? He'd confidently said he could do it, the web whispering strength to him, telling him he could.

He wasn't sure if it was real confidence or fake. If he really believed in himself. Maybe he needed to.

"It's broadcasting."

"Put it on."

More of the bell-like glyn language. Gleeeen. Each vowel extended, each consonant clipped.

Broadcasting. Words they could not understand. Threat or apology?

No. There was...it was repeating.

"It's on a fairly short loop. It's..." The comms officer frowned. "Wait. I got it."

Translation might not be possible. Pattern reading was, especially with the *Endeavour*'s AI to help.

Pattern reading. "It's more like a beacon, I think."

"So it's broadcasting our location to them." Chang frowned. For a moment, José was expecting her to order Weps to take it out.

"Marin, get ready to get us out of here."

José nodded. He'd been ready for hours.

"Weps, get me a real good scan of the probe. Make sure it doesn't look like it's going to blow up."

How did the *Atlantis* crew feel? One of them had appeared at the back of the bridge. The XO, a tall Russian woman.

"Are we about to be shot at again?" she asked, if politely. Probably, she couldn't stand sitting around waiting any longer. José knew he would probably have hit his limit of such too. Could he have stood this from the robot workshop?

Yes, because he would have had to, because a soldier did what was necessary. And right now, what was necessary was sitting here, on this bridge, sweating hands on the controls. Plotting. He had no idea where to take them.

Back to Earth was where he wanted to go, even if he was not now or ever welcome, even if there was no place for him there anymore.

Back to Earth. Because then the others would be safe, except they wouldn't be.

"Stand down," Chang said, quietly. "No, we are not about to be shot at again."

The glyn ship was still outside.

And it hit José. The glyn ship wasn't designed to be flown in an atmosphere even in an emergency.

Neither was the *Endeavour*, but they had designed her so that if there was no other alternative, she could *land*.

The glyn ship couldn't take any positive pressure. It wasn't built for it.

"They can't get to us," he whispered.

"Indeed they can't, and that probe doesn't have much longer. They can wait for us to come out, but they can't get to us."

Chang turned to her comms officer. "Broadcast this to the probe."

She tapped on her console. José could not hear it, but he suspected it was some kind of number sequence.

How could you communicate with just numbers?

The answer was you just kept sending them and hoped that the other side had a breakthrough. "And keep analyzing their broadcast. See if you can work out what they might be trying to say."

It did occur to José that some kind of depth charge could hit them here. But that would already have happened, he was sure of it.

He was back to waiting for orders. Sometimes it seemed…

…that he'd spent his life waiting for orders.

He remembered, in this dead time while they hid, while they talked. He remembered boot camp. The desert training.

"This is the closest we have to the surface of Mars."

They hadn't been saying war at that point. Heck, some people had never stopped calling it a police action.

The Martians had always called it war.

Police action. Back by Christmas. Hadn't they said that during World War I?

Christmas, when the entire war had nearly fallen apart. What would the world have been like if the Christmas Truce had held. If all of those men had simply refused to pick up their guns again. The officers couldn't have shot all of them. They couldn't have done anything to those men, and the war would have been over. It was conditioning and fear that had kept them fighting. It was…

They hadn't had the webs. He'd tried to refuse orders, he'd tried, and he'd learned that he couldn't. Which was why he wasn't in prison. Why he was not being blamed for all he had done.

Spiders did what they were told or what they were told was done to them. The web whispered. He wanted rid of it, he always had, but he needed it now, he couldn't live without it. He couldn't *fly* without it. He had to learn to stop hating it.

Spiders couldn't go back to being men. He remembered Obadiah, reaching down from the rubble, stronger than him even then.

It's the little ones you have to watch. He knew a few of those.

And when he'd started working with other countries, he'd realized who you really had to watch.

The 'ladies.' There was nothing nice or delicate about women in combat. Or women in the center chair. Without that experience, he might have bought into Reclaiming stupidity and not respected Chang.

With it…

She was just sitting there, remarkably still. She was an oasis of calm, the anchor that kept them all from panicking. "Two and a half hours," somebody reported. The time limit before they had to leave. He felt the ship creak slightly, like a submarine at depth.

It essentially was one right now, except submarines could be allowed to leak. Starships couldn't. They had to leave soon. Or not soon.

Had he really been sitting here for two and a half hours? Panic started to rise within him, was he losing track of time?

Was his brain just shutting down?

No, he realized.

He'd fallen asleep. And nobody had woken him up, he'd been in that drifting doze when you are asleep but don't realize it.

No doubt they'd decided to leave him. Or not noticed. Sheepish, he shifted positions into one which was less comfortable, intentionally letting the seat dig into his back. Checked his harness.

They'd have woken him if they'd needed to move, surely.

"We should leave," said the *Atlantis* XO. What was…Slava, that was right. Slava Koroskeva.

"No," Chang said. "I leave nobody behind."

Perhaps that was a daydream, but it sounded like a promise. It elicited a murmuration of sighs on the bridge. It was a promise to her crew. A promise José hoped she could keep.

"We could all die."

"Trust me," she said. She was waiting. And José knew why she had let him sleep. So he would be fresh. But it needed to be Lieutenant Lauxon here.

His genius only worked in hyperspace. In real space he was only competent. A thought rose up, as if it was the web's or the ship's not his own.

Jumping out of an atmosphere.

Jumping *into* an atmosphere had to be possible too. Dangerous, but possible. He could see it in his mind.

He started to calculate where to jump to. Out and back, into the atmosphere. But they would have to...they didn't have...

...and that was where the time had gone, at least some of it. He hadn't been here two and a half hours. Because they had to jump out of atmosphere, into atmosphere, out again.

It was the only way.

They still, though, had to leave the Verrans behind.

16

The captain stood and walked up behind his chair. "Mr. Marin."

He hadn't realized it until now, but she was treating him like an officer. He wasn't one, and wasn't sure he wanted to be. He wanted to be...he realized he *was* where he wanted to be.

Habit for bridge crew. "Yes, ma'am."

"How do you feel about trying to jump *into* an atmosphere?"

"It can be done," he said evenly. "I was thinking about it."

"It might be the only way to get us away from the glyn without leaving Lauxon and Jordan behind."

She didn't have to tell him that they didn't want to leave the women behind. And who was the third person with them? One of the *Atlantis* crew. Purcell, that was it. "Or Purcell."

She nodded. "Exactly. So, I need you to be ready to try it."

Even if it got them all killed or...was there a worse fate that might come from misjudging? He thought, for the first time in a while, of the tiny black hole in their back pocket. The controlled singularity.

If it imploded, they might be frozen at the event horizon forever, and he didn't want to think about that.

Didn't want to, but his palms were sweating again. "I can't promise it will work."

He didn't tell her the consequences. She knew them better than he did, likely. She was practiced at this. And she was weighing the risks.

She was risking the ship to save three people.

And he found he was perfectly okay with being risked. Maybe not everyone on board was. Or maybe it was easier when you were the one who had to get them out of it. In control. Like not being travel sick if you were the one driving. But he was a soldier, a veteran. You didn't leave a man behind.

The web whispered at the tips of his fingers. As if it thought it could. For almost the first time, he smiled at it, inwardly. For once the web and he were on the same side, together.

Maybe *Endeavour* thought it could, but the ship didn't think. One day, perhaps, ships would think. Not this one. Not even as much as a dog or a cat or a horse thought.

He'd gone riding a couple of times as a child, on the beach. On quiet mornings before the sunbathing crowd emerged. The power of the animal between his legs, the feeling of having something so large under his control. He could see why some people became all but addicted to it.

He wasn't one of those people. But he could understand it. The ship. The animal.

Chang nodded. Went back to her seat. Trusting him, or perhaps trusting the web. It was the web more than him.

He was a tool of it, and he shivered.

You couldn't disobey orders. It would flow through you, it would affect adrenalin levels. It would, if it had to, make you hate. The web and the conditioning working together, so that you hated.

Then you came out of that hate and the thing you hated the most was yourself.

He waited, his hands on the controls. The probe was still sniffing around them.

Chang sat back down. Strapped herself in. She turned slightly to the woman still standing in the back. "Get to a take hold point. Now."

Comms, over the intercom. "Take hold. Take hold."

Breathe, José told himself. If he failed to do this, this thing which had never been attempted before by a human, they would all die.

No pressure, he thought, wryly.

"Now, Marin."

No Mister this time, saving those two syllables.

He brought the controls backwards. In a crackle of orange lightning, *Endeavour* jumped.

Crackling. Storm extending away from them, and what damage was it doing to this already ravaged world?

José didn't want to know. At some levels, he didn't want to care. The fact that there would be nobody under it made him feel a little better, a little less like he was ruining everything for them.

There was very little down there to ruin, at this point. Gravity, inexorable. Like a black hole, like the singularity that let them punch through into hyperspace.

Hovering in the atmosphere. Positive pressure, still, but not nearly as much. Come on, he mentally willed the people on the surface. Get your butts up here so we can leave.

Leave the Verrans to their fate?

Hope the glyn could...but maybe nobody could. Worlds had lifespans. The universe had a lifespan. Somebody had told him that before he was ready for the knowledge.

He'd been terrified of the Big Crunch happening tomorrow for months, of being crumpled up like paper.

There it was, the shuttle. Their missing crew members. The bay would be opening for them, operated automatically. A computer could handle that, opening doors, closing them once the shuttle was inside.

He didn't take his hands off the controls. There was a headache forming behind his eyes, but he didn't and couldn't.

Had to be ready to jump, ready to dive towards the planet, to bounce off it, to slingshot into hyperspace. Where the stars promised and whispered to him. He was sure he could hear them even now, even in real space.

He was going insane.

That was the logical explanation. Going insane, but it didn't matter. As long as he could save them all, he'd give up what remained of his sanity. A madman wouldn't have to live with what lay behind his eyes. A madman could simply enjoy flying. Yet he wanted to be sane, now he had a purpose to his sanity.

The doors closing, he could feel it through the ship. He jumped without being given the order. Jumped to another system, the next one over. Not further from Earth, but kind of around the curve.

He felt real space coalesce around him, released the controls and slumped. Not quite passing out, but on the edge of it, a wave of exhaustion and starlight washing over him. Whatever was going on, whatever he was becoming, he had given everything he could. "Ma'am...permission..."

"Go. Mr. Taylor, take over."

That was the navigator, who could presumably handle the ship until a pilot got there.

He staggered from the bridge, he needed a headache remedy. A shower, but he couldn't luxuriate in one. A nap.

He felt as if his skin was sloughing off, so dry it had become. Exhaustion. Just exhaustion, but there was something else.

The web was so silent that he felt almost as if he was a boy again, no cares. No worries. A trail that ran through the jungle, wooden with those low rails on the side. No mud. Nothing at the other end but his mother.

Well, no, almost no worries. Even then there had been worries. About money. About survival. Would they have enough to eat? Were the megastorms really over? They had stopped, but nobody ever believed they had ended. They had stopped and there had been enough food, finally. The tourists had come back. But then, as a boy, they had not known whether the island would survive.

Had feared exile or worse. There had not been enough food, then, in those dark times. There had not been enough of anything.

He couldn't abandon the Verrans.

He had to.

Ocean and beach and sky and the heat of the subtropical sun. Everything a boy could need, if it didn't come with that sense of dread.

Had their world had oceans, once? It must have.

He made it to his quarters. Made it to his bunk. Even got his shoes off before he sank into it, just the way he was.

José slept.

He was not sure how much time had passed when he woke up. When he checked, he had slept for twelve hours.

Nobody had disturbed him. Perhaps they had put a medical hold on, not to wake him until he woke up on his own. Perhaps everyone was too busy.

His bunkmates were absent. He slowly got up. Showered and changed. Headed for the mess hall. Now he was awake, he was hungry, almost ridiculously so, but he had to shower first. That dryness of his skin was still there.

He was sick, he decided. He was definitely sick. Maybe Lauxon would know something about it, maybe he had just made too many jumps, too quickly, and none of them easy. Wearing against his brain and body. Wearing him thin.

He didn't care what the food was, he just grabbed some stew which the galley had put out, not even looking at it.

It was just fuel at this point. But he was alive. More to the point, so was everyone else. He wasn't the most important person here, not by a long shot.

Obadiah, stepping inside. "You're awake."

"Spying on me, amigo?" José asked, weakly. Friend. Sometimes he wished Obadiah had been more, but friend would definitely do.

"You did sleep for twelve hours. I'm supposed to tell medical if you have any symptoms other than exhaustion."

The web whispered. José knew he should speak up, should talk about it. About the dryness of his skin. "I think I just made one jump too many."

"That'll do it, I'm told. Your brain uses a lot of your body's energy and you were working it pretty hard. Much harder than we ever did on Mars."

A joke, that, that infantry didn't think. "Speak for yourself. *I* was doing robot repair.

Obadiah laughed. "Yeah, when we weren't...ya know, it doesn't take much smarts to point and shoot."

"You don't want smart people," José said, bitterly. "If we were too smart, we'd think about what we were doing, and if we thought about it... So...where are we?"

"A binary star system with no planets. Good choice, I reckon."

"I wasn't choosing. I was jumping blind. Just trying to get away from those aliens." The crazy, beautiful. "What do you think was with them?"

"I think they had a rogue subordinate who didn't like the look of us. Or they didn't like the look of us at all and were stalling until they got into position to fire."

Obadiah would think like that. José nodded. "But why would they not like the look of us?"

"Same as the other guys, I reckon. We're upstart newcomers in their territory."

It didn't ring true, not quite. "I doubt they all have the same motives. I mean, humans have a crazy enough variety, people from different planets?"

People who had evolved in different ways, on different worlds. People who thought differently, ate differently, mated differently.

"True. But it does seem like..."

José shook his head. "They were peaceful, then they weren't. I'm thinking rogue subordinate."

Maybe every species had its xenophobes. "Maybe they had a

closeted Nazi or similar on board."

Obadiah shuddered. "Space Nazis. That's the last thing we need."

"But from what the Verrans said..." From what they said, they had people like that. Maybe, probably, every world did...

17

José recovered. For now, at least, he felt as if he was a person again, not just the web supporting him, puppeting him.

Just like during the war, except there had never been that feeling. No, it had been his own idea to lift the weapon. This time he was more aware of it. This time he and it were partners, if aggressive ones.

What if they had lied? What if they had blamed the web for the things he had done to get him off, to help him avoid being arrested and tried for war crimes?

Blaming the web made everything tidy. It was nobody's fault, it was the eggheads and they just hadn't planned for all of the variables.

Maybe they hadn't planned for the kids.

But this had been different, this was the web having a mind of its own, the ship having a mind of its own. He remembered that ride again, along the beach. Petra's horse had developed such a mind of its own, had taken off up the beach at what he later found out was actually a slow canter, not a flat out run.

It had looked like a flat out run at the time.

The ship could not have a mind of its own, nor could the web. Hallucinations. The observation lounge, dimmed to protect from the radiation of the two suns. One white, one red. No planets, no life. Nothing here but a way station, a place you could jump to on the way to some place else.

He supposed there was no need for interstellar truck stops.

Or maybe there was no somewhere else. A backwater. A place between nowhere and nowhere, like the tired old diner that one time, when some of them had gotten a three day pass and just driven, a day out, stay there, a day back.

Driven at random through the landscape of Chile. Eaten in a little restaurant, the food far too spicy for the white guy with them. They'd teased him, called him Mayo for the only condiment he would use, until he became proud of it. It hadn't been nice of them.

Where was he now? José let his hands curl on the rails as he remembered.

Mayo was in a shallow grave on Mars, as were so many. Where they would not even decompose unless the Martians put them under their gardens.

Not until and unless Mars was terraformed, and there were fights, arguments. Whether it was the right thing to do.

Whether any of this was the right thing to do.

Some people thought humans should have stayed on Earth, but he wasn't on Earth. He was here, listening to the stars in his web and wondering if he was dying or going mad.

"Penny for them?"

Cecilie Lauxon. He turned, slightly, to face her. Taking in her pale face and dark hair, an almost Snow White variance in coloring. "I don't know if they're worth a penny."

"An austerity penny," she quipped.

He laughed, weakly. "Still. I was thinking. I was remembering a guy I knew," he finally admitted, honesty winning out. "A guy from boot camp."

"What did he do that was memorable?"

"Try to eat Chilean food. I think he was one of those white guys who thinks non-spicy chili is a thing."

Cecilie laughed. "I never cared much for chili. Don't like beans."

José nodded. "I think it's my favorite American food. So much of what white Americans eat is boring. But yeah. Mayo, we called him, because that was the only condiment he could tolerate."

"Bad race joke." She made a bit of a face. Then, quietly, "Feeling better?"

"Yes. I wore myself out."

No, the web whispered through him. Liar.

But if he told her, if he told anyone, they would…would what?

Would run tests, would find out. Would…probably never let him jump the ship again.

So, he didn't tell her. He couldn't. He was happy for the first time since his boyhood. How could he give that up?

* * *

Taking his turn on the bridge, José was starting to think that was a bad idea. He was sure and certain that the ship *wanted* to jump, wanted him at the controls.

Just like that horse that day on the beach, it wanted to run away.

He was hallucinating.

No, he thought. He was explaining. He had feelings that didn't translate well, and anthropomorphizing the ship explained them as well as anything. It was the stars that called to him, and the darkness between them.

Some writers of horror put monsters in that darkness, things older than man and indifferent to him.

Things like what was destroying Verr.

Sensor alert. A ship coming out of jump.

"They found us," comms said, evenly.

He kept his hands where they were; he thought if they were on the jump controls he might twitch. He twitched anyway, but nothing came of it. Wishing Lauxon was up here.

Wishing got him nothing.

"Let's try talking to them again." Chang kept her own tone equally even. "But from a nice distance, this time."

A nice distance would mean time lag, but perhaps it was worth it, given the alternatives. A few seconds of lag would even give the computers time to handle their translations.

Then their message came over comms. In very broken, simplified English.

"Sorry. Crewman. Trouble."

Well, that was progress. They must have, José thought, better AI, more able to work out language from what the *Endeavour* had sent. Maybe if they had Earth's television broadcasts they could talk like 1920s gangsters.

He'd have to share that line with Obadiah, the one person he was sure would appreciate it. In the meantime.

"We understand. No damage was done."

"You jump. Planet."

"We had people down there."

There was no response, not even after the minute or so lag, not even after several times that lag. José started to relax. No response was good and bad, or maybe it was simply no response. Maybe they had stumped the glyn.

Maybe it wasn't in their makeup to risk the entire ship to save three people. Maybe they didn't have quite the same social sense.

Heck, maybe they were some kind of hive mind, or they had everyone's minds uploaded so it didn't matter if people died. The old cyberpunk wet dream.

José was not sure he ever wanted his mind to be uploaded. But he didn't want to die either.

The web whispering, not wanting to die. Maybe…no.

Hallucinations. Rationalizations. There was nothing spiritual about this, consciousness was electromagnetic.

So was the web.

So was the ship.

So were the glyn. They had to be, that crystal coating, conducting. He would have to talk to Jordan. Maybe she had some idea what it was made of.

Exoskeleton.

That was the word. Finally, a response. "Send us. Words."

Chang glanced at the others. Made a cutting gesture at comms. "Send them words."

"So they can run them through their translation algorithm. They must have a good one."

"Anything we send them."

The navigator looked sheepish. "Send them my collection of romance novels."

"That's…brilliant."

Romance novels? José side-eyed the man. Not many men admitted to reading romance novels. It took courage to admit to it, courage José respected in somebody who, from his knowledge, had grown up during Reclaiming, when men were men and women…

José didn't really like any kind of novel, himself. He was a visual man, who preferred his entertainment on a screen.

But…romance novels would reveal human culture without showing any Earth secrets.

"Go ahead, but pull out any that describe constellations."

Let's not give them the location of Earth, José translated.

Abruptly he wondered if the glyn would reciprocate.

And what constituted romance to them.

Whatever the glyn were doing, it was taking a while. José admired Chang for her ability to look past what had happened.

Then again, believing them, or pretending to, might be the most diplomatic choice under the circumstances.

You believed people, you extended that bit of trust. You set aside the fact that it might have been a test.

Maybe the glyn had been all set to destroy them and changed their mind when they saw them risk the *Endeavour* for a couple of stray people. Maybe that was heroism to them. Maybe it was behavior so inexplicable that they wanted to study humans.

José didn't mind being studied if they could get some studying back. Shift over, Lauxon on the bridge, he made his way to the mess hall.

He almost went to sickbay instead. He felt a little stiff. It was probably just putting in too much time sitting in a chair.

He probably needed to get on the exercise bike once he'd had something to eat.

Obadiah, in conversation with one of the *Atlantis* people. It looked heated, and José gave them a wide berth, instead putting together a sandwich from galley stuff. Cheese and bread. Simple supplies. They had to be getting low.

Or maybe the cheese wasn't really cheese. Not having major food intolerances or allergies had been one of the criteria for even getting on this ship. In the future, they could accommodate stuff like that.

Right now, it was just one more problem factor. He sat down, took a bite. Yeah, he was pretty sure the cheese was as fake as an American excuse for queso. He didn't really care.

They might be able to...no. He was pretty sure whatever the glyn ate wouldn't be palatable to humans, and vice versa. There was protein chirality, too. If the proteins mapped the wrong way, the good news was that you couldn't be infected by anything. The bad news was you couldn't digest anything you ate.

Maybe they would negotiate with aliens about that. You have the right proteins for this world, we don't; what will you give us for it? Haggling over planets.

Haggling over real estate, which had to be valuable. Real estate, knowledge, trashy romance novels.

Art.

We should send them pictures, he thought. He looked around, feeling abruptly alone, isolated. Wanting company with his food after all.

Humans, social creatures. Especially when it came to eating. What was that old story about the species who ate in private and mated in public? He didn't remember. He'd never read it. It was just something tossed about.

In the barracks, in Chile, when they'd jokingly speculated about alien contact. Somebody'd brought that up.

Somebody else had brought up cannons being out as a sign of respect. Misunderstandings that could get people killed, could start wars.

Could destroy worlds.

That was the stakes they were playing with elsewhere. It was easy to destroy worlds.

It was far, far harder to save one.

18

A knock came on the door of the robot workshop. José was mostly there to...

...hide wasn't the right word.

Think. That was it. Think, in private. Which meant hiding, on a ship this size. He didn't dare ask them to go away.

"Who's there?"

"Me," came Lieutenant Lauxon's voice. She slipped into the room. "Just making sure you were decent."

He couldn't argue with her, not given how the chain (or in some cases braid) of command worked around here. "What do you need?" he asked, keeping it appropriately polite.

He couldn't snap at her either, no matter how much he wanted to.

"Nothing too onerous, I promise," she said in her French-accented voice. "We need to talk."

"I'm fine," he said, too quickly.

"Well, about that too. I can tell you're having web problems. Pretty soon, everyone else will be able to tell too."

José let his head sink into his hands. "I don't think there's anything that can be done. A reset didn't help at all."

"And infantry webs can't be removed." Lauxon took a deep breath. "But I respect you. I know you might be stubborn as they come, but I also know you're smart."

He was.

But there was, he was sure, nothing that could be done about this kind of subtle overload. The web couldn't be removed...any attempt to do so would leave him dead or paralyzed. The overload would simply continue until it killed him. He had already started to accept that. He wanted to keep this life, this purpose while he had it. "I really don't think..."

"I think your web needs to be reprogrammed. But I don't know if anyone on the ship could do it," she said, finally. "But this really isn't about that."

"Is it about Verr?"

She nodded. "We need a plan, and neither Chang nor Wilson thinks anything can be done."

"Meaning we need to sneakily come up with a plan, make it really good, then hand them a fait accompli." That was sometimes how things worked in the military, and he'd heard it was pretty much always how they worked in the navy.

Lauxon grinned. "Exactly. Are you in?"

"I'm a mechanic. I don't know how much help I'll be."

"You know robots. And you're the one who mentioned railguns."

"So does Doctor Jordan, or is she..."

"Jordan's more than in. She's determined. She won't let a civilization be destroyed before she's had a chance to fully study it."

José laughed. "Does she realize it's going to end anyway? That even if we save them, what they've built...unless we really do find a way to move their planet."

"Moving their planet would probably have the same effect as the gravitational tug anyway. No, you're right. The Verran civilization is doomed. But we might be able to save their people."

José nodded. "Railgun."

"That's the best idea we have right now. So, talk to me about railguns."

José shook his head. "I only know the basic concept. I know that it's not really feasible to build one on Earth, but possible on Mars."

"Except the Martians won't. Because they don't want to use their best site because..."

"Because they want to keep Olympus Mons pristine for tourists," José quipped. "I mean, if it's not a Martian National Park yet..."

"I actually heard they designated the Opportunity lander site as their first."

José grinned a bit. "Of course they did. But I thought that was already done, and just reconfirmed."

He forced himself back on trail. "So, railguns."

"I don't even know the basics. Educate me?"

"Hold on here. I can actually do a demo. Anyone else need to see?"

She considered. "How about after dinner? Will you need more space?"

"A bit." He grinned. He remembered his high school science teacher doing this one.

It was kind of fun.

"So, the basic principle is simple. It's used on naval ships and sometimes on military ships. Doesn't have the controlled range of a missile or torpedo, you can't change trajectory mid-flight," José explained to the group.

He set down the somewhat cumbersome device. "This is a demonstration gun. It won't fire anything fast enough to damage the hull, but everyone should stay behind him."

What he'd put together had about the same kind of force as an air rifle, deliberately. "The current running through the rails creates a magnetic field, which launches the projectile." Making sure everyone was behind him, he fired. The small metal pellet went across the room and landed by the far wall.

"Naval railguns can blow the top off a mountain. Space railguns can do a lot of damage to another ship, but with the limitations I mentioned. Easier to dodge than missiles."

"And railguns for space launches?"

"Normally prohibitive. The amount of energy you need to store would require capacitors the size of a small city. They've done some stuff with small projectiles from Luna."

"Verr has Earth gravity."

"Verr also has a problem." José pulled it up on the screen. "Namely Lucifer. What we actually do is fire the payloads towards the gas giant. Get the angle right, and they won't go into the other planet. They'll just go into space."

"What about the G forces?" Obadiah asked. "That's the other issue. Artgrav won't give that level of inertial protection."

"That's all in the projectile design. But we'll probably need the G-tanks they were experimenting with. The gel. Which we can make easily enough."

Obadiah nodded, satisfied.

Lauxon walked over to the demonstration gun. "May I?"

José stepped to one side.

She fired. "Always wanted to play with one of these."

He laughed. "They didn't turn out to be as useful in space as we thought they might be. But the concept is fun. The other advantage, you aren't shooting as much fuel as payload."

Obadiah nodded. "What about keeping the railgun in one piece down there?"

"It's more efficient to put most of it in a tunnel anyway. We'll need a mountain, but the locals can help with that." José had to assume the locals would help.

"That might be more of a challenge than you think." Jordan, from the doorway. "They aren't universally going to want to leave."

"I know that," he said.

"As in, some of them think this is God's judgment on their sins," Jordan said, sadly. "I wish we could...but we can't." She smiled. "I got enough of their language to know that there are doomsday cults down there. Which I'd find amusing, but..."

"We can only save people who want to be saved." José tapped the gun. "But we need the means to do so. And once the station is built..."

"Then panic will probably take care of getting as many people up there as possible. But..." Jordan frowned. "There's something about this I don't like, but I can't put my finger on it. You're right, though. We have to try."

Which meant, José knew, getting the plan past Chang and Wilson. He firmly believed they would listen.

Chang, he knew, cared.

And they did have other help. Or did they?

Lauxon flew the jump back to the Verran system. The glyn were slightly faster in hyperspace, it seemed.

José wondered how long they'd been doing this for. He wondered what humanity would turn into, doing this, being out here. Working with these people. Learning not to be xenophobic.

Of course, they'd done aptitude testing. They'd tested people for xenophobia as best they could before letting them on this ship.

José was surprised it had worked as well as it had. The multi-ethnic crew probably helped. A rainbow slice of humanity. All the shades of brown and tan there were.

Which might give the aliens too good an impression of them. Or would they understand they were seeing a carefully chosen elite.

But he was still waiting for the other shoe to drop. For somebody to say openly that they should not even talk to the Verrans, let alone try to help them.

For somebody to say… He shook his head. If there was anyone who felt like that on the ship, they had the sense not to voice it.

Somebody on the glyn ship had fired on them. Somebody over there had failed whatever test of xenophobia they put their crews through.

Or it had been some kind of weird test. He wasn't discounting that, he wasn't assuming they told the truth. But now they were in the Verr system again.

Well, the…had they gotten their word for sun? The sun might not be hugely important to people who lived underground, but once they had walked proud on their world's surface.

Once, they must have appreciated the sun. Or perhaps the stars. Had they had a moon, which had already been swallowed by Lucifer?

That world was both well and poorly named. It was bringing Armageddon, but it was not its fault; it was the inexorable laws of gravity. Still, it was El Diablo in so many ways, if not like the devil of his childhood.

You couldn't mess with gravity. You could fake it with magnetic forces, which was about how artgrav worked.

But you couldn't change it. It was the weakest and strongest force in the universe, reaching out into hyperspace. Affecting everything, affected by everything. Mass seeking mass.

He wondered if the glyn knew what it was. He stared at Lucifer.

"Makes you wish we could put that thing back where it came from." C.T. Wilson, of all people, pointing at the gas giant.

"We can't," José said. "Maybe one day. But at that point…I think if we had the ability to move worlds around like billiard balls? At that point we won't be human anymore."

Wilson looked thoughtful. "Maybe we won't be human for much longer anyway, in the way we think of it."

José shook his head. "As long as we love, as long as we struggle. As long as we at least occasionally have to face our own mortality…"

"By that definition the Verrans are human."

José nodded. "They are. And maybe evolution doesn't matter."

"Of course, do they…" Wilson paused. "They must love, because that's just how a social sense looks from inside. But do they fall in love?"

José considered that. "As far as I can tell, no." He glanced at the XO. "Who is it?"

C.T. laughed. "That's none of your business, Mr. Marin."

He knew it wasn't. "I know, but I couldn't resist."

"I want you to keep your eyes open. Somebody on this ship isn't behind helping the Verrans."

José nodded. "I already am. There has to be at least one."

"There has to be," C.T. agreed and then vanished.

José wondered if this was him hiding being the one who wasn't behind it.

Or maybe he wasn't, but was doing it anyway. He might never know.

19

Wilson's words did have José looking for trouble.

The obvious center was the XO of the *Atlantis*. Slava Koroskeya. He found her sitting in the mess hall, fidgeting with something small.

"Hey."

She looked up at him. "You. The golden child pilot." The sarcasm in her tone melded with her accent. He could understand her bitterness. She had gone from XO to superfluous.

José shrugged. "I can't exactly help it." Maybe he would get more sympathy if he told her what was going on. About the web whispering to him, about the growing feeling that the stars wanted him. About how that might relate to what had happened with the first webs. He knew they'd tested the technology on criminals. Or on people in vegetative states. He knew what it had done to them, hallucinations, madness, death.

They'd saved some of the latter. Allowed them a half-life. Some, they could even give a full life. Except on Mars, where the fledgling republic had banned web technology. She wasn't webbed. She wouldn't be sympathetic. He dismissed the idea as born out of his own fears rather than whet he needed to talk about.

She shrugged. "Doesn't matter whether you do it on purpose or not. You're going to be an officer if they can get Earth to sign off on it."

José shuddered. "Not if I have anything to do with it."

Her eyebrow arched. "You don't want..."

"What I wanted was to be left alone, to fit back in. To go home," José said, glancing at his hands. "When I couldn't have that, I decided I'd settle for being wanted out here. Being useful. I found myself more useful than I expected, but what I want is...I want *this*. All of it." And it would not, could not last, but that bittersweet feeling was leaning towards the sweet.

"So why are you going around tossing out ideas to save a bunch of furries?" she asked, finally.

"Because it's the right thing to do." He couldn't say more than that.

"They're not human, and we probably can't save them anyway."

A pause. "We're not glyn," he said. "We're not…whatever they are that blew up your ship."

She shuddered. "Monsters. They're monsters."

"What makes you say that?"

She turned towards him. Something in her eyes. "You haven't seen them. You don't know what it's like."

"Tell me."

"They look at you. They breathe. They don't even have a nose, they just have a mouth. No, they have a maw, it's full of teeth, and they move, and all you want is to find a gun and shoot!" Her voice rose.

"Then I know exactly what it's like." He reached out to put his hand on hers. "I know *exactly* what it's like, except they were human. As human as me, as human as you. They just made them monsters to me."

He took a deep breath. "That's why you fired. Because you saw monsters, because you saw something you couldn't understand. But that doesn't make them monsters."

What did it make them? Products of a different evolution. A pause. "It makes them predators. You felt like prey."

"I did."

And that was the key thing about the conditioning. The thing nobody understood. It didn't turn you into a predator.

It turned you into prey.

He watched her go, but there was a thoughtful expression on her face. So, now he knew.

Now he knew what the brass was sitting on about the Eridani aliens. He knew why there was a war. Because they made everyone who looked at them into conditioned spiders.

Maybe that was what they needed to talk to them. Could he overcome it because he'd learned to overcome the other? Could he… but the Verrans didn't have that effect. Nor did the glyn.

It was something specific. Something that could and had to be overcome. Knowing what it was gave him hope that there could be peace. "They must think we're barbarians" he said to himself, or perhaps to the *Endeavour*.

He was starting to think he loved the ship more than any woman or any man he had been with. Which was probably bad. The web instead of sex.

Maybe that was what he needed. Maybe he needed to get laid, but he'd been trying to avoid it. Fraternization brought complications. It created the kind of drama they couldn't afford out here.

He glanced at where Koroskeya had gone. Wondered about her. Of course she hated the aliens; she might never stop hating them. But maybe she could learn not to be prey.

Anyone could learn not to be prey. He remembered sometimes back on the island. He remembered a man smelling of smoke, of tobacco and of something else. Might have been crack. Certainly wasn't weed. He knew that sweet smell. Smoking wasn't really socially acceptable anymore. It was something only assholes did. He remembered the faint sound of reggaeton in the background, he wasn't sure if it had really been there or if it had been some melody stuck in his head, some mental soundtrack to the scene. No, likely it had been real, drifting out of the window of a house from which nobody saw nothing.

How he'd been pushing a woman up against the wall. José, on leave, the web sparkling in his hands. Seeing this.

Seeing a monster, seeing a woman turned into prey, he had lost control.

He had killed the man.

It had been the last leave he had before the war. The last leave any of them had. They'd ruled it justified, he'd been stopping a rape.

But they'd also said he couldn't control himself. That wasn't true. He could. No, he couldn't, but it wasn't the web making him do it.

It was the web empowering him to do it. He remembered how the man's throat had felt when his hand had struck it, the faint crunch. The...he had no idea what to call it.

He had no idea. So, he sat there, pushing aside those memories. He had killed that man, not the web.

And he would do it again, if the circumstances were the same. But there was nobody to kill here, nobody to fight. The web's excitement for it died down slowly.

He thought of the stars, and it died down further. Focused on them.

Obadiah came into the room. "What did you say to Koroskeya?"

"I told her that thinking an alien looks like a monster isn't much different from being conditioned to see humans as monsters."

Obadiah blinked, laughed, then sat down. "The aliens look like monsters."

"The Eridani aliens. The ones we're at war with. That's what the captain isn't telling us."

"Maybe she doesn't want us to react the same way."

He considered that. "No, I think she just wants to sort out what's going on." Chang was a secretive woman. A good captain, but not prone to socializing with her crew. "She'll tell us."

"When the time is right. Or maybe when we aren't thinking about so many other things. She's talking to the glyn."

José hoped that there would be no terrible mistranslations.

He hoped they could work together.

The glyn were on board the *Endeavour*, thus proving they could survive in the same atmosphere and gravity as humans.

Specifically, they were in Chang's office. José knew better than to try and eavesdrop, but as he started to go past, "Mr Marin."

He turned on his heel and poked his head into the room.

"Come in, please," Chang said.

He slid into the office. The two glyn, being longer and shorter than humans, took up an inordinate amount of the available space. "Hello," one of them chimed.

They could speak English then, or at least a few words of it. Maybe they'd do better with Cantonese, he thought with amusement. Or maybe however they produced sound…it seemed to be by rubbing things together like a cricket.

"Hello," he said, feeling his heart rate increase, feeling the web whisper worried nothings under his skin.

They were beautiful and terrible and they were utterly alien.

"Mr. Marin is the one who suggested railguns to use the gravitational flux to get payloads off of the planet."

The glyn tilted part of itself, perhaps a head, but they didn't really have a head. He definitely was sure what eyes it had were on him.

It was unfair. They, he switched in his mind. You didn't think of sentient beings as its. "Uh…yeah."

"It might be workable. From the math we have done, we have ten Earth years before the atmospheric loss renders the surface uninhabitable. Their domes might last as long as thirty."

José reached up to touch his hair. "That's time."

"It is. The ky'iin would be great help, if we can convince them to stop fighting you."

So, the Eridani aliens had a name. Ky'iin. José stored it in his brain, did his best to replace all other thoughts with it.

It was different enough that it had to be their name for themselves. And did...did the glyn just offer to help stop the war between them and Earth?

It seemed like they did. "Can I ask...do you care about us fighting, other than this?"

The glyn chimed at each other. "War bad for trade," the other one said, a bit brokenly.

José decided that was fair enough. "Except trade in weapons."

That got a higher, brighter chime. Was it a laugh?

Chang was laughing too. "Certainly true. But war is bad in so many ways. I think even aliens can agree on that."

What else could aliens agree on? He wasn't sure, although he did at least get a good look at their shining exteriors. They were more pearlescent than translucent, he decided.

"Railguns are a thought. But we have a better one, if it can be done. Using some of the same technology."

José held his breath. "You do?"

"Reinforce their city so it can hold against vacuum and just fly the entire thing off the planet."

He stared at them. As if they thought that could be done. But the tinkerer part of his brain could see it.

He could see it. It could be done.

The web whispered treacherously, about how he could never trust these people.

He ignored it.

20

"They're crazy," Obadiah said. "The issue would be..."

"No they aren't. Remember that we used Mars' moons to create bases. Admittedly, that's..."

"They're already in orbit," the head of security cut him off with. "It's the idea of trying to sustain structural integrity through the lift. Even if we did it by weakening the rock so Lucifer could do the work for us, which might be possible, we'd still have to keep it in one piece."

José tapped his fingers on the table, feeling small shocks run through him. The web was getting worse. He had to admit it.

It needed to be reprogrammed. But he couldn't bring himself to ask, to see if anyone here could fix it.

Was it because he was afraid that if it was fixed, he'd lose everything? Or was he afraid that it couldn't be? He was afraid the web was going to kill him. "We do. How about...hrm..."

He frowned a bit, and pulled out his phone, activating the display. "If we created snakes of metal and wove them down through the bedrock..."

"...making a net."

"I was thinking a web." Their eyes met. It was all about webs and spiders, wasn't it?

"I think I prefer net," Obadiah said wryly. Then, "You really need to talk to somebody about yours. I can tell it's not working right."

"Do you think anyone here can fix it?" José sighed, pushed himself back. "You're right."

"Are you afraid that if it's fixed you'll be back to being just a mechanic?"

A pause. "No," he said finally. "I'm afraid that if it's fixed I won't be able to get us out of the next tight spot. I thought I wanted to go back to being the guy who fixed robots. Maybe I don't. But more than that...." He could never have what he had left again, they had made that clear to him. The streets of San Juan, taking money from the tourists in exchange for the kind of local color even their AR units couldn't give them, making that bit of extra cash. Being island color in a brightly colored shirt, after high school. Things that changed and stayed eternally the same, a city rebuilt to look as if it had never been destroyed. As if Leonidas had never come.

He wanted the hurricane-torn sands. The things he could never go back to. That might not still be there.

If the aliens started using kinetic weapons on Earth, then nothing he knew might be there when and if they ever got back. If there was...

...no. He doubted the ky'iin had planet busters. If such a thing existed, they might even be able to use it to solve this problem. "Altering the planet's orbit isn't going to work," he added.

"No. It's not a bad idea, as an idea, but it won't work," Obadiah predicted, a little sadly. "I think we should go back to railguns."

"I think," José said finally, "we need to go down there and talk to them. We've got an entire planet full of people down there. Some of them are geniuses." By the law of averages, some of them *had* to be. They could be wracking their brains and ignoring the Verran Einstein.

No, they didn't need Einstein.

"We need to know where their biggest university for engineering is," Obadiah quipped. "Their equivalent to MIT."

"You're right. We do." A pause. "What do you think our chances are of being allowed to go look?"

They were still...he frowned.

"Let's talk to Doctor Jordan. She may already have thought of it."

José had the fleeting thought that they would be quite screwed without Jordan. He dismissed it, for now.

There were others who could manage if she was gone.

As the walked into the city, José looked up. The dome kept out the weather, kept in a cleaner atmosphere.

Could it take the sort of forces the glyn thought it could? The air was definitely cleaner in here, but what about the pressure? He thought about the *Endeavour*, its double hull, its design to keep air in.

The dome hadn't been designed for that, it had been designed to keep weather out. Because that was what the locals thought they needed.

That the climate had gone to pot. They thought it was their fault, they carried some kind of guilt with them.

More guilt than the people responsible for Earth's climate going to pot, which really had been their fault. It was good now, a new equilibrium, civilization adapting to the fact that there were days on which it was simply too hot to go outside.

Día de playa hirviendo, they called them where he was from. When standing on the sand would give you burns. A term coined during the worst of the climate crisis, when they had feared they would lose everything. When they feared there would be nothing of their land and people left but dismal refugees on northern shores. Día de playa hirviendo. Boiling beach days.

But it had got no worse than that. And one day it would probably cool off again. Heck, one day there would be an ice age.

Verr was going to die.

And it wasn't their fault. It was ill luck, it was the universe against them. It wasn't even a test of resilience because, by definition, the test of Job had to be something you could survive.

But he was making notes. How did they keep this place intact? The web whispered, as if it had an answer for him, but that answer was in no language he spoke or had even heard, it was in the chimes of the glyn.

Doctor Jordan was speaking with the Verrans, gesticulating. Struggling across a language barrier. They - he still was not sure how to sex Verrans - were gesticulating back. Pointing up at the dome. Their university affiliation was visible in medallions they wore.

He stepped forward. "It's theoretically possible, but it's going to take years of work." How much they understood, he didn't know. He couldn't tell. He pointed at the dome, then at the floor beneath their feet.

They had ten years to make the city airtight. Twenty more to teach it to fly.

And then the rest of their lives to decide what to do after that.

The Verran turned to him. "And those who won't?" they managed.

"You can't help people who won't be helped." He was likely reminding himself. There were other Verran cities. Other places where these people lived. And they didn't like each other.

Perhaps the disaster had stopped a war, but if so it hadn't done it by bringing them together. Quite the opposite.

They were at peace because there was no way to fight a war.

"And if they attack?"

José had no answer to that. He glanced at Jordan. This species couldn't afford violence.

It certainly could destroy itself in the very moment of escape from this dying world.

Jordan glanced at him. She brushed back a braid. "My feeling is that we try to help all of the cities. And then, perhaps, we can get them to go in different directions."

The cities couldn't leave this system, though. The people could. "If Earth and Mars can fight..." He tailed off. "It's not our problem, is it?"

He'd gotten what he wanted, to come back down here and talk to these Verrans. And they seemed to be on board with the glyn's radical idea.

Which made it an engineering problem.

He glanced up at the dome again. And heard a faint booming thud, a sound he knew only too well.

"Me cago en ná," he swore.

"What was that?" Jordan asked.

"A bomb," José said, shortly. Civilians often hesitated. If you'd been in a combat zone (or raised somewhere with active terrorism problems) you didn't. You knew. He'd known instantly what it was, and that it was far enough away for them not to be in any danger.

The question was: who had blown up what, where, and why.

The Verran's rodent-like ears had swiveled towards the sound. They produced a long string of chitters.

José didn't need to speak the language or understand the species' psychology to recognize expletives when he heard them. "What blew up?" he asked, once the Verran had wound down.

But they weren't answering. Rather, they turned and ran towards the sound of the explosion. With a glance at Doctor Jordan, José followed.

It was not an easy task. Panicking Verrans were, of course, running the other way, not wanting to be caught if there was another bomb. Others were just standing in the street. The explosion had been of considerable size, and he couldn't blame them for their fear.

But he was going to get to the site, and he was going to help. If only to prove that humans were worthwhile allies to those who might still be hesitating about the matter.

His breath came a little short. The web was helping, but not as much as it should. He felt as if it was arcing inside him. As if it was leaping across the gaps between itself, making a network of stars within him.

There was nothing he could do.

He was running towards the center of the city. On the ground, it was a surprisingly short distance. The Verrans built up and down, not sprawling in their underground dens. The road became a bridge above burrows below, below skyscrapers (roofscrapers?) above.

And the explosion had happened below them, well below. He could see where the wall of a building had been blown out.

He could see bodies.

That angered him. They weren't even of his species, but terrorists were terrorists, and this was an act of terrorism. Or of war.

Or of both, and he ran down stairs that led down to that level. People gathered around the fallen forms to administer first aid or last rites.

He realized to his horror that some of the bodies were smaller and naked, furless.

Children.

The bastard had blown up a *school*.

José didn't know how to apply first aid to a Verran. He ran into the building, looking for people who might be trapped in the rubble, for places where his enhanced strength would prove useful. There was a soft keening around, perhaps from parents.

There was a huge Verran, twice the weight of any he had seen, trapped under a beam. He frowned. "Hey! Should I move the beam or not?" He pointed at them, pointed at a nearby Verran. He didn't want to move it and end up with them dying from shock. It could happen.

The Verran frowned. They moved to rest their hand on the other's arm. Shook their head.

He knew that head shake. He moved the beam anyway. They might already be dead, but the body needed to go to its family.

"Teacher?" he asked.

The Verran was reverently adjusting the position of the body, shaking their head again.

They didn't understand him, he realized. They didn't know what he said, he couldn't know what they said.

But he knew grief when he saw it, grief and respect. He remained silent for a moment, then moved to see if there were others he could dig out.

Bastards.
You didn't blow up schools.

21

"That's from what I understand," Jordan was saying, her voice quiet. Obadiah had joined them along with a younger scientist. "It wasn't exactly a school. And the bombing killed four of their queens."

José thought about the extremely large and heavy Verran.

"They have a monarchy?" Obadiah asked.

José nudged him. He'd heard the word queens before and wondered that, but now had it worked out. "Queens as in breeding females, Obadiah. Am I right?"

"You are. Only a tiny number of the population achieve sexual maturity, and then only when there's an...opening. The queens and drones mostly raise children. Which they consider to be the most important task in their civilization. They aren't in charge, but they..."

"Preserve and continue the culture," José said. "Grandmothers."

"Grandmothers indeed," Jordan said with a smile. "But attacking queens is a major no-no. It's even worse than killing the kids."

Guarderia, José realized, was a better word than colegio. A nursery or a crèche. "I suppose..."

"There will be new queens," Jordan said. "I don't think I envy them. I don't know. I don't understand what it is like to live in that system."

Especially, José thought, as you couldn't tell the sexually immature apart. Did they even know whether they were male or female? Medical scans could presumably tell, but maybe they didn't care until they matured.

If they ever did.

"They are, of course, blaming their closest rivals."

The city next door. José rolled his eyes. "Without evidence, I'd blame their further away rivals. Great way to damage both cities, right?"

Obadiah nodded. "Absolutely. They shouldn't assume anything or attack without proof."

"I think most of the talk is of demanding compensation. Or hostages. Or, somehow, both. I don't understand their culture well enough yet," Jordan said. "Or even their language."

"I suppose there's not really anything we can do."

"We can keep providing technical assistance. If they all die, it won't matter," Obadiah said grimly.

Hostages. Compensation. José thought he understood what they were asking for from their neighbors. Babies young enough to be imprinted with this dome's culture.

He wanted to judge that idea. He couldn't. He'd fallen into the trap of thinking Verran morality would be human morality.

Of course it wouldn't. It couldn't be. They didn't have marriage. People grew up not knowing or caring what gender they were or, presumably, the genders were queen, drone, and worker. Babies belonged to the city, not to their mother. Or perhaps to their mother but to the city through her.

"They aren't a dang thing like us, are they?"

Jordan shook her head. "They love. They desire knowledge. They build. Their family arrangements are what's different." She added. "The glyn don't even *have* sexes."

José shook his head a bit. "I guess…"

"Biology informs culture informs technology informs culture. Climate informs all of it." That was the younger scientist. "Anthropological principles still apply to things which aren't anthro." She laughed a bit.

So, she was an anthropologist. "You're a xenoanthropologist."

"No, I'm not. Anthro is the study of men. I came out here to study those who are *not* men. Xenosapiologist, thank you very much."

José tried to get his thoughts around that word, which he rather thought was a coining straight out of her own mind. That wasn't his problem, though. "I suppose that…"

"I didn't even know it was a field, I just hoped. The universe is too big for us to be alone."

José knew she was telling the truth.

Dr. Jordan rolled her eyes. "The term is xenologist."

He could tell this was an ancient argument. Or at least one which had started before they left Earth. He decided he didn't really care which word they used.

He cared that something had happened that might change their mission.

Or make it impossible.

The Verrans held a memorial two days later. They asked the humans to stay.

They composted their dead. Maybe they hadn't done that once, before the domes. Now, it was the most efficient thing to do.

There were four queens, three drones, and no less than thirty children of various ages. They didn't seem to get their fur until they were close to full grown.

The surviving children huddled around their parents or caregivers, he wasn't sure which. He wasn't sure they particularly cared who was who's biological offspring. It takes a village to raise a child.

The children clung to each other and keened softly. Tears for emotion were apparently not part of their biological makeup.

José found he had plenty for them. He didn't even know these... Doctor Lawrence, the young scientist, had reminded him they were not men and women...people.

He didn't care. They were victims of the kind of act he had done, had been involved in. He cried as much for himself as for them, knowing that nobody was going to criticize him for losing machismo here.

The Verrans didn't even know what machismo meant. They didn't have the same concepts of masculinity and femininity. Not even twisted in the way an alien human culture might.

They literally didn't have the same idea of gender, at all, and there was nothing he could do which would make them understand it at anything more than an academic level, any more than he could understand having a life, living it, and then suddenly growing teats and discovering you had to be a queen, had to give it all up to bear and raise children.

Like you were a character in some old story where the heroine, inevitably, found the man she loved and suddenly discovered that a clean kitchen and babies were all she cared about. But if it was biological?

He realized that the only answer to that was to talk to the queens.

Find out how they felt. There had to be traditions, there had to be ceremonies, there had to be...

He cried for them, for the queens and for those about to become queens. How would they know? Was there...was there any way to control it, to give people the choice?

Did they...

He had to stop thinking they even saw free will the same way, that they even saw *choice* in the same way. Maybe they did choose, but it was deep inside, where it could not be seen.

Obadiah squeezed his shoulder. He turned and was not entirely surprised to see tears in the black man's eyes too. "Kids," he said, softly.

"Thirty kids." José managed not to swear, not like Obadiah would have cared. The f bomb was still there in the gap between the words.

"Yeah. I can see why they're spoiling for blood, although it seems they might..."

"...settle for thirty kids," José said, quietly.

"Yeah. That's kinda weird, but I suppose..."

"I was just thinking what it would be like to become a queen and have to give up your life to have babies."

Obadiah shuddered. "That's enough to make me glad I'm not Verran. And I suppose becoming a drone wouldn't be much better."

"Maybe they have themselves well trained to see it as an honor."

The last of the sadly small wrapped bundles was being removed now. The funeral was over.

José had to think about the living.

"They're going to make their demands. They suggested we might not want to be here," Jordan added.

José frowned and nodded, then headed for the shuttle. They shouldn't take sides. They shouldn't even take sides against the person who had blown up the guarderia.

They should be saying it was more important to save the species.

José didn't want to save people who blew up kids. But what did that mean for him?

Maybe he had to pay this back by helping even those he didn't want to help.

An entire species. Some of them were going to be bad.

Some of them were going to be just following orders.

They hadn't caught the bomber.

The shuttle lifted off through the storms. José would be glad never to see the surface of this world again. He wished they had transporters. Gateways so they could just go from the ship to the clean cities.

The atmosphere whistled around him. He imagined could feel Lucifer's pull, devouring. Claiming.

Some of those kids would barely have time to grow up.

The ones that still got to grow up. "You know what we really need, I hate to say it."

Obadiah from the back seat, "A Martian or two."

"Exactly." They knew how to build domes. Could it...no. Lucifer would eventually destabilize the planet itself.

Eventually.

Maybe all they needed was to build domes, keep the atmosphere in, then slowly pull the population off planet.

Maybe all they needed was... The shuttle landed in the *Endeavour's* bay, and José ducked into the robot repair workshop.

He needed to think, and he needed to both put those small bodies out of his mind and put them in his mind's eye. They were motivation, at some levels.

No, he didn't want to save terrorists, but there was far more than one good "man" in this Sodom. So, if they could seal the cities, they might not need to actually fly them.

And he pulled up his computer. There was the system survey, such as they'd done. There was the inner system. Verr and Lucifer, crossing each other, tearing at each other in a battle Verr was guaranteed to lose.

Ten Earth years to the next conjunction, and the next conjunction would leave Verr without enough atmosphere. And that was assuming Lucifer did not...he frowned. There were multiple possibilities.

But if they could make the cities capable of being separated from the planet, could they make them survive it being torn apart? They'd still need some...that was the rub of it.

The real problem was getting the cities to maintain structural integrity. Four cities. Only about a hundred thousand Verrans, total, remaining. Enough to ensure species survival.

But how many had there been? He brushed back the tears that wanted to come.

They had to make the domes of the cities into spheres. That was ultimately what they had to do. The glyn thought they needed the ky'iin to help.

Maybe they did.

He needed to know what was going on on Earth.

22

"I don't like what's going on down there." Doctor Lawrence, talking to Doctor Jordan. José was pretty sure the two women were not aware that he could hear them.

Or if they were, they didn't care.

He wanted to know what was going on down there, so he drifted closer. Of course they were spying on the Verrans. He decided that wasn't entirely ethical.

He decided it was entirely necessary. The circumstances made it such. He wouldn't even mind if the circumstances were the reverse.

Humans would be fighting down there too. Had they made things worse by telling them this couldn't be fixed, telling them they had to get off their planet? He didn't know, he couldn't know, and he was afraid that was exactly what had happened.

Afraid they had made things far, far worse for these people. The bombing indicated there were spies.

So, of course, all of Verr knew.

"It's inevitable," Doctor Jordan was saying. "They're going to fight each other, then they'll make peace. Maybe make an example of the bomber."

"They aren't humans. We can't expect them to think like humans."

"They know their survival is on the line." Jordan tapped on the table, her neatly trimmed nails making a rat tat tat sound.

"That doesn't mean they'll react the way we would, or in any sane way."

Queens. Babies. Drones. Something niggled at José's mind, but he didn't cut in.

"No, they'll react in a way that's sane. And they have to protect their…"

"The only thing that they are going to care about saving is the queens and drones," Lawrence predicted. "Women and children first is one thing, but they only *need* the queens and drones. Everyone else…"

"We still don't know what decides which workers change. I'm still trying to decipher their genetics from a couple of fur samples I snagged."

"No, we don't. But from their attitude, it appears that…twenty queens can sustain a twenty thousand worker population. Or thereabouts. Twenty queens and maybe five drones…more's good for variety, but…"

The two were talking about the Verrans as if they were animals, but that made sense. They were animals, after all, just as human beings were.

"The queens and drones…"

"…all used to be workers. Just because all they do now is look after kids doesn't mean they couldn't crew a ship."

"It's a moot point," Jordan said. "We aren't only rescuing the queens unless we have no other option."

José thought that might end up being the case. No other option. How many queens did they need? If twenty were enough for a twenty thousand person colony. "I think you're missing something."

They both jumped.

"If there aren't enough queens or drones, workers go through puberty, correct?"

Jordan nodded.

"So, any group of workers that was isolated from the queens and drones completely…"

"May well produce the queens and drones they needed." Lawrence was the one who nodded. "Mechanic's got a point."

"If we understood the mechanism…"

"It would help them rebuild their population from the bottleneck this is going to create." Lawrence shook her head. "There's only a hundred thousand of them. So, something might be limiting the number of individuals maturing sexually. Something to do with resources."

"Space?" José suggested. "Or maybe it's something they have to, like, do. We'd have to ask them."

"There's a ceremony, I asked, when somebody starts to show signs of changing. But I'm not sure the Verrans themselves understand it."

Jordan glanced down, at the floor. By symbolic extension, at the planet.

If they didn't, then maybe they would have to learn. "So, if we can only take a few people, we should make sure at least some are queens and drones, just in case you need a queen or a drone to make more," José mused.

"The *Endeavour* can't take them. Neither can the glyn ships. I think the idea of lifting their cities away from the planet would save the most people, given we can't just go find a starliner."

José had an image of a starliner at that, a cruise ship in space. It would be perfect. But, no, they didn't have one.

"But if flying the cities isn't possible, then…"

"Then we have ten years to solve this."

José felt a prickling at the back of his neck.

As if the web was suddenly not sure they really had ten years.

He ignored it, of course. The web wasn't sentient, but maybe he had seen a pattern.

If he had, though, it was a face on Mars. Orbital mechanics gave them ten years. Every ten years there would be a conjunction with Lucifer.

It couldn't happen faster than that. There ws no force that could make it faster.

But there were forces on Verr that could still bring about destruction faster in other ways. Maybe that was what he was seeing, hallucinating as the web talking to him. That the Verrans might destroy themselves before Lucifer did.

But what could they do? Nothing was the sharp and clear answer, if not the one he wanted to hear.

Can only take a few people. What was the minimum? At least one queen, just in case there were no female workers in the bunch. At least one queen, at least one drone. He didn't know.

But they had no space. If they hadn't had to take on the *Atlantis* survivors, they might have. But they had.

And they were under strict instructions not to go back to Earth. Not to seek help.

The glyn seemed to…José frowned. The glyn didn't have another ship in the area, was the logical explanation. Or they didn't think they could sustain Verrans.

He closed his eyes. Opened them again. The mess hall had not changed, the people eating breakfast around him hadn't.

Slava sat down next to him. Uninvited. "So, the moles aren't exactly acting rationally."

"Seems to me that makes them more like humans, not less."

Unexpectedly, she laughed. "You're right, it does. And at least we seem to share the idea that it's wrong to blow up kids."

Unless those kids were... José shook his head. He didn't want to talk about it and did, and definitely didn't want to talk about it with her. "The future of the species is going to be important. That *has* to be universal."

"So, how do we get them to play nice?"

"You care now?" he found himself saying.

She shook her head. "I don't know. It seems like a lot of effort to try and help. But at the same time, they *do* grieve like people do."

Maybe the dead kids had achieved something. José forced aside that particular cynical thought. It was true that good could come of evil, but it didn't make evil any less evil. "And commit evil like people do."

"Oddly, that almost makes me feel better about helping them."

"Any social species is going to commit evil, I think. Just as universal as protecting kids."

"What about non-social species?"

"Talk to Doctor Lawrence, but I'd lay bets she'd tell us that a non-social species has no chance of becoming technologically dominant. If you can't cooperate..."

"If you can't cooperate you don't fight wars, but you also can't build anything that takes more than you and maybe your family. You're probably right."

A non-social being could be sentient, but could not build a civilization. "How are you holding up?"

"Tired of being a backup. Of not having a job." She let out a breath. "I want to go home." She lifted a hand. "Not home home, not to stay. But home so we can regroup and rebuild."

"That might have to wait." He hadn't heard any news of the war.

"It might. But if we wait too long. They blew up Ganymede, José. My *brother* was there."

No wonder she was so angry. José didn't know anybody on Ganymede. "I'm sorry," he said, the lame sorry of somebody who knew he could not, truthfully, say anything to the grieving.

It was the best he could offer.

Obadiah shook his head. "They're still wrangling down there.

Koroskeya's right, it is a very human situation."

"I'd like to think no sane people would kill kids when facing planetary extinction, but people aren't sane, are they?" José looked up at the dome.

Doctor Lawrence stepped in, her blonde hair neatly pinned up close to her head. "If you guys are finished, I'd like to talk to both of you. You both have on the ground combat experience. On Mars."

Obadiah nodded. "Sure do. What do you need to know?"

"What's the chance of dome damage from a conflict between Verran cities?"

José knew the answer to this one. "Low, thankfully. The size of their domes and the mud piled on top of them makes them even more resilient. A bomb like that right next to the dome could cause a small breach, but it would be repairable. And right now, they do have atmosphere on both sides, so there wouldn't be decompression."

There had been blown domes. Small ones. Larger ones tended to stand firm. Orbital bombardment would make it different, but the Verran space program hadn't reached that point yet. "Even after the next conjunction, they should have enough atmosphere to avoid explosive decompression. Worried about more bombs?"

"Very worried about more bombs," she said. "Okay, so best as I can tell through the language barrier, there's been a conflict between two of the four cities for generations. We, of course, happened to show up at one of them. This appears to have triggered the attack."

"Colonialism again," Obadiah said. "I mean, we don't have much choice but to try and help, but...we seem to be messing up just the way white folks always have. No offense."

Lawrence laughed weakly. "None taken, given most of that was before my grandmother was born. But yeah. We blundered in and triggered something and we may have doomed these people instead of saving them." She looked away. "We're never going to get it right."

"Oh, quit the white guilt," Obadiah said before José could say anything else. "No, we may not be able to get it right, but we have, have we not, given them ideas for how to get out of their situation. We can give them tools."

"We just have to give them the tools they want. And there are four *different* cultures down there," José cut in with. "Which might mean four different solutions."

Lawrence lifted a hand to her head.

"I'm from the Caribbean. My people lived through the megastorms.

The solution for Puerto Rico was not the solution for Haiti was not the solution for Cuba. You know that. And it wasn't just because of geography. It was because we're *different people*. Aliens aren't going to be some kind of Star Trek monoculture. You should know that."

"I suppose."

Obadiah laughed. "I always thought we needed Vulcan ethnicities, but even when we saw a black one…then again, with that climate and planet, they should *all* have been black."

José rather thought Obadiah was right. Or brown, at any rate.

"And I do know that. It's just that it's not theory any more. It's real, and there are lives at stake, and I don't know how to…"

"None of us do." Obadiah, José realized, was the oldest of the three. "Because it's not theory any more. But what we need to do is talk to each city separately, lay things out. Not try to mediate, unless they ask us to. Not try to solve this. Just tell them it needs to be solved."

This time, José did not just think he was right. He knew.

23

The surface of Verr roiled beneath them. From the shuttle, José could not see where there might be cities, or roads, or any of the other trappings of civilization.

He saw a river of mud, he saw all the signs of an unstable world. Even far from the conjunction.

He saw the megastorms again.

Lauxon was at the controls. He was flying literal shotgun, armed just in case. They trusted the Verrans they knew.

They didn't trust the ones they didn't know, the different cultures. He didn't plan on letting them see the gun, though. That struck him as decidedly unwise. They would recognize the weapon, he was sure of it.

They also already knew that the humans had talked to their enemies. Hence why there were five people in the shuttle. Doctor Jordan, himself, Lauxon, Obadiah and one of Obadiah's security people, a woman of mixed Asian descent named Shen.

These people were going to die. "From the maps, the city is down there," Jordan said. "I'm not clear on what caused the rivalry, but I'm assuming it's just over resources or similar, not...ideology."

Hopefully not ideology. Resources would become a moot point, one way or the other. Of course, so would ideology. "Or both. Ideology as an excuse for resources. Your god is bigger than my god," she added.

José laughed. The white people had indeed made their god bigger. Of course, he was Catholic himself. Nominally.

Atheist in truth. He wasn't sure he needed any god except the stars.

Except the stars and they were burning him, threatening him with destruction.

"There. Put us down there."

He could see the door, eventually, as they landed. It did not look like it had been used in a very long time.

Door or hatch. An opening into the city, from when the surface had been more habitable. Perhaps not used in a conjunction or two.

He and Obadiah stepped forward to get it open. It was not locked, but it was very stiff. Even with the web, the effort set up the kind of almost instant burn in his muscles that told him he would be regretting this tomorrow.

The door slid open, and a bit of air came out. Cleaner than the outside air. Once they were inside, he pulled it closed. Carefully, as he didn't want it to close such that they couldn't open it again.

But he didn't want to let in any more mud than was necessary.

They were on a sort of platform above the city. People were moving to and fro. They wore a lot more bling than the other Verrans, and their fur seemed to average darker. Definitely a different culture and ethnicity.

The bling had something to it. "Militaristic," he asided to Obadiah. "They're wearing rank badges."

"So they are. Maybe this place was a military base before things went to heck."

José wondered why he didn't swear. True, there were women present, but that had never stopped Obadiah before.

He had the gun behind him. And then the Verrans swarmed them.

He didn't use it.

The cell was clearly built to contain a Verran. It was not quite the right shape for José...ironically, he might actually be more comfortable than one of the moles would have been. He sat up against the wall. They'd taken the gun, of course.

The gun had been a bad idea. But now he was trapped. He might die down here, and the ship needed him.

He liked to be needed. He didn't need it the way some people did, but he liked it. It felt good. It felt worthwhile.

But he didn't have the choice to escape. No, he did. He had to work out how to talk his way out of this when he was dealing with different people, whose language was only similar to that of the Verrans they knew, not the same.

He was no linguist to guess how far apart they were, but he had tried the few words he had, and only gotten head shakes and chitters.

Or perhaps he was being judged for his accent. More likely he was being judged for his alienness.

They'd taken a blood sample. He wondered what they would, or could, do with it. Learn quite a bit about alien genetics, he supposed. Learn that there was such a thing, that lifeforms could have different proteins.

Learn how to make a virus to kill humans. He wished he hadn't had that last thought. It was a military thought.

But they did look like military people. They had colored bar insignia that they wore around their necks on loose chokers, rather than on the clothing they, like the others, did not bother with. Different colors and numbers of bars no doubt told a story, but it was not one he could read. He could have watched their body language, likely, looked for signs of deference. Of hierarchy.

But not from inside a cell.

Two Verrans showed up at the door. They opened it and gestured. Come, was universal. Or at least it was when you had hands.

He came. Not doing or trying anything. Oh, if he had a good opportunity to break out, he would take it. Maybe.

Maybe this was the best place to be. They led him down the corridor and into a room which immediately made him think 'Star Chamber.' Six Verrans with lots of bars.

Generals? Diplomats?

They chittered at his guards, then the guards stepped back. They didn't think it was necessary to cuff him.

Which said they were confident. He let the chittering die down. Looked at each of them in turn. Wondered if the others were still alive. Whether or not they were, he was in a position where he had to try and make contact.

He lifted his hands. Showed them clearly. Then pointed to himself. "José."

They probably couldn't pronounce it. But names were always what you started with.

And perhaps it achieved something. The chittering started up again. He listened for patterns, for words similar to the few he had picked up.

That was all he could do.

The others were escorted into the room. Guards kept them slightly apart. Apparently, José had done something either right or very, very wrong.

More chittering.

Then one of the Verrans stepped forward. They walked right up to Jordan. Got in her face. To her credit, she didn't step back or so much as flinch.

Sniff.

The Verran stepped back. Then they pointed to themselves and chittered something. Ikkik was the closest José could get.

A name.

Or a title. He couldn't be sure which.

They had to work out communications, and fast. "I wish we had universal translators."

Jordan quirked her lips. "So do they, I'd imagine."

Assuming they had the concept.

"Likely," Obadiah said. "Likely they're also trying what AI they do have. It's somewhat helpful."

Would be more helpful if they stole the data from their rivals, José mused. Maybe they should have...but that would have been betrayal.

The general, as José couldn't help but thinking of them, stepped forward again. They pointed at the sky, then at the humans.

"Yes," Jordan said.

José shot the young security crewman a reassuring look. She looked very nervous and uncertain.

The general nodded. Then he signaled one of the others. They pulled up a hologram.

A virtual orrery. This wasn't something he'd seen in the other dome, but it looked pretty good. He stabbingly pointed at Verr, then at Lucifer. Then pointed at the humans again.

It was obvious. He wanted a solution, and that mattered.

Then he pointed at Verr again, pulling up the globe. He chittered something angry as he indicated the other city.

Jordan shook her head. She pointed at each of the cities on Verr, then upwards.

The chittering became even angrier.

José shook his head. He too indicated the cities. The he pointed upwards, but he also made a sweeping gesture. He hoped it would be read as there being plenty of space.

Plenty of space for them to get distance, but not so much they wouldn't be able to trade. That was what he could hope for.

The general gave a sort of grunting sound.

Jordan was now pointing at a third city. She made it a stabbing motion too.

The general grunted again. Oh, for language. But without it, they were making a remarkable progress on communication.

It helped that everyone had hands. Hands meant something, they gave a commonality. Maybe even a commonality to the brain.

Then the general nodded. He indicated the aides.

The humans were escorted to a kind of ground car, and taken across the city. The windows were closed. These Verrans were, apparently, suspicious enough that they didn't want the humans seeing the layout.

José couldn't blame them, but they would have to get over it. At least their destination seemed to be further away from the cells.

The vehicle moved with an electric hum. "I think we made progress."

"They want just them to be saved," Jordan said. "Not happening."

No, that was not happening. Definitely not. But what was going to happen was unclear.

The car stopped and the doors opened, revealing the interior of a garage. José stepped out and looked around.

The two guards, plus another Verran, this one with fur pure black. And this one was, obviously…male.

24

Where did you take people to learn? A school. And the guarderia in this city was more...hierarchical. Children, grouped by age (or at least size), moved from class to class in silent groups.

José did not see any queens, not when he arrived, and certainly not right away. Instead, the drone took them to an unused classroom. One clearly intended for young children.

It was a brilliant idea, because there were pictures on the walls. None showed anything of life outside the city, perhaps because the adults knew the children would never experience such or need to know about it.

But they showed all the basics of life inside the city. Enough to trade words and vocabulary. The guards didn't leave. Drones, José supposed, might be less valuable than queens in some ways, but they were certainly valuable enough not to leave alone with offworlders.

The drone put the guards to work helping with words, though. He put José in mind of certain professors he had had, of the more absent-minded variety. Perhaps the black-furred male had been chosen for this *because* he was absent-minded. Because he cared more about teaching than who he was teaching or what for.

More organized and sensible than the others, less individual freedom. But then, José couldn't judge.

They got the name of the city, Kirkit, and the name of their teacher, Miri. They even got names for the guards.

It all made them more human, but building vocabulary took time. José still thought he liked the other city better. They seemed freer, more like home.

The sad part was that this one seemed more likely to survive. More likely to reach beyond what they were now and become something new. Whatever that would be without a homeworld.

"Miri," he said finally, now they had some vocabulary. "Why city like this?"

He could almost see Jordan holding her breath.

"Survival," the mole chittered. At least he thought that.

"Others...other ways."

"Our way works."

That might be the simplest and most pragmatic answer ever given to such a question. Their way did, indeed, work. Perhaps not well, but the important thing was... "But you fight war."

"Not if I can help it." Miri sounded angry for a moment. "No war."

So, not everyone here was a hawk. And perhaps that was another reason they had chosen this particular teacher.

"You didn't blow up the...nursery." José nodded. "We didn't think so."

"So, you came. Find out. Make peace?"

He nodded again. Obadiah cut in. "We caused it, we want to help fix it, but if you want us to go away, we will."

They didn't quite have a word for leave. Go away. José wondered. If the Verrans asked them to leave?

He thought about it. The white man had never left when asked, his own white ancestors hadn't, that was for sure. He was the island mix, white, taino, probably some black, he didn't know for sure. He'd never had his DNA tested, even if it was pretty accurate these days. It didn't matter. The lines had braided and made him.

Maybe he hadn't wanted to know.

But no, they had to leave if asked.

"You would just go?"

"If you asked us. But we want you to live."

Miri pointed at a picture on the wall. "Kvyt." He used their name for Lucifer.

"We can't stop it from happening. We have to get you off the world."

He didn't have the word for planet either.

He wished he did.

That idea had caused Miri to fall silent for an extended period of time. José took the opportunity to pick up a child's book from the shelf and flick through it. With enough time, he could probably use it to learn to read their language.

Right now, that didn't seem necessary, so instead he looked at the pictures. Pictures of buildings, of machines. There were, he realized, no domestic animals down here, only wild ones and vermin in the darkest tunnels. Had they never domesticated animals? Jordan said they had no small livestock. Maybe there had been large ones on the surface, before it became a hellhole where only the toughest survived.

Perhaps not. Or perhaps they hadn't thought them important enough. There were cats and dogs on Mars.

None on the *Endeavour* but maybe the next starship could have a ship's cat. "I see the big difference," he murmured to Obadiah.

"What?"

"No domestic animals."

"I noticed. The glyn at least...I think I saw a picture of something pet-like."

"Sure it wasn't a baby?"

Obadiah laughed. "It was...no wait, some people put their kids on leashes. But no, I think it was a pet. So, no pets."

"Or no pets anymore." He kept his voice down. "For some reason, that's starting to bother me. Maybe it's that other animals are so important to us..."

"We would never have left them on the surface to die, but maybe they would have."

"You don't get it. We bond with other animals. They don't. What do they see us as?"

Obadiah frowned. Then he nodded. "Strangers, I suppose."

"Aliens in the true sense. But in this case, a resource. Something they can use. They want our help, but we don't know what they *feel*." José thought that was true anyway, but a species which didn't form pack bonds with other species might have difficulty forming alliances with them.

Maybe the only reason they were even still alive was the disaster. He thought about the DNA samples.

He thought about biotechnology.

"They understand trade. That will have to be enough."

José nodded. There was nothing they could do about Verran psychology, except try to understand it, and that was the xenologists' job, not his.

His job was to...get back to the *Endeavour*.

His eyes finally fell on Lauxon. She had been incredibly quiet through the entire thing and still was. He wondered if being captured and locked up was wearing on her.

Or if she just wasn't the best person to be here. "Cecilie?" He didn't use her first name, generally.

He used it now, to get her attention.

"These people remind me of Nazis," she said, finally. "I can't...I don't know."

There were always Nazis. They seemed to show up every few generations. "Just remember that they aren't human."

It had to help, surely.

The Canadian woman nodded. "I know that, but did you see they have rank badges on the kids?"

He had noticed that. He thought of history studied, not studied, and repeated.

Then Miri came back and their break was, apparently, over. The two guards were with him, and they had brought plates of food.

José glanced at Jordan. She nodded, and he munched on the bread. It tasted oddly bland and bitter at the same time.

It tasted like hope and fear.

They let them go. Well, after indoctrinating them with language, after explaining what they wanted.

Which was to be left alone by the other cities, essentially. José believed them when they said they had not bombed the school. It did not seem like something these people would do.

They were borderline fascists, or at least...he did not know quite how to put it. The weird thing was that they seemed to be happy.

They also did not seem to know what to do with the humans. He was relieved when they got back to the shuttle. "Phewf."

"I don't trust them," Obadiah said.

"They want peace but to be ready for war," Jordan opined. "But I think we're right not to trust any of them. Any Verrans."

What could they do? José thought. They could have killed them.

But that, he realized, would have gained them nothing. Killing the humans would only have got them angry humans.

Which was what Jordan had been counting on. He studied her braids as Lauxon prepared to lift off. She was still quiet.

He decided she might just be a little bit xenophobic, not in the sense of wanting to hurt the aliens but in the sense of being made uncomfortable by them.

He could not entirely blame her. He had been fine until he had hit on a reason to be uncomfortable. Now, he was inclined towards Jordan's opinion. They could not be trusted.

Landing on the *Endeavour* he, for the first time, wondered if they should just fly away and leave the Verrans to their fate.

Not that he meant it. They had treated him well enough, he decided, once they let him out of the cell. And the first city had welcomed them.

He put his feelings down to residual xenophobia combined with an ambiguous feeling about the desirability of helping people who had not, in the first place at least, asked. Was he a colonizador again? He wasn't sure.

He wasn't sure at all and he didn't want to be one, not again. The red sand of Mars in his boots. Between his toes.

Dust everywhere, dust sometimes in people's lungs. He'd gotten lucky. He didn't have asbestosis. Some did.

Some had wrecked lungs, broken by the dust.

And many more had wrecked minds, broken by the deeds they had done. He had no clue how else to put it.

Wrecked minds. He thought of the device he'd had to wear to sleep, the one which supposedly chased nightmares away. It worked. He didn't need it any more. Most of the time.

But now he was having all new nightmares, ones in which he dreamed of Lucifer pulling the atmosphere off of Verr. It kept getting embellishments.

He saw the small bodies. No. "We still have to help them. If we can. But how do we do it without…"

"We don't. We will change them. We already have. Maybe the Prime Directive is a good idea after all."

He looked at Obadiah. "Maybe." Then he fled to his usual refuge in the workshop. Where a robot looked up at him accusingly, like a neglected pet.

He thought of cities flying.

He thought of them being pulled into Lucifer's maw.

25

"It's over," Chang said as she stepped onto the bridge. "The glyn apparently went and knocked everyone's heads together or something."

"The war?" Comms' voice was incredulous.

"The war. More than that, Earth is now officially allied with the ky'iin, the glyn, and a race called the tyrar."

Would they add the Verrans to that list? José didn't need Obadiah to be present to hear the Federation joke he would make at this point.

Verran probably wasn't right, either. But as nobody could pronounce their name for themselves, it might stick.

"Thank…" he tailed off. No, he didn't have God to thank. He had the glyn and whatever diplomats on both sides had worked to stop the war.

Maybe they would even help rebuild the outpost on Ganymede, but nothing could replace the lives. Nothing ever could. People, any species, so unique and precious.

He forced his breathing back to a normal pattern, remembering another time when the war was over. Remembering that he had literally been in a drop pod.

Get out he had heard. *You aren't dropping.*

Relief and disappointment, and the web wanting to go anyway. Some teams, he had heard, had. Some people had died after the ceasefire.

Wasn't that always the case in war? And in a war where they had to rely on not-always-reliable ansibles or ships, it seemed more likely.

It seemed like interstellar war was a bad idea. Supply lines too long. That was why they had lost Mars, after all.

Supply lines too long. Distances too great. Field too large. Or perhaps technology would shrink the solar system and then the galaxy. Perhaps they would travel to the ky'iin homeworld, wherever it was, for weekend breaks, one day.

"So, we carry on with what we are doing, but we can hope for more resources. We have contacted all four Verran cities. Only one rebuffed us completely."

Maybe they would listen to their own kind once there was a plan in place.

Maybe the ky'iin would show up to help. If so, would they be able to talk to them?

Would Koroskeya be able to handle it without trying to blow them up?

They were now allies. They'd not just ended the war, but they'd come to the realization that...

"Space is big," he murmured, a bit too loudly. "Best to gather around the campfire with everyone who is friendly."

Chang shot him a look. "Indeed. And there may be worse things out there than the ky'iin."

Or worse things out there than humans, José thought. He leaned back in his seat a little. The ky'iin probably weren't bad.

Klingons. Kinda like Klingons. Not evil, but antagonistic because of all of the cultural differences, and cultural flotsam. And language barriers. And misunderstandings.

"So. Mr. Marin, I want to hear more about your net idea?"

"Here?" he found himself asking.

"As good a place as any."

"Well, the idea would be to reinforce the bedrock under the cities with a net, created by small robots that would...you know, the ideas for a space elevator?

The space elevator hadn't worked, but extruder robots existed.

"Extruder robots. Yes. And that would..."

"It should reinforce the bedrock and start to...ease the cities away from the planet. In theory..."

"What," Comms said, "if we don't ease them away from the planet. What if we just reinforce them. Then when Verr breaks up." She moved her hands outwards.

"Hrm," Chang said. "Might work."

"The real challenge, regardless, is going to be keeping them from falling into Lucifer." His nightmare. He shuddered.

The web whispered opinions that did nothing to deny that possibility.

The one thing they had not realized was that the fourth Verran city, the one which did not want to talk to them, had plans of its own.

José knew he should have. After all, everyone did, all sentient beings.

Unfortunately, the first expression of those plans came in the form of an attack. It was a rocket, and it was, of course, no threat to *Endeavour* or its crew. But it was a rocket nonetheless.

The other cities did not appear to have rocketry, although José suspected that was already in the process of changing.

This one did.

"I'm thinking," Obadiah said, leaning over the tactical board at the back of the bridge, "that we ignore it. Don't even bother to swat the fly."

José was inclined to agree. The rocket did not even have the range to reach them, although its trajectory and payload made it clear what they intended. The payload probably would not have breached the hull.

"I don't think it would have done much damage...to our paint job," he added, a little sardonically.

Chang laughed. "No, it wouldn't have. They don't, thankfully, have nukes."

José shuddered at that. The last thing Verr needed was nukes.

Or maybe...nukes could be used to separate the city from the planet. But that would involve giving the Verrans nukes.

If they hadn't worked it out on their own, it was best not to try.

"We need in that city."

"The disadvantage," Obadiah said, "of them being aliens is that we can't easily spy on them."

"Nanobots?" Chang suggested.

"Possible, but they have reasonable computer technology. And good noses. We could try it, though. They're already mad enough with us."

José thought that true. When somebody is already shooting at you, you didn't really worry about upsetting them further.

"However," Chang added. "I suggest we wait a little. Maybe when they realize they can't shoot at us they'll try talking."

Ignore them, then. It seemed wise, but José wanted to know what they were thinking too. Did they want the *Endeavour* to go away?

What if they all wanted it? It was the same question again. He was repeating himself.

"We are certainly not leaving," she added, as if reading his mind. "Unless all four cities ask us to."

That answered that question at the practical level. Chang had made her decision, and the *Endeavour* was not a democracy.

It didn't answer the ethics. The rocket, having fallen short, had exploded in space.

So, they waited. They waited three days, with no response from that city. They had given radios to the other three, radios and machine translation algorithms. Uncertain ones, half-coded, but they were better than nothing.

The other three cities were using them to talk to each other. It was progress.

The next rocket was aimed at one of the other cities.

Had they had more warning or understanding, maybe the *Endeavour* could have intercepted it.

ICBM was the more accurate word. They had ICBMs. The payload was heavy enough to dent the dome, but not crack it. Even from orbit, José thought he could see the damage, but that might just be knowledge and experience. His prediction had been accurate. It was unlikely they would seriously damage a dome. But minor damage, with rockets... "*Now* can we spy on them?"

Chang templed her hands. "Part of me says we shouldn't interfere with this war unless asked. The rest of me says screw them."

That wasn't language he'd heard from her before. Well, he'd heard some muffled Cantonese words he was suspicious of, but she had never got this close to swearing in English.

José let out a breath. Their captain was angry, and she was not prone to anger. Which meant she was a very dangerous woman at the moment. He was glad she was on his side.

"We're not going to attack them, because their species might not take the loss," Chang added. "But..."

"It's a shame we can't take them somewhere and leave them there, isn't it." Maroon them. Except that...well...if it was a nice planet where they could rebuild.

"Sometimes I think there are some people on Earth who need to be left somewhere," Chang mused. "Of course, the English tried that and ended up making Australia."

Was that a bad thing? José didn't know many Australians. They tended to focus their attention entirely on keeping their country from becoming completely uninhabitable. They hadn't contributed to the war. New Zealand had some, but not Australia. "Maybe we need space Australia."

Chang laughed. "Well, mostly the people they left somewhere were criminals." She smiled. "To your duty, Mr. Marin."

It was probably the most personable she had been to him. Perhaps her anger was making her more human, less just "the CO" as she tended to be.

Perhaps.

Still. "So, what we're going to do is blow anything like that out of the sky. We're capable of doing so. Regardless of which side sends it."

That did seem like the best thing to do. Neutral, but saving lives. That vague feeling of discomfort with the situation was still there, but José respected Chang.

He had to. If he didn't, he shouldn't even have been on the ship.

"We just launched a shuttle, ma'am," Comms said abruptly.

"As in…"

"As in we launched a shuttle."

"Find out who is on board." Another flash of anger, this time clearly aimed at whoever had disobeyed orders and taken off like that.

Then she added, "And get Lieutenant Lauxon, assuming it wasn't her, in another shuttle to go after them."

José watched the sensors. Unless they needed to move, there was no other purpose for him up there.

The shuttle wasn't going to the targeted city.

It was going to the one that fired.

26

Obadiah was on the shuttle with Lauxon. Chang had give José a look.

He was not going.

She did not, apparently, want too many pilots off the ship right now. So all he could do was watch as the second of their four shuttles…five with the one fully working one from the *Atlantis* arced down into the turbulent atmosphere in pursuit.

Electric storms seemed to gather around them. It matched his mood. It matched his fears.

Two of his closest friends were on that shuttle.

"I identified who was on the shuttle. Lieutenant Commander Slava Koroskeya from the Atlantis and Crewman Charles Borke…"

José arched an eyebrow. Borke was their cook. What was he doing in on this? Only person Slava could get?

Or maybe they were involved. Stranger things had happened. He couldn't see what anyone would see in Charles Borke, but he had had a boyfriend that had elicited that reaction from others before.

Or…

"Well, huh. I wonder what they think they can do."

"They took some of our demolitions explosives."

So, they wanted to retaliate. They had taken sides, but who wouldn't? Who wouldn't take sides when fired on? People who hadn't seen what had happened on Mars. People who didn't know that there were more important things than retaliatory strikes.

"Let's hope Lauxon can catch them," Chang said softly. "We stay on shift for now."

It should have been shift change, but Chang didn't want to vacate the bridge when she had what was at least insubordination, if not mutiny, on her hands.

There was a difference that civilians seldom understood. It was insubordination if you disobeyed. Mutiny was getting other people to.

José felt his mouth dry. There was only one punishment for mutiny, even in time of peace. Only one…

He'd seen it carried out before.

What could he do, though? He could do nothing except sweat, wait, and swear under his breath in Spanish.

Well, no, he couldn't do that. He was fairly sure Chang didn't speak it, but one could never be *totally* sure, and she was the type of woman to keep exactly which languages she understood under wraps. He would do the same, in her place, especially if it was a tongue that people would not assume he spoke.

Like, say, the basic Cantonese he had picked up during the war, not exactly fluent, but enough to get by.

The first shuttle vanished into the clouds.

"They're down," Comms said, no doubt relying on the shuttle's transponder rather than visuals. Certainly there was no way to see it from the visual cameras that gave them a view of all that surrounded the ship.

"And the second shuttle?"

"On their tail, but…oh crap. The first shuttle is now buried in mud."

They'd triggered a mudslide, whether intentionally or otherwise. José frowned.

That shuttle might not be able to take off.

And if it was intentional? It would make them hard to see on the ground, that was the only reason he could think of.

Either way, it made the situation worse, as did each passing moment. He could imagine Lauxon fighting with the yoke to get the craft down, its autopilot unable to deal with the unpredictable weather.

The mud and, judging by the clouds above them, the driving rain, rain which had nothing to nurture and feed.

"I hate this planet," he said, finally.

"Don't we all?"

"Can you get anything from Lauxon?" Chang asked.

"They're down. Wait, she's responding. Says she, and I quote, can't see a thing."

"Put her on speaker."

José tensed. He wasn't sure he wanted to hear her voice.

"Like I was saying," her voice said, "I can't see a thing. Driving rain, wind whipping up the mud, it's a mess down here."

Calmly, Comms informed her, "The shuttle is fifty yards...no, wait, that won't work. Start walking, I'll give you warm and cold."

He heard Obadiah cursing in the background. He, apparently, didn't care what language the captain heard him using.

Or maybe he figured that anyone would understand why somebody might be using that language down there.

"Cold," was the first thing Comms said.

"Got it."

There was silence. Chang leaned forward, saying nothing, not wanting to disturb the two humans on the surface of a world hostile to them.

Well, except that the comms weren't quite filtering out the faint whistle of the wind, and José knew how loud it really was. It was a wonder she could hear a thing, let alone see.

Many, many reasons why the Verrans had moved underground. After the next conjunction, they wouldn't have these problems any more, if the math was right.

There wouldn't be enough atmosphere for rainstorms.

There wouldn't be enough water. The world would dry out, become Mars-like, but with ongoing seismic instability.

Then the next conjunction would deal with, likely, the rest of the atmosphere.

"Warm," Comms said.

More silence. More whispering of the wind. Maybe they should try and get a video link, except Lauxon had already said she couldn't see a thing.

"Any better visibility?" Chang said, finally.

It was Obadiah who responded, "Not at all. I can see my hand in front of my face, but that's about it."

José thought about the megastorms again. This entire planet was a megastorm, one which would only end with death.

Even if somebody could move a planet, he rather thought it was too late. There was no ecosystem left.

There was no way to save this place short of the kind of terraforming effort the Martians argued about.

"Found the other shuttle," Obadiah said. "Hatch is closed. They can't have gone far, though."

Comms couldn't pick up on the other two. They must have turned off the transponder feature on their radios.

Like good little mutineers.

He reminded himself this wasn't a mutiny, yet.

"I think there's a hatch into the…"

There was a sound as of a tremendous rushing of wind from the comms.

"Lauxon! Smith! Respond!"

Obadiah's voice. "We're alive. Thanks to all the mud!"

José managed not to laugh. This was probably one to laugh with Obadiah about later, not laugh at him about now.

But there would be a later.

"They booby trapped the hatch," Lauxon said, with disgust. "Our people, the Verrans, I don't know which. And I can't see their footsteps."

The mud would have covered them. But either they had set the booby trap or failed to find the hatch.

"I have an idea," said Comms.

"What's the idea? We can't override their radios."

"Did anyone remove the probes we put in shuttle 2?"

José blinked. "Not as far as I know."

"Shuttle 2 is the one they took. Lt Smith, you have the override."

Robots.

Robots were such useful things, really. And sometimes they were useful for things other than what you initially planned. José could actually see what Comms had in mind.

"I'll get them," Obadiah said.

"We'll get them," Lauxon cut in. "We are not getting more than five feet apart in this."

Smart, José thought. They could apparently see the shuttle now.

"Going to have to dig," Obadiah said, with another word that might not generally be considered acceptable in mixed company.

Lauxon produced one of her own, albeit in French, proving she was no kind of a lady at least where language was concerned.

It was going to take a while. José settled back in his chair, tried to relax. Of course, bridge chairs were deliberately designed to be a little bit uncomfortable. Just to make sure people didn't relax too much.

The people who had made that design choice were not familiar with the ability of ground troopers to sleep anywhere. Not that he intended to sleep.

Just relax, just save his energy until and unless it was needed.

"I have the robots," Obadiah said, eventually. "I assume you want…"

"Mr. Marin, I believe you're familiar?"

"You'll want to open the panel on the back. Turn the infrared gain up to maximum. Then tell them to find human heat signals other than yours."

Obadiah had worked with robots before, there was no need to explain how to instruct them to him.

He could hear Obadiah doing just that, and he was doing it right. Simple, literal, precise; that was how you instructed simple AI. Like telling a dog what to do.

He did sometimes wonder if they had some self-awareness, just like dogs did.

If it was something that was needed even to be able to follow orders.

The wind seemed to be dying down.

"It's not raining as hard," Lauxon said, sounding grateful for the fact. "Still coming down, but not in quite as big buckets."

José smiled a bit. If the storm ended, that would help. He wondered if the mutineers had chosen their timing carefully.

He had thought he'd gotten through to Koroskeya. Or maybe he had, just in the wrong way. Maybe this was in part his fault.

Nah, other people's actions were only your fault if you were the one giving the orders. He hadn't told her to go down there.

She had been, in fact, told not to. Explicitly.

So, no, this was not in any way his fault, but he felt he bore a tiny part of the responsibility.

"Got it," Chang said. "Find them, get them back to the ship."

There was another sound. A startled yelp from…he was sure it was Lauxon. Another curse word from Obadiah.

"What's going on down there?"

There was no answer.

27

"Lieutenants. Respond." Chang sounded crisp, businesslike.

Obadiah's voice. "One of the Verrans emerged from the hatch, grabbed Lauxon, disappeared."

Chang swore fiercely in Cantonese. José was familiar enough with the words she was using to wince. Of course, the captain could get away with it.

"Okay. Try to find the other two. Maybe they'll be sheepish enough to help."

Or the same thing had happened to them, José couldn't help but think.

"Maybe."

"Otherwise, we're going to have to go in to get her."

And that would mean sending down a third shuttle. Or Obadiah would have to come back and get people. At many levels, the latter made more sense.

"Which might be their intent."

José shook his head. "The other Verrans wanted to study us. These guys may be isolationist, but they might not be able to resist."

He tried to imagine that way of thinking. They wanted only them to survive.

Or they thought...maybe what they thought was quite sensible. Human influence would cause problems.

"Likely not," Chang said. "But that only means we have to be even faster to rescue her, before they decide dissection is a good way to find out about humans."

José winced. She was, of course, right. Dissection was a very real risk, and a risk that they had known about going down there.

Heck, he was pretty sure that if Doctor Jordan happened to get her hands on a Verran corpse, she'd do just that. For science. She wouldn't hurt anyone to get one, but she wouldn't be able to resist finding out where they kept their various internal organs.

"So, Lieutenant Smith."

"I found them," he says, wryly. "They went the wrong way from the hatch and are huddled under the mud."

Hopefully regretting that they had ever gone down there. "Tell them that if they help you retrieve Lieutenant Lauxon, we might just be able to forget this little incident."

Might, not would. It would probably depend...it was basically 'come back with her or not at all,' from the tone.

Obadiah was likely immune to that tone, mostly. But then, he didn't need to be. Obadiah had been on Mars.

He wouldn't leave a woman behind in the hands of the enemy, not under any circumstances. No more than José would.

No, this was aimed at those who had either been in the navy or sat out the war in a cushy civilian job.

José's lips quirked, thoughtfully. "I wish I was down there."

Chang turned to him. "So do I. But we are not going down there. What we are going to do is position ourselves right above their city."

José couldn't help but smile. Chang would never order an orbital strike, but these were the kind of people who *would*, and they might just be intimidated by the *Endeavour*'s Independence Day-like presence above their heads.

Heck, he would, if he didn't know that they were essentially a lightly-armed scout, an exploration vessel not designed for war.

He nodded, and did exactly as she said, positioning themselves in the lowest orbit they had fuel for.

Right over the Verran dome.

José went off shift with the ship in that position, relieved by Alice Foreman from the *Atlantis*.

He went to the mess hall. He was tired, but food was more important. A sandwich. Fuel. It wasn't anything he really wanted to eat, but he didn't care. He was in one foot in front of the other mode, forcing himself to eat because he knew he needed to rather than enjoying or savoring it. Even if it had been good food.

Supplies were good, but variety had gone down. Even with raiding what had survived in the *Atlantis*. And asking the Verrans for food?

Not after what they'd fed him. He closed his eyes. Almost fell asleep right there in the mess hall seat. Forced himself to finish his sandwich.

"Do we have to carry you to your bunk?" came a voice.

He laughed weakly. "I think I can make it. If I collapse in a corridor, just roll me there?" He turned to see who had spoken.

It was a couple of the younger scientists. He had to think for a second for their names. Charlton Marrow and LaVonte Washington, that was it. Marrow was the one who had spoken, the larger and paler of the two.

They were, as he recalled, geologists. Or whatever you called it when you weren't dealing with Earth. Planetologists, that was probably it.

"Will do," said Marrow, weakly grinning. "What are the moles up to?"

"Being...scared," José finally decided on, after running through several other words which might well be descriptive of their behavior. "Their world is ending and they don't know how to make a new one."

"I'm sure humans wouldn't do any better," said Washington, "even with all the disaster movies."

He laughed at that, tiredly. "We do seem to enjoy telling stories about the world ending."

Washington checked off disasters, "Climate change. Global plague. Comet strike. AI deciding that the only way to stop violence is to kill everyone. Kaiju. Don't forget the kaiju."

José would probably have joined in if he had had the energy. He didn't.

"Of course, they might have disaster movies too."

Maybe that would be a trade good, José thought, but even his thoughts were getting sluggish. The web was utterly silent. "I...think I need to get to my bunk," he added. "Before somebody really does have to carry me."

He made it there, barely. He did not manage to undress, but rather just lay on it, on top of the covers, drifting immediately into that halfway state between awake and asleep, and then into true sleep. He was so tired he did not even dream. Yet, he was remarkably content.

Which was, perhaps, for the best, given the recent content of his dreams.

He slept until he was awakened by the alarm he had set for his next shift.

* * *

The next day, or rather shift, they were still hovering over the city. Wilson had decided, it seemed, to put José in the regular rotation, at least until they had Lieutenant Lauxon back. He changed into coveralls he hadn't slept in, got breakfast, and went to the bridge. He took his place, trying to feel like he belonged there.

He failed. He felt like a blue collar guy who had been given an office job and forced to wear a suit. Yesterday, during the crisis, he had started to feel something more like part of the system, but it hadn't lasted.

The web whispered seductive opinions. Reminded him of why they wanted him here.

Would he find an officer's badge when they got back to Earth? Earth, which was now at peace. He'd missed an entire, brief war out here. Brief, nasty. Mars now only had one moon.

Chang was taking over from the officer of the watch. "Any change?"

"Lieutenant Smith got into the city. We haven't heard from him."

The thickness of the rock was probably blocking his radio. José frowned, worried for his friend, then forced himself to relax.

Not because he shouldn't worry, but because he trusted Obadiah. He would, in fact, trust him with his life, so it was easy to trust Obadiah with his *own* life. But he was in hostile territory, where he would be recognized instantly.

José had to worry a little that he was now in a cell next to Lauxon. And that one or both of them was already dead.

He could not do anything but trust them. He hated dealing with aliens. Not the aliens themselves.

Just the dealing.

"We're getting some kind of incoming radio call."

"Is it from the city?" Chang smiled slightly.

It was the same Comms officer, the one everyone called Comms. José hadn't even heard her name. Maybe she liked being called that. "It is."

"Then let's hear it."

There was an explosion of clearly angry chittering. Then, in very broken English, "We have person. You want back?"

"Yes, I do." Chang responded. Keeping it simple.

"You come here. We talk."

"I don't leave the ship. You can talk to my people."

José suspected he knew the meaning of the chittering that followed.

There was silence. "Like other person just found?"

"You can talk to him." Chang still kept her tone even.

"Him." As if the pronoun was an alien thing. Perhaps it was.

Perhaps it changed something. "We talk him. Then we talk you."

That sounded like a promise. Would they try and get up to the ship? They had rockets, but that didn't mean they had anything man... Verran...rated.

It did mean they could build them, though, and now they had such clear knowledge that it was possible.

Silence. They'd hung up. Chang nodded. "Hopefully that keeps our people safe."

And they might even get information. "How did they get so much English?"

"I assume by spying." She sounded thoughtful. "Or they have really good translation algorithms."

They definitely had higher technology than the others, but translation algorithms? They'd have to be good...

They'd have to be very good.

28

Two hours passed. Then the radio crackled to life again. "Hello, Captain."

"Hello, Lieutenant Smith. You've been busy. Is Lieutenant Lauxon alright?"

"Mostly. They didn't deliberately harm her, but apparently something she ate disagreed with her."

José winced. Alien food might, he supposed, easily give one problems. It was something to think about.

"And they took samples, but they did so without doing real damage. They don't want us here, but they want to die less, I think."

"How about the other cities?"

"They don't want them to die. They don't want to merge with them. At least that's what I can tell."

"A natural worry. It's a shame there isn't another planet they can just move to."

José had been thinking that.

"Well. Can you extricate yourselves from there? And what about our wayward people?"

"They're back with the shuttle. Supposedly."

Why they hadn't come back to the ship, José didn't want to know. They were still up to something.

Maybe they'd gotten what they wanted. Maybe they'd booby trapped the hatch from the outside so Cecilie and Obadiah would not be able to get back to the *Endeavour*.

José had started to trust Slava. He'd stopped again. Whatever she wanted, she hadn't gone about it the right way. They had to work together.

So did the Verrans.

These people had rocketry. The other two cities...one of them had organization. The other appeared to have...better agriculture. Better food.

If they worked together, they increased their chances. But those chances might increase from zero to minimal. Or, well. "X percent of zero is still zero."

"What was that, Mr. Molin?"

"Just thinking that they would increase their survival chances if they worked together, but if those chances are zero..."

"Which we know they might be."

And they might have lived in peaceful ignorance until the end. José thought about it, then decided he sure wouldn't want to live in peaceful ignorance.

He would want to come to terms. He would want to rage at the uncaring skies.

To rage at the laws of gravity.

Obadiah again, "I heard that. Thankfully, I don't think they understood it. They seem to think their chances are rather better than that. But we may have them convinced they're even better with us."

"If they have a plan, I want to hear it. And no, I won't promise not to help the other cities."

Chang was going to make that the price, José thought, of their assistance.

We won't leave anyone behind.

She was so reserved he didn't feel as if he knew her. He had heard something about a partner or spouse, but no details.

And whoever it was, they were on Earth. And she had brought nothing of her personal life with her.

He rather thought it was an ex-partner, that she would not have left somebody she loved to come here. Or would she?

But he trusted her. She would not leave anyone behind. That was all he needed to know about his captain.

"I will see if I can get it out of them before we leave, one way or another."

Obadiah was a man who would make a false promise if lives were at stake. José knew that much, and that meant he trusted him too.

Trusted him to get this done. It felt good.

Both shuttles arced up from the surface. "Well, this is going to be fun."

Chang again, reaching out more than normal. Because apparently the lieutenants had a guest...one of the Verrans. A representative.

A response to their refusal to send Chang down alone, they were sending one of theirs up alone. José thought they might have missed a vital cultural signal there.

Open gun ports.

But it hadn't resulted in any more shooting at them. It hadn't resulted in any more of the kind of crap that had happened before.

Just that they were going to have a Verran shedding all over the ship. He shook his head at himself. That was a rude thought.

But then, furry things did tend to shed. Humans shed, it just wasn't that noticeable.

And Verrans did smell just a tiny bit, although not that bad.

"Bring the Verran to the meeting room." Chang glanced around the room. "Kirk, relieve Marin. Mr. Marin, you're with me."

José stood up, wondering why the captain wanted him along. Or maybe she just wanted an escort.

Maybe. She was smarter than he was, he knew that, and she likely had an insight into Verran psychology he had not just totally missed but not even got in the area of.

"Him." The way that pronoun had been delivered.

Males important. In the other Verran cities, both of them, drones had played important roles, but mostly in child rearing. And, of course, child siring. José wondered for a moment what it was like to live perhaps your entire life without not only ever having sex but without ever wanting it.

Some people didn't. But this wasn't the same thing. This was that as a norm. As part of society. Mother and father as distant things, important and not at the same time.

But Chang wanted a man next to her. Just in case.

Just in case it made a difference.

They got to the meeting room before Obadiah and the Verran did. Stood as the two arrived.

"I am Chang Yi Hui," she introduced.

"In charge?" the Verran asked. They had pale grey fur, and it seemed a little thinner than most.

Old, José decided. Old and never having changed. Expendable and knowledgeable. Perhaps the perfect choice.

"Yes. This is José Marin, one of our pilots. He knows something about engineering."

The Verran nodded. "He. She." Their nostrils fluttered. "Pilot."

"We do not change as you do."

The mole seemed to think about that. Then abruptly they nodded. And sat down. "Why help?"

"Because on our world you help people who...who have disasters. And they repay it, in the end, to you or somebody else."

"What payment?"

"Nothing. You may one day be in the place where you can help us. That's all we need."

José was pretty sure the Verran didn't believe it. Perhaps didn't believe anyone would do something without payment.

Perhaps didn't believe they could survive.

"What want?"

"I want to know your plan."

They laid it out on the table.

And it was something out of Jules Verne, but something that had the core of something which could work. They were working on a giant cannon which would, they hoped, shoot large payloads into orbit right at the next conjunction.

"We can't save all, but can save some."

José wanted to pull out his demonstration railgun. It would allow them to fire... "What if you could fire three times as often."

"Could that be done?"

Chang looked at José. Then she nodded. "I think so."

"Still couldn't save all. Save the children, the shes, the hes."

"Wouldn't new people change if there were none?"

"Yes, but you can't predict it without a..."

So, somehow, the queens or the drones or both controlled what sex somebody changed into? Pheromones? Something like royal jelly.

"At least one he. Good to take shes too, start the breeding."

The drones, then.

The drones who watched the kids, watched them develop. Did they take notes? Did they trigger the change itself or just guide its direction?

It was starting to make sense, but he didn't understand it all. Couldn't. They needed so much more data.

"Plus, got to raise the kids."

Poor kids, José thought. But the kids and the...breeders...would go. The workers would die. And this old Verran thought that fair.

Women and children first, he thought, when there weren't enough lifeboats. It was sexism, but there was also something behind it, a faint knowledge that males were expendable.

Old workers, past the age at which they could change, had to be the most expendable of all, if he had any understanding of their society and biology.

But they would have knowledge, too.

"It's not so far from some of the things we have thought. Why not help the others?"

"Because they aren't us." Then a pause. "I suppose they look like us to you."

"They do." José suspected the Verrans could not even see the obvious ethnic differences between him, and Chang.

Obadiah finally spoke up. "That excuse darkens the history of our species. Any time you other people, it will come back on you. Your species needs to grow past that to survive."

"Spe…" The Verran shook their head.

José took pity on them. "Species." He pointed at the others. "Human. Species."

"Ah. I see what you say."

Apparently, the concept was fine, but the word had not made it into the limited shared vocabulary.

"They are not you, but they *are* you," Obadiah said. He pointed at José. "You see how much lighter he is? And he's still darker than some."

They would understand skin color as a differentiator.

"It's not just color."

"I wasn't saying it was. Just, different." There was always difference, there was always separation.

"They took our kids. Without agreement."

That was, well, that was pretty damning. And Obadiah flinched. The obvious answer was to tell them to get over it, but who could think about the history of humanity, of child thefts and slavery and genocide in all of its terrible forms and still say that.

Maybe a white man.

Maybe. But then he recalled that demanding children as compensation was part of their society. Was kidnapping really another form of theft?

On Earth, stealing children was genocide. Here it might be more like cattle rustling.

29

"Bridge to Captain Chang."

Chang turned to José. "Get up there."

He got, and thus did not hear what the problem was. It was like she was just assuming that he would be needed. Jane Kirk got out of the pilot's seat as he arrived. He strapped himself in, frowning.

"Got it," Comms said.

"What happened?" José asked, feeling he had every reason and need to know, especially if he was about to have to try and fly them out of there at full speed.

"Another explosion on the planet."

José sighed. "Are they fighting each other again? Still?"

"No, we think it might actually have been a launch, but if it was, it didn't get off the pad."

José winced. "Where from?"

"What we're calling city three."

José nodded again. "Thanks." He then turned his attention to the controls. He didn't want to ask more. Chang emerged onto the bridge not long after.

"Just in case that was something we need to worry about...I want you to hold position right now, but do the math to get us over that site."

What could they do? Orbital bombardment could only make things worse.

If there were Verran astronauts in uncontrolled orbit, though, they might be able to grab them. It seemed distinctly unlikely.

José thought he should at least try and think of them as one of the sets of chittering clicks, but which one? And did they mean species or ethnicity or nationality or something else altogether? They could pronounce English, humans couldn't pronounce their language.

Always going to be at a disadvantage. Or not. Humans could presumably learn to understand it.

There was another explosion from the planet, close to the first one.

"Or we have a small war going on down there."

Three was the city that had blown up one's guarderia and blamed it on two. One and two might have gotten together for a little bit of vengeance.

Any death either mattered not at all or hugely.

Comms frowned. "The explosions are both at the edge of three's dome. I think somebody's overkilling trying to blow a hatch."

Or maybe three had managed to build full blown pressure hatches, which would be very hard to blow on that kind of scale. José didn't say it out loud. He just frowned. Thinking tactically, thinking like he was still a soldier.

You blew a hatch to get in, but you also blew a hatch if you didn't care about using what was on the other side of it.

If you had suits and they didn't, but that didn't apply in this case. Yet. He shuddered, the image of the atmosphere being pulled off back in his mind.

So, why would they not care?

Unless their goal was to cause expensive damage.

"Send down a probe. Now."

Weps, currently Jane Kirk, nodded and hit a few buttons to launch one. José was glad they had one ready. He wanted to know what was going on down there, wanted it to the point where his fingers curled a little towards the controls.

You couldn't save a divided world.

They had to unite. But there was no enemy to unite against.

You couldn't unite against an enemy you literally couldn't fight.

"So, what appears to be going on is that they blew open a hatch and are going into the city. Clearly they don't intend to sneak around."

Comms fiddled, and got the video from the probe on the front screen, although it took her a moment.

They could clearly see the blown hatch. "What can a small team do?" Comms added.

"Blow stuff up," José said, grimly. "Blow up something really important if they can, like the power plant. From the way they went in,

I'd say this is a damage team."

A team that would just...destroy infrastructure until they were killed. Tactics they had used on Mars, seen again here. And in the same context, with civilian lives at stake.

If anyone was a civilian on a dying world. *That* was not a good way to think José told himself.

These people were none of them innocent and none of them villainous.

"How would you stop them?"

"From here, I wouldn't. Down there? You kill them, and fast." He answered Chang almost without thinking about it. "You take them out before they can do any more damage. They'll be ready for that, though."

From here, though, there was nothing he could do. The web *itched* under his skin at the thought of ground combat, at the thought of going down there, taking a rifle and shooting a few people. Killing them.

Killing them before they could take out something really bad like, say, a power plant. He hadn't been inside Three, only One, Two, and Four. He didn't know the layout.

He wanted better names for them. With just the numbers, they sounded like something from an early twenty-first century young adult dystopia, from that very specific subgenre that had been, for a few years, popular. Until, of course, everyone had enough of it.

The probe was following them into the city. "Wait," José said.

"You have an idea, Mr. Marin?"

"Can the probe broadcast?"

"Sound only."

"It'll have to do. Send it ahead of them...see if we can find their police before we lose signal."

Comms smiled. "Captain?"

"Do as he says. I like it."

They would lose signal, but hopefully they could get enough through the hatch to...see and identify the cops. Warn them. Annoy them into doing something.

He couldn't be down there, but they could.

There was a group of Verrans. They didn't look like police, they looked like maintenance workers.

Comms had the probe produce a series of chitters, computer generated Verran speak. Hopefully it said something meaningful, not a bunch of swear words or a meatball recipe.

It certainly got their attention. Comms repeated the chitter, a little different.

They ran, one of them pulling something akin to a phone out of his pocket.

"Well, hopefully they're calling the cops, even if it's on us," Comms said.

"What did you say to them?"

"What I *tried* to say was 'Enemies at the hatch.'" They were probably investigating the explosion anyway.

So, it might only have bought a few minutes. And possibly the lives of those Verrans, armed only with maintenance tools.

They'd left their truck behind, with the tools in it. But it also blocked much of the corridor.

All José could do was wait and hope.

The fight, when it came, was short and nasty. And that corridor was now blocked with rubble, although two of the intruders were under it.

"Maybe we shouldn't have taken sides," Comms said.

José shook his head. "They were going to go for an important soft target. Power plant. The creche again. No, we had to stop them."

He looked to the captain. She had her hands templed in front of her again, something clearly personal in her repertoire of gestures.

Part, he suspected, of how she thought.

"Mr. Marin is right," she said, simply. "Protecting civilians is not taking sides."

Sometimes it was. But he didn't voice that. The civilians had been protected, the only damage was that corridor and the hatch. Would make it hard to reinforce it, but they had time. They still had time.

Time and that whispering in the web that maybe they didn't have enough. Certainly, they weren't going to sit here for ten years.

That was probably what was bothering him. The Verrans had time. The *Endeavour* ultimately didn't. She had been designed for a nine month voyage, and it was more like six with the *Atlantis* survivors eating their food.

Longer if they could find a nice uninhabited terrestrial planet with compatible plants on it, but that seemed decidedly unlikely at this point.

Nice uninhabited terrestrial planets didn't seem all that common, in this part of the galaxy at least.

Maybe all the really nice terrestrial planets were inhabited. That wouldn't surprise him.

Comms shook her head. "I think we should...I hate to say it, but we should write up the blueprints to a plan, give it to the leadership of all four cities at once, then skedaddle."

Chang nodded. "That's not a bad idea, Ms. Kruger."

So, she did have a name.

"But it's only one prospect under consideration. The other is to keep an eye on them."

"For ten years?"

"Not with one ship, not consistently. We can leave probes..."

"We can start building a station." José was surprised by his own words.

"We...hrm. Not without help."

"Help could be sent," José said, finally. "Look, it's the next step anyway. Build an outpost here. Make a destination for some of the Verrans to rocket up to. Eventually, we hand it over to them."

Bring them into the Federation, he thought. The alliance. Whatever it ended up being called. There might be Verrans on Earth one day, taking photos of the monuments.

It was the first truly positive image he'd had in what felt like a long time. Verran and glyn tourists exploring Earth.

Verrans building out from the station, abandoning their doomed homeworld to build a truly space-based civilization. They were used to living underground. A smaller step for them than for man.

If humans could do it, they certainly could.

"We have another incoming radio call."

"Put it on," Chang said, simply. "Let's hear what they have to say."

30

"You said you were…not…fight."

Chang shook her head. "We will protect anyone who is in danger."

José thought about that for a moment. But he was not going to argue with her. She knew what she was doing.

If she didn't, then it certainly wasn't his place to talk to her, it was C.T.'s.

He wished he knew the XO a little better. He wasn't as reserved as Chang, but he tended to stick to the company of the officers and scientists.

"So, we are not to be allowed to…solve…problems."

Chang stood. "Your entire world is in danger, your species is highly likely to become extinct."

She was probably using words that were too long for them.

"We can fix it."

"You have ten years to get your cities sealed, thirty to get enough people off planet to ensure Verran survival."

"What if don't want to?"

"You can make that choice for yourself. Not for anyone else."

She was right on that front.

And then the proximity alarms went off. José threw the *Endeavour* to the side. Their missiles were getting better, or…

No, it was a missile. It exploded harmlessly somewhere off their stern.

"Also, if people are going to keep shooting at us, we do have the right to defend ourselves."

"Or you could leave."

"Not unless all four cities ask us to go."

José's hands began to sweat. True, their weapons were not a threat to the *Endeavour*, but the anxiety rose nonetheless. It didn't matter whether the fire you were under was super soakers filled with plain water, it was still fire. You didn't not dodge, because that trained you to not dodge.

"The next one will be something which can damage you."

Chang shook her head. "Cut them off," she said. "So, one of four asks us to leave. Three of four ask us to stay. Two want help, the third just us to go over their plans." She sounded like she was thinking out loud.

"We stay," she said, after a moment. "We stay, and we go over their plans, and we leave as soon as they don't need us."

It all seemed fair. Then Weaps spoke up. "Three ships just came out of hyperspace."

"Can we identify them?"

"Not yet, they came in a way out. All I saw was the flares."

There was a bit of an energy release when a ship came out. So, they knew three ships, but not whose. Glyn? Ky'iin? A new player altogether?

Likely not human, even with the military retrofits.

What could they do in this situation? Maybe the ky'iin would build a station for the Verrans.

"Tell me as soon as you have a clue who they are," Chang said, then turned her attention and templed hands back to the planet below.

"Okay, so, the railgun plan and building a station seems like the best first thing to push them towards. Making the cities airtight should not be a problem, but getting them away from the planet is beyond our current engineering."

With a station, they could build ships, could slowly move population off planet.

José rather thought they needed a ship design that was a lot bigger than the *Endeavour*. They needed a colony ship.

"I have an idea," he spoke up.

"Yes?"

"There are colony ship designs on Earth, right?"

"Those are classified, young man."

José's lips quirked. "There wouldn't be any point in us coming out here if somebody wasn't working on ways to move a few thousand people to a nice uninhabited planet."

"No, there wouldn't, I suppose. You're suggesting we give those designs to the Verrans."

"Yes."

"And what do I tell the brass we are getting in return?"

"An ally that is grateful to us. An outpost in this system. If they can't think about what..." José tailed off. "You mean the military types."

"I do indeed. Truth is, I already asked. And that was exactly what they want to know. They're not willing to give designs we haven't even built and tested yet to aliens."

José smiled. "Haven't even built and tested. How about...how about we make use of the xenophobia generals always have."

Chang's laughter was ringing.

"I'm not saying, understand," José was saying to Chang, "that we should really make the Verrans take all the risks."

"But that we can sell it to the military as...the Verrans take all the risks."

Weps cut in. "I believe they're ky'iin ships. A task force."

Chang nodded. "Okay. So, we can't look the ky'iin in the face without wanting to punch them. We can't do audio only. What they are suggesting is that we send notes. Which wasn't thought of because the ky'iin aren't, apparently, big on writing."

That was interesting, José thought. An entire civilization without writing? He could see that it could be done, but the Verrans had writing...

"So," she continued. "We're going to exchange written communication in English. Comms, I also want you to get ready a package to send of all the video we have of the Verrans, the map we have of their world."

Comms nodded. That alone should be enough to get the ky'iin up to speed.

"Also, from what I'm told, ky'iin are matriarchal. Assume the captains are female."

José nodded a bit. He wondered what else they had found out about them. He also wondered if sticking to English was the best idea. What if Spanish ended up being easier for them to learn? Or Chinese. Perhaps if they weren't big on writing they would do better with a different alphabet...who knew. He didn't.

"It's possible for humans to learn their primary language, and people with certain learning disabilities are immune to the provocation effect," Chang continued.

José thought for a moment. She had to mean autistic people, or rather that subset that had difficulty naturally reading body language. Maybe kids introduced to the ky'iin young would also be immune.

He thought of the Verran talk about trading babies like they were commodities.

He thought of older ideas of fostering kids so they would build a lasting peace.

"Okay," she said, finally. "Also, they outgun us. José, I want you to be ready to jump out if they decide that they aren't going to abide by the treaty."

He nodded. He didn't think it was likely, but three military vessels versus the *Endeavour* was as uneven a contest as the Verran missiles.

"Should we warn them about the pot shots from the planet?" Weps asked.

"I'll compose our message real quick, but yes, we should. It won't be a threat to them, but they should know things here aren't peaceful."

José let out a breath. Be ready to jump. It was a good thing he was used to ninety percent boredom and ten percent sheer terror.

Not to mention to hoping that his superiors didn't screw up the correspondence. Exchanging notes with people who didn't speak your language just struck him as...

...as something for the kind of AI nobody wanted to build. Maybe now they would have to.

"Another missile from the planet. This one's bigger."

José dodged it. The explosion was quite a lot bigger. "I suppose they thought that would hurt us."

"It might have in a direct hit," Weps said grimly. "Should I target the launch site?"

The idea of dropping something on the launch site appealed for a horrifying moment. But if they did, this became war in truth. Was it the web again, expressing its opinion through him, the old conditioning. He saw the tactics, and he hated them, hated himself. Reached instead for the connections he had built. Not just with the ship but with the stars and this world.

"No. We wait for the ky'iin. They are much more experienced with this kind of thing than we are."

José wished he thought that was a good thing.

The three ky'iin ships, as they came close, looked like warships. They bristled with visible sensors, perhaps scanning the planet below.

José wondered if they had come here before and decided the Verrans were not worth saving. If they had tried and given up. If they needed human help coming up with more ideas.

He thought it more likely that they had been trying, but not enough. Or maybe they hadn't thought it was worth leaving a ship here.

Or maybe *they* couldn't talk to the Verrans.

Exchanging notes. The first response had come, and it translated mostly as, "Why do you want to help them?"

Chang had already given an answer to that. And it hadn't seemed like the wording meant that the ky'iin thought they were crazy, so much as some kind of test.

"It's a lot of resources," came the next note.

It was a lot of resources. What could they give the ky'iin? What could they trade with these people?

And Earth had its own rebuilding to do after the war, a war which had cost the ky'iin only, perhaps, ships and trained personnel, not entire outposts.

Launchpad was gone, and that hurt a little. A station could be rebuilt, but it would not, could not be the same place from which they had left what felt like a lifetime ago.

It was hard to believe events were counted in weeks, months if you were generous. Maybe that was the real reason he couldn't imagine that the Verrans had years.

Well, Earth years. Verran years were...similar, but not the same. Local time.

Chang was typing on her console again, writing another note for the ky'iin. "I told them we can learn a lot from this effort, and that the Verrans, some of them, are worthy allies."

She was being open and transparent, at least to the bridge crew. Likely to the scientists, who were still poring over all of the data from Verr. Trying to work out what kind of planet it had been before the weather went crazy, before climate became something of a myth.

A lot of resources. But this system had them. There were metals in the outer system, out into the oort cloud.

If the Verrans could mine them.

"So, the ky'iin suggest that we start by working with them on a station and better ground to orbit. Which was what they had already decided to do, but they hadn't got the resources together."

It felt more like confirmation than anything. "Can they do anything for large ships?" José asked.

Maybe they wouldn't have to give the Verrans plans for untested prototypes after all.

"Maybe. I can ask."

The faster they could move population off planet, the better. And it would have to be stations, ultimately.

Because they didn't unite against external threats, José realized. They didn't unite. They scattered, and would scatter themselves to extinction without pressure in the other direction. Would separate themselves off from each other such that they didn't have the genetic diversity to survive.

Chang smiled at him. "Be careful, or I'll leave you here in charge," she threatened Marin.

He realized that she wanted banter, managed, "I thought you needed me to fly this crate."

She laughed a bit. "Maybe I'll leave Lieutenant Smith."

He thought Obadiah wouldn't actually be a bad choice. But what about the *Atlantis* XO?

Or did she want to get back home as quickly as possible?

José thought of his home. The smell of his father's cooking (never his mother's, she had been prone to burning water). Seeking shade in the heat of the day. The sound of Spanish, not the English overwhelmingly spoken on the ship. Voices raised in anger or in joy. Walking along the boardwalk, ignoring the tourists, tuning out their congratulatory talk about how Puerto Rico had recovered, how resilient they had to be. His home.

The Verrans would never see theirs again. It seemed worth the sacrifice of his to give them some future.

31

They only had Verrans on the ship once. Now the ky'iin wanted to meet Verran representatives.

On *Endeavour*.

José was not in a position to question why. But he was in a position to make sure that nobody disrupted the meeting.

Which meant he was in a position to hear something of what was going on. And to glimpse the ky'iin.

That brief glimpse said it all. Ebon black, stalking, no nose on their otherwise remarkably humanoid faces. It wasn't the web that wanted to fight or flee, to do whatever it took to get away. It was José himself, pure human instinct.

He understood now. The ky'iin were apex predators, they reminded humanity of the time when humans had been both predators and prey.

They were big cats, but without the shared evolution that had led small cats to become humanity's friends.

And the Verrans were rats.

Was that the problem? Did the ky'iin get hungry when they saw Verrans, and were they trusting the humans to be a mediator, to be the species that could get on with them.

Three of the cities had sent representatives, collected separately. José had flown one of them up, but the mole had had nothing to say for themselves, rather clinging to their seat with an expression that, if he read it right, spoke of profound airsickness.

They made it without throwing up, but the way down would be worse.

The idea of not returning some Verrans to the surface crossed his mind. They would live, but he certainly wouldn't want to outlive his species, not without hope.

He shook his head. Turned his attention back to eavesdropping as best he could.

There was only so much he could drop. The occasional chitter, the whistling sounds of the spoken part of ky'iin language. They were communicating somehow and nobody was being eaten.

The ship shook.

Three had, it seemed, sent another missile up. José wondered if the ky'iin, military personnel and by definition more trigger happy, would take out the launch site.

They might need that launch site. Rockets were easier, cheaper, and faster to build than the spaceplanes the *Endeavour* used as shuttles.

Of course, any launch site might be transitory, with the shifting muds and earthquakes down there. There was nobody in there with them except robots recording the situation. He thought of the AIs on Earth, the sentient ones they hadn't brought out here, that were kept limited. Kept untrusted.

Treated like kids. Too precious to risk, too dangerous to trust.

He thought they needed one of them after all. Maybe the ship itself. Maybe the feeling from the web was the ship's desire to live.

But could they trust it? People on Earth had thought not.

Could an AI translate for them? Or were they best off relying on native human intelligence. It was a moot point.

Unless the ky'iin had one.

Obadiah came wandering over to join him. "Wish we could understand what's going on in there."

There was a flurry of very loud chittering that might or might not be shouting.

"Somebody's not happy."

The kerfluffle died down rapidly, though. José shook his head. "I don't think anyone in this system has a reason to be happy." He wished he was less happy himself. He didn't feel it was fair, but he couldn't quite help it.

"I don't know about that," Obadiah's voice had an amused tone. Then he asided. "I caught Comms and Jane Kirk kissing in the storage room."

José laughed. "I won't tell on them."

"I know you won't, or I wouldn't have said anything."

José shook his head. "As long as they don't affect the ship."

"They haven't so far."

There was another loud flurry of chittering, and a bang on the door behind them.

"I think somebody wants out."

Whatever was going on in there eventually calmed down. A bit later, three very chastened-looking Verrans came out of the room. José didn't want to stick around to see the ky'iin, even if he'd managed to restrain himself. With warning.

So, he moved to follow them, to escort them. Chang stepped out of the office. "Mr. Marin."

He turned.

"Please escort our guests to the mess. The kitchen has a list of things they can eat."

He could do that.

"How did it go?" he ventured, hoping that they would understand him.

One of the three grunted, one remained silent, and the third, "They help. Still worried they eat."

José hesitated. "Also worried they will eat me."

The Verrans might not be as badly affected, but they were definitely aware of the ky'iin predatory nature. José didn't blame them.

But at the same time. "What did they offer?"

"Mining," the Verran said simply.

"Mining the outer system for resources to build."

"And..." They looked away.

José realized what they'd thought of. That the and might well refer to what was left of their homeworld after Lucifer finally tore it apart.

He tried to imagine that. He couldn't. "We'll help."

It was a promise, one he technically didn't have the authority to make, but it passed his lips anyway. He could not keep it from doing so.

"You not in charge," the Verran pointed out.

"I know." He'd do whatever was in his power, though. The web whispered, it had been quiescent lately. Perhaps because they hadn't jumped in a while. Perhaps he shouldn't jump.

The inexorable laws of gravity. "I..."

He realized there was nothing he could say that would not be a human platitude, unwanted by humans and not even understood by these people. So, he left it at that, escorting them to the mess.

Slava Koroskeya was there. She'd got away with what she did. Mostly. He had seen her doing work normally given to robots as punishment, but at least it hadn't been called a mutiny.

Would Chang have spaced her?

Yes, José knew. Without any hesitation and with remorse only in her cabin. She would have had to.

Seeing the Verrans, she tensed, gripping the table she was sitting at. Her eyes flicked around, and it looked like she was considering panicking or fleeing.

José decided the best thing to do was to position himself between her and the Verrans.

"I see the moles are on the ship."

"We were just facilitating a meeting. They were afraid the ky'iin would eat them."

Slava laughed. "Are *you* afraid the ky'iin will eat you?"

"Only when I'm in a room with one." He stayed between her and the Verrans. He bit back 'stolen any shuttles lately.'

"So, now you understand."

"The web was holding me back." He kept his tone even. "We're probably going to have to raise our kids together or something to work together properly."

Slava shuddered. "No thanks. Can I raise mine somewhere well away from them?"

"That can probably be arranged," José mused. "I mean, we can't expect everyone to be okay with aliens."

He glanced at the Verrans, who were being shown pictures of food by the cook.

"And some people are probably going to try and mate with them."

It felt like an accusation. José laughed. "I'm not...I'm bisexual, not..."

A xenophile. Besides, he was pretty sure the various parts weren't compatible.

Slava arched an eyebrow. "Omnisexual is the word I think you're looking for."

"Yeah. That." He let out a breath. "Somebody will probably try the experiment, but I don't think they'll get very far. And can you imagine the glyn?"

She laughed. "Yes. No. No thanks."

He felt he'd defused things sufficiently. And he did like her, when she wasn't being an idiot. When she wasn't endangering the entire ship. He doubted she'd ever be XO of a ship again, even if they built many more. He had the horrible thought that *he* might be one first. No. He wasn't going to let that happen.

He turned back to the Verrans. Tried to see them as something to fear.

He couldn't. It was other humans that triggered the web and the fear.

Not them.

The Verrans eventually left. The *Endeavour* was now flying away from Verr, one of the ky'iin ships pacing them. José could feel the ship's motion, feel it entirely too keenly for a moment. He *knew* where they were going and he was afraid that he...not that he was hallucinating again, but the accuracy of it bothered him. Was it a hallucination if it was real?

ESP had been mostly debunked. But electromagnetic signals passing from the ship to the web, that was something they could build off of.

Could and would. He headed up to the observation deck.

Chang was there.

He assumed the Captain had no desire to socialize with him, no interest in doing so. She was standing with her hands clasped behind her back, looking at the system.

Had he not known who she was, she would have seemed quite... well...ordinary. Just a middle-aged Chinese woman looking at the stars.

He stopped, mid stride.

"Whoever you are, relax. We *are* off duty."

He hesitated, then walked up...not next to her, no, but in the same plane, looking at the same view. "Captain."

"Mr. Marin. You have caused quite a stir on my ship. But you also saved our butts."

"I didn't want to...I didn't...I don't." He couldn't find the words. Out here, the captain had the power of life or death, almost literally. He respected her, and that made it hard to explain.

"Don't want what?" Her tone became amused.

"People have been talking about how I deserve to be an officer."

"And you don't want that."

José paused. "I *like* being a pilot. I like being out here. I wish I'd passed the aptitudes during the war. But I don't want..." A pause. Then he finally admitted it. "I don't want to be in charge of a squad again. I don't want people under my leadership..."

"You don't want people under your leadership to die. That, Mr. Marin, is exactly what made you a good squad leader." She turned. "I've read your file. I read your file before I let them put you on my ship. I knew I had a good one."

He squirmed under her gaze.

"But your fate will wait until we get back to Earth."

He didn't want to go back. Didn't and did. "I wasn't a good squad leader. Men died."

"Not all of them. Sometimes we have to save what we can."

He had a feeling she was talking about Verr.

He had a feeling she was talking about *Atlantis*.

Maybe she was talking about all of it. All of this was under her aegis, and they were a long way from home.

The deck plating beneath his feet shook. He saw her face before she all but dived for the suit locker. Middle aged she might be, but she still made it there before he did. A crack was starting to form in the observation dome.

"Report!" She snapped as she tossed him a suit with surprising strength, then started to suit up herself.

"Explosion. Right below the observation deck."

"A bomb," Chang translated.

Who had put it there? José had no answer to that question. He pulled on his suit then tapped the radio. "We need hull repair robots on the observation dome."

Chang produced the patch kit. "I need you to do something."

He nodded. "What?"

She ran back out to the middle. He followed her. "Lift me."

She was the lighter one. And between them they could reach the crack from the inside.

Air hissed out through it.

Somebody was probably going to get spaced for this, José thought, before he focused entirely on the repairs.

32

Chang was as deft as putting on the patch as José would have been, if not more so. Apparently even the Captain had gone through this drill and, presumably, kept up with it. She stood on his shoulders to finish it, then jumped down.

How she was staying this fit he did not know. She looked at the deck. "That, we can't repair easily."

José studied the worst of the cracking. "Meaning we may have to live with it until we get back to Earth."

"I have a bomber to find," she said, briskly. "Mr. Marin, with me."

He followed her. All thought of being off duty was gone, along with any thoughts about finding out more about the enigmatic captain.

Well, except she was very fit. And knew how to fall. He wondered if she'd been an athlete in school. Maybe even a gymnast, if that wasn't too stereotypical based on her size.

Probably it was.

He opened his mouth to say something. Decided she probably didn't need or want his opinions right now and closed it again. She was in charge, and he had to let her be.

But the question on his mind was simple. Had one of the Verrans managed to plant the bomb or did they have a saboteur amongst the crew?

He dismissed Koroskeya right away. She didn't like aliens. She wouldn't blow up the ship she was standing on.

Who would be that stupid? That stupid led to the Verrans, who were not here.

Or the ky'iin. "Mr. Marin, has anyone been expressing discontent?"

"Only Koroskeya and I don't think..."

"She might be stupid enough to, but no. Not unless she could frame a Verran for it."

Now there was a disturbing thought. José had not considered that. *That* she might do, especially as...

"I...hate to bring this up, Captain, but I would note the bomb went off when *you* were in the observation dome."

"I had thought about that."

It could be personal, José thought. Chang was not universally liked amongst the crew, but he did think she was at least somewhat respected. But if she did have an enemy, then the timing was hugely suspicious.

"Somebody needs to talk to the ky'iin. Unfortunately, we don't have anyone on board who can do so without taking a swing at them."

José thought about whether he could avoid doing so, decided the answer was most definitely no. He would take a swing at them and he would make things worse. "And exchanging notes doesn't..."

"No." She spoke into the intercom. "The ky'iin representative is to be returned to ly ship."

She smoothly used the ky'iin third gender pronoun, with the ease of the multilingual. "I will be sending them a message."

Chang did not tell him what she had in mind. He did not ask. She strode to the mess hall. "I want everyone not on duty on the bridge in the mess hall, stat. And I mean everyone."

It was the only place in which they could all fit. With the extra people it would be tight.

He followed on, wondering what she had in mind.

Wondering if they could find the bomber before worse happened.

Over the intercom. Obadiah's voice. "I...need help."

José gave Chang one look.

"Go."

"Where?" he asked.

"Engineering."

He ran. Any kind of attack on engineering could result in the destruction of the ship.

Down through the tubes, not trusting the lift, running as the artgrav became unstable for a moment, his run became a kind of roll and tumble, protecting his head and landing running again.

Obadiah, outside engineering, engaged in hand-to-hand with Slava Koroskeya and another of the *Atlantis* survivors.

So, it was her after all. A spike of pained anger and José ran into the fray. The web roared in excitement at finally getting to do what it, what he was designed for.

He threw the second person into the wall like a ragdoll. They weren't webbed.

Neither was Slava, but at some point she received high level training. She really knew what she was doing, but with the other guy out of the way, Obadiah was holding his own against her.

Her style was hard, she chopped at him. He grabbed her wrist, sent her spinning away towards José.

With a grin, José caught her, getting her hands behind her back with web-enhanced speed. "Now, that was almost disappointing. Slava, what the heck were you doing?"

"I'm on your side!" she yelled. "There's a mole in engineering!"

Obadiah opened the door. "Let's see if she's telling the truth."

A Verran stowaway. In engineering. Where a wrong button could blow the drives. If she was right, then they had a problem. José kept a firm grip on her.

"Where did you see the mole?"

"I saw its tail disappear into the storage compartment."

José didn't argue about the pronoun. Obadiah went for the storage compartment. It was locked. He tried the code. "Somebody over-rode the code."

Could the moles do that? Maybe, if they had good enough computer knowledge.

Kicking in the compartment was too risky. Obadiah turned to Slava. "If…"

She pointed, as best she could, to the guy in the corridor, who was picking himself up and limping. "Spiders," he grumbled.

For once, José took the insult as a compliment. "Can you get the storage compartment open?" Obadiah asked.

Then to José. "Let her go. The two of you, check the consoles."

José didn't protest that he wasn't an engineer. He had enough basic knowledge to see if anything was redlining.

He looked at Slava. "Sorry about that if you're telling the truth."

"And not if I'm not."

"You already stole a shuttle." José liked Slava. He didn't trust her, and he hoped that when they went back to Earth…

What would happen then? He didn't know. He didn't want to know. He didn't want to worry about it until the time came. "Not seeing any red lines. Slava must have spotted them before they did anything. But where's the engineer on duty."

That was a good question. There should have been somebody here. At least one person on duty, if not two. And they weren't supposed to leave it unattended.

"Got it!" came a voice.

He turned to see what was in the storage compartment.

The engineer on duty was in there. Tied up. José looked at Slava. "Where's the mole?" he demanded.

Obadiah was already moving to free the man. Then a furry shape struck him from above.

"There," Slava said, wryly.

José was already moving to help Obadiah with the ambush. The Verran was heavy, and had Obadiah on the ground.

José took a risk and grabbed the alien's tail. He pulled. Hard.

He was rewarded with a yelp that indicated tails were every bit as sensitive as he had hoped. At least, Verran tails were. It was hard to keep a grip on it, though, as it swished around with him attached.

But it gave Obadiah an opening to reverse the situation.

José didn't look up. He'd work out what the mole had been clinging to first. But obviously, the compartment wasn't soundproof. The mole had ducked in and then gone up, where even trained soldiers sometimes forgot to look.

Which told him this was a trained soldier. Who was now on his back on the floor.

"Do you surrender?" Obadiah demanded. José was not sure whether the Verran could handle the word surrender.

But they could surely handle the concept.

"City Three," José guessed. "I guess we found our bomber."

"We want you leave."

"Others want us to stay." Obadiah looked at José. "Let him go.

José released the tail so Obadiah could pull the Verran roughly to their feet.

Slava was glaring. "Maybe we should leave. Leave you all to your fate."

"We save ourselves."

"I hope so, but…"

Slava would, José suspected, be quite keen on the Verrans saving themselves so humans didn't need to help them, work with them, or deal with them. It would definitely be her first choice of outcome.

It wasn't the outcome they had, though, and nothing was going to change that any time soon. José shook his head. "We want you to save yourselves. We're just here to give you technical assistance."

Which was clearly too many big words, from the look in the alien's eyes. They didn't understand.

"Tools," José tried. "We give you tools."

"And rule us."

So, that was what the Verrans were truly afraid of. José didn't know what the answer was. He was, after all, an araña.

He had fought in a war about just that. On the wrong side.

Then Obadiah spoke up. "There's three ky'iin ships to our one, to make sure we don't try anything like that."

But could the ky'iin be trusted? José found himself wishing that they were not outnumbered, simply because that way they could keep the ky'iin honest.

"We'll keep each other...honest," José said, softly. But he wasn't just talking to the Verrans. He was talking about his hopes for the alliance.

"And we're building something you can be a part of," he added.

Something that the Verrans would need. If they had to become entirely space-based, they would need trade. Without a planet...

"Trade," José said.

Slava looked at him. "Look, I don't like you," she then said to the Verran. "I don't want you. But that doesn't mean your kids deserve to die."

They didn't have kids. Unless they had some attachment to the kids in their city.

But there was something about her honesty.

Something that caused the Verran to kind of slump. Perhaps it worked better than anything that had been done before to get them to listen.

Perhaps, ironically, they needed to know humans didn't all like them.

33

Chang stood in the center of the bridge. They still did not have visual communications protocols with the Verrans, so José could only assume that she thought standing like that would make her sound more in charge.

"We have your...agent. They have not been harmed."

That was mostly true. Obadiah had administered a few bruises.

"Your attempt on our ship is an act of war," she added. "You can be thankful that we have learned our lessons well."

Was she about to say she would only help three of the four cities. "If you want any further help from us, you need to replace those behind this."

Ah, yeah. She was calling for a coup. One, Two and Four were not a problem.

Three was.

Three was going to be the problem, and leaving them to die...but no. There were kids.

There was a response. "Go to <chitter>."

She turned it off. "Well, then. We broadcast details of the plan to the other three cities. Let Three go to the trouble of stealing it if they want it."

It wasn't their responsibility to save people from themselves.

But José couldn't disagree. And he couldn't avoid hearing the anger in her voice. Anger that matched his own.

But they were afraid of losing who they were, of being taken over by humans or by ky'iin.

The plans had been finalized. A mix of things. The railgun. Space planes. A station, first, and then they could expand it into a habitat.

A place to flee to. It was, in theory, all done and handled. They could help for a bit longer, then hand things over to the ky'iin.

"What are we doing with the Verran prisoner?" C.T. from the door, sounding more curious than angry.

Chang frowned. "Treating them as a prisoner of war. We'll hand them over. I was thinking of just dropping them outside a hatch."

José nodded. In the mud.

He glanced at C.T.

"I'll find out who most wants the pleasure then." He tapped his forehead, not quite a salute, and left.

Chang turned back to the front. "I think we are very close to being done here. I would rather wait for another ship, but we may not be able to."

It felt wrong. It felt like they were not done, but José knew she was right. Done and ready to go back to Earth, to drop off the *Atlantis* crew.

And then what? Get repairs, come back out, explore? That was what José wanted to do. But what if he was the only one?

He shook his head. The *Endeavour* would continue to fly, and he could feel the energy that flowed around her, could feel just the whisperings of the stars.

"What more do we have to do?" Jane Kirk ventured.

"Make sure the Verrans understand what we gave them. Turn it over to the ky'iin. They have their own bad colonial history."

José frowned. Mentioning that made him tense up, for some reason. Or perhaps because there was a certain law about bad histories coming back to haunt you.

One of the ky'iin ships had, he recalled, gone to the outer system.

The second he thought that, Comms spoke up. "Distress call from the KY 3546."

Chang swore in Cantonese. "What?"

"They're under attack."

The other two ky'iin ships were already speeding towards the fight, at a higher speed than the *Endeavour* could manage.

But any fight would still be over by the time they got there.

Chang hesitated, then. "Follow them, Mr. Marin."

"We'll never get there in time," Comms pointed out.

"We are still going to try."

Which meant gun it. The *Endeavour* was slower than the ky'iin warships, less developed technology. They were not the most powerful or advanced people here, José knew, plain and simple.

The ky'iin were. But what about whoever had attacked them. A new player altogether.

"Do we know who attacked them?" Chang asked.

"They didn't say much. Something about rogue tyrar."

Whatever tyrar were. Another kind of alien, not doubt. And rogue meant that they were ignoring their own government and/or some kind of treaty. José found that somewhat heartening.

A rogue unit would not have the entire force of their people's navy behind them, no matter what. A rogue unit could be dealt with without starting a war.

Maybe they could jump. He considered it, then dismissed it. The ship wanted to, the ship was like a racehorse waiting in the stall, wanting to move.

Or no, he wanted to. And he was feeling the ship as an extension to his body, his own desire to fight expanding through the metal. The *Endeavour* was not a warship.

They did not want to get there in time. They wanted to get there late, to pick up lifeboats. That was what had to be on Chang's mind. The ky'iin streaking away from them.

But it was still a matter of hours at the highest speed of the ion drive.

"Mr. Marin, do you think a micro jump advisable?"

"No, ma'am. They're in the Oort, and we don't have the maps. The ky'iin don't seem keen on trying it either."

And, by definition, they had more experienced pilots. They knew better than he did whether this was safe. Despite that desire to fall and leap into hyperspace, he trusted their judgment.

"In that case, as nothing is going to happen for several hours, hand over to..." She paused, and then spoke into her intercom. "Foreman, when she gets up here. Try to get some sleep. I want you and Lauxon both on the bridge when we arrive."

It might be too late to change the outcome of the battle, but if the ky'iin lost, they would still have the tyrar to deal with.

If the ky'iin lost, then there was no way the *Endeavour* could win.

"Comms, please broadcast the package to every city but Three. It's not as ready as we'd like, but that can't be helped."

Alice Foreman, her blond curls bouncing, stepped onto the bridge. Relieved, José went to his quarters. Chang was right.

He should sleep.

And being a soldier, he actually could. He could feel the tension in the steel as he went down to his quarters, though. Could the ship sleep? He was suspecting, now, that it had enough complexity for some kind of vague animal sentience.

And he suspected that the next generation would have more. It was inevitable. But for right now, he was just worried about getting to his bunk. Throwing himself down on it and sleeping as best he could, trusting he would be wakened when he was needed.

He slid into sleep, but his dreams were haunted by Verran children with rifles. And finally he was standing on a beach, the water retreating rapidly away from the sand...

Tsunami.

He was wakened by his name over the intercom, as if his brain had been primed and trained to listen for it.

Straightening his coveralls, he ran for the bridge, sliding into his seat as Patrick vacated it.

Holy crap.

This was a rogue unit? It dwarfed the ky'iin ships. One of which, he presumed the 3653, was disabled. The ky'iin did not seem to name their ships.

The other two hadn't got there much ahead of the *Endeavour* after all. They were trying to fight the behemoth.

"That's a rogue unit?" he burst out.

"So it seems."

It was a battleship. There was no other word for it. Bristling with weapons. It had to be that an admiral or a long-trusted captain had gone rogue.

"The ky'iin said they made demands. We are to take the 3653 in tow and leave this system, never to return."

Comms sounded calm.

"Options?" Chang asked.

Leaving the system never to return seemed like a good idea to José. He had already been to the head, now he wanted to go again.

The Endeavour was a shuttle next to the scale of the tyrar ship. There was no way they could fight it.

Nor could they, from what José knew, tow the 3653 into hyperspace, the ky'iin would have to do that themselves.

"Stay quiet, see if they notice us, grab survivors," was what he said.

"Wise. They will most likely overlook us in favor of the warships.

What language are they communicating in?" she asked Comms.

"The message was text from the ky'iin. We'll have to trust their translation."

They would. They couldn't talk to the tyrar directly.

José kept his hands on the controls. He was ready to jump them out of there, back to the Hoth system, if they were in real danger. The ky'iiin couldn't expect a lightly-armed exploration vessel to take on that thing. Chang couldn't. They didn't have stray people on the planet this time.

The tyrar ship did not seem to have noticed them.

Kirk spoke up. "What about mines? If they aren't paying attention to us?"

"I don't think the mines we have would do anything against a ship that size. We'd have to get people on board."

José winced. He didn't like that option. It would likely be a suicide mission.

"We do have a volunteer if it comes down to it," Chang said. "But I think I like Mr. Marin's plan better."

An explosion blossomed on the side of the tyrar ship.

"We stay here, and we grab escape pods. From *any* of the ships."

Staying neutral? No, making sure they got prisoners. José's lips quirked. Lauxon was on the bridge. He yielded the primary seat to her, knowing she was by far the better real space pilot.

"You just get ready to jump us out if they start firing," Lauxon asided to him.

"I am."

The web wanted to fight. Something in him wanted to fight. Did these people intend to save the…

"That ship…it's large enough, isn't it," he said, suddenly. "That's the design the Verrans need."

"Observant, Mr. Marin. Unfortunately, capturing it is out of the question.

His mind was churning. Another explosion. The great ship was taking damage.

But not as much as the ky'iin.

34

"We have an escape pod," Kirk said, simply. "Not entirely sure who's."

"Have security check it."

Chang watched the screen. The ky'iin appeared to be losing. If they could convince them to end the fight, then…

José shook his head. The ky'iin, who could communicate, had to do that.

Why did the tyrar want this system?

"Tyrar. Two individuals. They're fuzzy," security reported.

Maybe they felt mammal kinship with the Verrans. "Escort them to the brig. See if you can find out what they eat," Chang instructed.

"We're being painted."

Apparently, picking up the pod had been seen as a provocation.

"Hold firm."

"And locked."

"Mr. Marin."

José reached for the jump controls, and the *Endeavour* dived amongst the stars. Chang hadn't given him a target. The system they were calling Hoth was as good as any. Diving, twisting, and then they were out. Out and safe. There was nothing but duty and alliance to get them to go back.

"Don't suppose the ky'iin sent us a tyrar dictionary?"

"No, but the tyrar are apparently signatories to the treaty. We could send to Earth," Comms said. "Heck, we could *go* to Earth. It wouldn't take that much longer than getting a response."

Something in José's stomach lurched. He both wanted and didn't want to go to Earth.

"Negative," Chang said. "We send to Earth, and we try to talk to them in the interim. I don't want that rogue ship following us."

Or rather, if they did, she wanted them to follow them here. José rather thought they wouldn't. It was the Verrans they wanted.

But then, they had two of their people. Two people who should be returned. His palms were sweating.

Starlight whispered through the web, but it wasn't as bad as it had been, perhaps he was adapting?

But it felt interrupted, it felt weakened. He knew why he wanted to go to Earth.

To get himself checked out or to stand on a beach or both. Were there beaches on the ky'iin homeworld?

Were there beaches anywhere but Earth? Were most of the habitable planets marginal things like Hoth?

He leaned back. He hadn't been dismissed, and he felt preternaturally aware. Making another jump would not just be possible, it would be easy. That worried him, because it didn't feel right. It felt as if he was in very real danger, at this point. Of losing himself. "Captain, I...permission to be relieved, ma'am?"

"Are you okay, Mr. Marin?"

"I think so."

"That's not good enough. Lieutenant Lauxon, take over the jump controls. Mr. Marin, go do whatever you need to know you're okay."

He knew what the first thing he needed was. The shower he had not taken, considering sleep more valuable. Probably something to eat.

If that didn't help, if that didn't make him feel as if he was the starlight merely wearing his body, then he had to go to sickbay.

He couldn't get away any more from the fact that something was wrong with his web.

Something was very wrong.

"Is that better?" the doctor asked.

José considered. "Slightly."

"Bluntly, your web is doing things it was never designed to do and shouldn't be *able* to do. You need to stop."

"Stop flying." José thought about that. "What if I'm the only one who can pull it off?"

"That's your call, but every time you jump, you're wearing the web thin here and here." The doctor waved his hands at the screen, showing an image of José's body. "One jump too many and you *will* be dead or paralyzed. We don't have...I can't fix it."

José knew the answer. But he was a soldier. He'd face death or paralysis if he had to.

"And before you get any ideas, I'm reporting this to both Wilson and Chang."

So, no, he wouldn't be able to hide it. He could never feel the stars again. Except perhaps if...

...he shook his head. "I'll do what I need to do."

"I know you will. I know your kind. Which is why I made sure to tell Chang myself. She won't let you kill yourself."

He nodded. He stood and left, his movements feeling stiff from the web reset. He went to the robotics workshop. Sat on the jump seat there, sank his head into his hands. Locked the door from the inside so nobody could disturb him short of an emergency override.

If he couldn't have that feeling again and couldn't go home? He would have to settle for being a good mechanic. And at least this probably meant that Chang wouldn't try to put him in officer training, formal or informal.

But he found he liked the idea of being on the bridge. Not in charge, no, but there was nothing like the feeling of jump. Even the feeling of flying in real space, the thing they had denied him for what he was now suspecting were reasons that had nothing to do with a failed aptitude test. They had needed boots on the ground more than another average pilot.

The ship whispered through the web. He didn't just need to stop.

He needed to be put ashore, because the web was primed now, nothing was going to stop it from pulling energy from the ship.

Something it was never designed to do.

Something it should not be able to do. He wished he could ask the ky'iin. Did they use webs?

Did they have alien spiders on their bridge, feeling the stars? Did they know how to do this right?

If they did, then maybe he could be...upgraded. Or maybe he would always be the prototype.

They used to call it beached. The image of sea and sand flowed through him.

The sea receding away from him. The tsunami in his dreams was the war, was the tyrar, was all the threats out here and all the beauty.

And he had to go home, he had to go back to hearing the jeering cries of *Araña, Araña*. To being something to be at best pitied, at worst mocked.

War criminal.

Should be in jail. Should be locked away. All of the things he had run from, but he had found so much to run to.

The surface of the Verran world, haunting in its storm-aftermath beauty. The chill of Hoth. The stark beauty of the glyn.

He could still be useful for the rest of the mission, but once it was over, once it was done, he had to go home.

He had to forget all of this existed.

Men didn't cry.

José did, sobbing, letting the tears fall when nobody could see them.

Men didn't cry. But he remembered a man who had failed a medical crying, crying for the things he would not be able to do.

José cried for the things he would not be able to see.

"I heard you got a downcheck."

José looked up. Cecilie Lauxon was, perhaps, the last person he wanted to see and talk to. Or perhaps the first one. "I did."

"Do you know if it's permanent?"

The web whispered. "Probably. I'm probably leaving the ship as soon as we get back to Earth."

What other choice did he have? But the web didn't want to, he felt the ship around him again.

"Dammit," she cursed. "You belong out here, José."

"I don't." He did, but he had to stop belonging, had to think about how to build a life. Maybe he would, could move to some new colony if one was ever founded.

But no, it was back to being... "I can't."

"What will you do?" She slid to sit opposite him.

"I don't know," he admitted. What could he do? The problems he had left to get away from still remained. The inability to find a job, the inability to find a girlfriend or boyfriend. The lack of friends outside his family.

"There..." She tailed off. "Those putain de infantry webs."

José was not sure what "putain de" meant, but he could guess enough to flinch a little. He hadn't really heard Cecilie swear before. "You know I'm safe."

"But most people don't." She looked at him. "And I bet if I walked in wearing a Martian Resistance uniform..."

"Point taken. Thankfully, people don't do that." But that was why he couldn't go to Mars. He would never trust himself there. They were right to ban his kind. "Off of Mars anyway."

She closed her eyes for a moment. "Is there anything I can do?"

He wanted to say 'leave me alone,' but he didn't really want her to leave him alone. He liked her, even if they couldn't work together. "If there's an emergency…"

"It could kill you."

He spoke over her a little. "If there's an emergency…and we'd be dead anyway…" Would he take the risk? He absolutely would. He had to.

Anyone would.

"I know." She looked at him. "I know how you do it. I can handle it. I promise."

He couldn't tell her he didn't trust her, especially as he wasn't sure it was him talking, not really. Him or his destructive desire, no, need to feel the stars like that again.

There was a very nasty word for it. Addiction.

Which meant it was right to cut him off. But could he even…could he not reach for the ship when they jumped.

Could he survive long enough to get back to Earth. He should ask for a sedative, a fast-acting one.

"I know you can handle it. But in my place…"

"I'd worry too." She reached for his hand. Sparks crossed the gap and she pulled back. "Oh, that's not good."

"Just in case you didn't think I was down checked for no reason."

"Can you even…never mind, there's no alternative, is there."

She was having the same thoughts he was. Could be survive another jump? Several more jumps? There was no way to evacuate him, no facilities in this system. A colony world was equally beyond his reach. If he survived to reach Earth, then it would be Earth forever, no job, no nothing. No. He would find something. But that was assuming he survived.

They would have to jump back to Verr.

Or would they?

"Lauxon to the bridge."

The intercom interrupted them. He watched as she stood to go, wistfully. Then he shook his head and went to the robot repair workshop.

It was a good place to hide.

35

The *Endeavour* jumped. José still felt it, like a lover's touch, if more distant. A lover he had to break up with, for his own good, but could he? Was it even physically possible?

He didn't need to ask where they had gone. Back to Verr, he was sure of it. He could feel it.

He knew where they were. It couldn't be turned off. Maybe if he hadn't embraced it, hadn't used it.

If he hadn't, they'd all be dead. If he didn't again...no. He had to trust Cecilie.

When had he started thinking of her by her first name? He wanted to stay friends. Maybe they could be penpals of a sort.

Maybe.

Part of him did not want to leave. No, none of him wanted to leave. Part of him was not sure he could survive what had been happening on Earth, not knowing there were alternatives. Not knowing that he could come out here.

But he'd be shipped off as soon as they got back. They'd make sure of that. Put him back on the beach, let him stay there.

The sun and the sand no longer called to him. He could not remember what it was like to see plants that weren't in pots. Or rather he could, but he just didn't care anymore. He didn't *need* Earth, that was what it was. He needed the next star, the next planet. To see what was over the next hill. He had never been one so prone to passion de viajar, but he was now. It had taken this to bring it out in him. And soon it would be over.

It had been a shock coming back from the war. It would be the same thing again here. And this time there was no way forward, he'd exhausted them all.

Starlight whispered along the web, a desire to give himself to it, to let himself be consumed by it, to let himself flow into it.

To go so deep he reached that mythical place where the universe became a point. He closed his eyes and he saw stars.

Addiction. It was definitely addiction. But the fact that he had no answer as to what to do next was aside from that.

He unstrapped himself, looked at the robot he had just finished, then pulled up his computer terminal. The *Endeavour* had the entire library as of the moment they had left Earth, all of human knowledge for their use or for, if the worst happened, its salvation.

Or both.

Earth was safe for now. Earth was part of an alliance. But one day humanity would need to expand to survive.

Why not now?

He pulled it up and started to search. Looking for other things he could do. Checking the law.

He had to declare himself, he couldn't just move somewhere else and not tell people he was a spider. He already knew that.

But where could he go, on Earth, that wouldn't care?

Where he would never see another ship, never be tempted. He wished the web could be removed, but it couldn't.

Not without leaving him dead or paralyzed.

It whispered to him. It promised, it threatened. It tied itself all up with memories of the war. His own voice shouting as part of a dome tumbled down on him from above.

Obadiah, responding.

He couldn't talk to Obadiah about this. Obadiah would understand. Obadiah had been through all of the options. But Obadiah had chosen this sooner, had proven himself.

Had gained an officer's billet. Maybe he hadn't gone through the list after all.

There was always crime, José thought wryly. He was pretty sure that criminals would hire spiders to do the physical dirty work. Would and did.

Maybe he could become a cop.

No, that was one of the professions explicitly barred to him. It wasn't discrimination, or so they said, because it was based off of a choice.

It hadn't been a choice.

They didn't care about that.

"Mr. Marin to the bridge."

He didn't want to even see the bridge right now. He couldn't not do what the captain said.

He couldn't ask her what she wanted. He could only zip up his coveralls the rest of the way and go. Step out onto the bridge, feeling uncomfortable. Lauxon was in the pilot's chair. The second station was empty.

He stopped, hesitating in the entrance. "Mr. Marin, I want your opinion."

There was no place but that station to sit. He sat, but kept his hands away from the controls. He didn't know how he looked, he didn't want to know. But he was sure the tension was visible in every motion he made, in every breath he took.

"The tyrar and ky'iin are talking now, and the tyrar build the kind of large ships we need. But they want us to leave the Verrans strictly alone."

"We should," he said. "Look. You know what humans are like."

He didn't say especially white people, but caught a look from Cecilie. She knew he was thinking it.

She was probably thinking it herself, even as white as she was.

"I do. And the tyrar think they're immune. So, the question is, do we trust them?"

Why was she asking him? A fresh brain on the matter.

To make him feel more useful? He hoped it wasn't that last. "I don't know, ma'am," was all he could say.

Chang nodded. "None of us know."

Cecilie asided to him, "She's asking everyone. Basically taking a poll."

That made him feel less singled out. But he knew she had her reasons for asking him up here, when she knew he shouldn't be anywhere near the jump controls. Had no place here.

There was silence from the captain. "Which is why we're in full emergency mode. Marin, I would rather not ask you to do anything that could endanger you."

But she wanted him here in case he was the only one. "I know, ma'am."

"But my first priority is this ship."

It had to be.

"And as nobody is sure whether to trust the tyrar or not, I want you here. I know what I'm asking."

Did she? She was waving an addict's bottle in front of him. Or maybe it wasn't that good a parallel.

"With all due respect," Lauxon said. "I can handle it."

Lauxon was trying to protect him. And he knew she could, and he knew if he was up here he would interfere whether he wanted to or not.

He also knew. "Lieutenant, it doesn't matter where on the ship I am." He said that softly. He appreciated her efforts.

He knew they were real, that they came from a place of caring.

Cecilie frowned.

"I know that. That's why you might as well be up here." There was a note of sorrow. "I would put you ashore if there was a place." A pause. "We're already making use of the fact that you can be anywhere on the ship." She didn't say how.

He did not want to be put ashore. He was going to see this through, to whatever fate it led him.

"The tyrar are hailing."

"Put them on."

José wanted to ask Lauxon if they had sent back the tyrar prisoners yet.

"We want people."

Chang nodded, even though it was audio only. "We will fly them back to you." She considered. "No strings."

No strings was good. No strings was the best way, given they had plucked the two tyrar out of space.

Not intended to kidnap them. It had just kind of ended up that way.

But now he had to take them back.

"I don't get why we got stuck with this," Obadiah mock-complained. José knew him well enough to know it wasn't anything close to a real problem.

"I think Chang wanted me off the ship after something I said to her," José quipped. "So it's my fault."

They were trusting that the two tyrar, who huddled together in the back of the shuttle, clinging like drowning men, wouldn't catch any of it.

"It's always your fault."

The shuttle made its rather awkward way across. Close up, the damaged tyrar ship seemed even larger. But something like that could hold…how many people in a configuration designed to hold lots of people? José shook his head. A shuttle bay, looking like an insect hole, opened, and he slid the shuttle into it.

If it was just that he couldn't do jumps, he knew he could stay out here. But it wasn't. It was more than that, and as the shuttle touched down, he almost felt that he sensed something, something deep and rich and alien.

It was probably his imagination and expectations, though. And then…he couldn't feel it.

Or that faint whisper of stars. His eyes widened, as he stepped aside.

The tyrar ran past, to be greeted by a trio of their crewmen, but José was staring at first the ceiling, then the floor. No doubt it looked like he was being polite and not looking at the reunion.

The size of the ship? Something else? Something they needed to know about. It brought him the vaguest sense of hope. What if they could shield him from the resonance? He put the thought aside.

One of the tyrar stepped towards them. "Thank you," she managed. She was pressing a hand on a small box at her waist.

A translator? "You have…"

He pointed to the box.

She took her hand off it. Spoke. He could tell she was speaking. Her mouth moved. But he could hear nothing. Put it back on.

"Audio frequency transposer," Obadiah whispered. "They must speak below our normal hearing range."

Just like dolphins spoke above it. Easy enough to get around.

She put her hand back on. "You speak high."

"We can get something like that," Obadiah said, pointing at the box. It wouldn't be hard.

"Heck, we can probably make it." Now they knew why their tyrar had been quiet. It hadn't been because they had been refusing to talk. José glanced at Obadiah.

Engineering could make frequency transposers, surely. It wasn't exactly complicated technology.

The tyrar nodded. "I am…I can show you ship?"

A tour? That seemed like a gesture. Maybe the tyrar thought humans were more trustworthy than ky'iin.

Maybe it was compensation.

As they moved further into the ship, he felt that deep presence again, but it was muted. There were so many questions he wanted to ask, would ask if it wasn't for the fact that he couldn't really ask them. They didn't have the words, the language in common. The tyrar were a little larger than humans, and their fur scent was all around him, lingering on every surface.

He finally realized what they smelled like.

Horses.

They smelled like *horses*.

36

There was, it turned out, a quite logical reason why the tyrar smelled like horses. They were herbivores. That meant that their sweat smelled more like that of a horse or a cow than a human. José was still mad with himself for thinking that, though, for comparing people with animals. That was rude.

Of course, who knew how he smelled to them. He wanted to ask if they could look at the drives, but he knew better than to push it. The ship was more advanced than the *Endeavour*, though, and he made mental notes about everything he saw. Had they resolved some of the issues with artificial gravity?

Did their pilots have webs, or did they have something else? He recalled Chang's assertion that they had found a use for the induction effect.

He wondered what it was. The web interacting with the ship and pilots getting webs designed for it, made for it.

If they improved this technology, a paraplegic could fly a ship. A quadriplegic. Disability would not matter.

"Do you know what Chang meant about uses for the induction web?"

"Oh, well. Human pilots may be obsolete," Obadiah quipped. "They got a dolphin to fly a ship."

"A *dolphin*?" Dolphins had turned out to be at least as intelligent as humans, but a dolphin as a pilot?

A dolphin pilot would likely be better than a human one by the simple measure of natural ability to think in three dimensions.

"A dolphin. So next time we come out here, we might have dolphins with us."

"That would..." José tailed off. "We probably should have brought them anyway." They were part of Earth, and while not everyone agreed they should have rights, anyone who didn't agree wouldn't survive out here.

Can I go to a planet where I don't have to deal with aliens? Slava. That might not have been exactly what she said, but he heard it in her voice nonetheless. And maybe it might be necessary. To set up some kind of enclave.

"Why did you ask?"

"I was wondering how other species navigate jump space."

"I'd lay bets the tyrar have multiple pilots in tandem. Have you noticed that you never see just one of them?"

Obadiah had a point. The tyrar moved through their ship in twos and threes.

But the muting effect, the... "They use induction webs," he said softly.

"How do you know?"

"Because I can almost feel their ship, but it's..."

"It's an alien ship."

José shook his head. "It's basic electromagnetic patterns interacting. Or I wouldn't be able to feel it at all." He examined the wall. "They have it shielded."

"Duh." Obadiah smiled. "We need *that* technology."

A dolphin using induction...you could set that up by taking advantage of the conductive ability of water.

A human using it would want to be...you could shield things so what was happening to him didn't happen. So they felt the ship only when they needed to.

"Maybe," José said. "As you said..."

Their tyrar guides turned. "What talk about?"

José considered his answer. "Flying ships."

"Ah!" the tyrar said. "We can't let you see the bridge, but..."

"But our scientists can talk to your scientists." He hoped that word was in their vocabulary.

"Yes. What we learn from you?"

José thought about that. Glanced at Obadiah.

Obadiah spoke grimly, "Fixing planets."

Ecological remediation? Was that what he meant.

"Can't fix this one."

"True."

They meant Verr. But there was something in Obadiah's tone José resolved to ask him about.

Later.

The tour finished in the mess hall. Like humans, the tyrar cooked their food.

Unlike humans, they were as herbivorous as he had been told. José suspected that small amounts of animal protein found their way into the diet, much as horses were sometimes caught munching on eggs. Or fed them deliberately.

He suspected you didn't talk about eating eggs around the ky'iin. Or did you? Whale fetus was supposed to be a delicacy, after all. Albeit one it was no longer socially acceptable to serve.

The mess hall was huge, but mostly empty, presumably due to the shift timing. He tried to imagine serving on a ship this large, bigger than anything Earth had.

He could only go back to old science fiction for his answers. The *Enterprise D* was, if anything, smaller.

Maybe Battlestar *Galactica* was a better parallel.

The tyrar offered them some kind of grain salad, no doubt aware that omnivores could not digest the higher cellulose vegetation that seemed to form a bed under their meals. José sampled it and found it not bad at all.

"I see a trade item if it doesn't make us sick. Whatever spices they're using are quite tasty."

"Except not to white people," Obadiah quipped.

José laughed. "I don't know, I've met some white people with asbestos gullets and some Asian people who order off the "mild" part of the menu. Of course, then there's Mayo."

Obadiah had a point, of course, about white folk and bland food. And the spice was pretty...it had a bite to it that reminded him of pique. Spicier than anything his mother would have made, but he had developed a taste for hotter food as an adult. And been mocked for it, for the amount of pique he added to his food, sometimes preferring it to sazon.

"You have a point, but let me have my white people jokes."

José realized one of the tyrar was watching them with an expression he could not help but think was amusement. "I think they gave us spicy food to see if we could take it."

Obadiah laughed. "Wouldn't you do the same thing?"

"It's tempting." Puerto Rican food tended not to be quite as hot, although it was certainly well-seasoned, but testing aliens to see if they could take your cuisine? Or just to see what they would do?

If they were being tested, then it would also explain the tour, it would explain why they were even here. The tyrar wanting to know more about humans. Seeing what they would do in different situations. Seeing if they would try to push for access to the bridge or to engineering.

Seeing what kind of humans the humans would send. It all made sense, and it wasn't like they hadn't poked and prodded the aliens they had met. Everyone would. It was not going to be possible to stop it.

Just keep it in acceptable bounds.

It was so hard to tell, though. The flat, furry, Bigfoot-like faces were not easy to read. Probably, he wasn't easy for them to read.

But if he could be shielded from the ship, he could stay. He'd still never feel the stars again.

Then he felt the faintest shimmer of starlight. "Obadiah."

"What?"

"I think we just got kidnapped."

"What?" Obadiah said, incredulous.

"Shielding or no shielding, I felt it." He kept his voice very quiet, and would have switched to Spanish had Obadiah spoken more than a handful of words of the language. "We jumped."

Obadiah bit back whatever he was going to say. "What would get them to jump?"

"Could be a test. To see if we react." Could be a test of him, even, if they used similar web abilities, or something akin to it. "Could be an emergency. Could be that they're getting revenge on us for kidnapping theirs. Making a point."

He looked at the older man. "Making a point is tempting."

There hadn't been a takehold warning. There hadn't been any of the normal turbulence of a jump. José wondered if it was more advanced technology or the sheer mass of the ship.

Both, he decided.

"I didn't feel the jump…"

"The ship's mass smoothed it out. Could also have been a micro jump."

If it was a test, then it might be. Jump to the far side of the system, see how the humans react. See if they could handle it.

Their guide looked at them. "So..."

"We jumped," José said. "You can't hide that from us. Why?"

"To get something. You will be returned."

Obadiah growled under his breath. "Why trust you? We returned your people."

"So you should trust us."

"You didn't trust us enough to ask if we minded," José pointed out. The tyrar tapped her speech box.

They could talk without the humans even hearing them. The reverse was, apparently, not true. José thought about that for a long moment, then mentally shrugged.

And wished Obadiah spoke more Spanish.

"You might not have agreed."

"What do you need from us?" Obadiah, finally, fixing the tyrar with a chief of security look. "We're just a couple of..."

"Your captain not send..."

"Stupid people," Obadiah finished.

"Send pilot." The tyrar looked at José.

"I can't fly," José said. He would risk his life and health for the *Endeavour*. He wasn't so sure he'd risk it on some tyrar errand he didn't, at this point, properly understand. Didn't and couldn't.

"Why not?"

José didn't know if they had the words for medical or doctor, and he wasn't sure he cared. "Can't," he reiterated.

"We want you on...we bring something to Verr, we want you..."

"You could have asked."

José couldn't fly. And why would they ask him to do something? Because it was dangerous? As a test?

"We could. But you didn't ask our people." The tyrar said that evenly.

"We were saving their lives," Obadiah growled. "We would much rather have given them back before we jumped."

José felt something else. He frowned. Then the great ship did indeed shake, it shook like a giant hand had grabbed it and waved it around before setting it down. Starlight shimmered. A second jump...

Obadiah clearly felt it too.

And he fancied that the look on the tyrar faces was alarm.

37

José knew that had he been able to, he would have grabbed the ship and done...something.

Were they in real space? No, they were still in hyperspace. The web vibrated slightly, but he could feel it becoming more intense. Shielding or no shielding, this was going to affect him if it continued. Affect him in what way? He didn't know.

He couldn't afford to be afraid. "Take me to your bridge."

The tyrar looked at him. "Please. Do it."

The ship shuddered again. Drive malfunction? Some kind of weirdness in hyperspace itself? He didn't and couldn't know.

He really couldn't know. All he did know was that the ship was in trouble and he couldn't help unless he could get out of the shielding.

And there might be a thousand tyrar. No, a thousand *people* on this ship.

The tyrar presumably consulted one another. He could no more hear them than he could fly.

Then one of them grabbed him and set off at a run. He could barely keep up with the larger being. Tyrar could *move* when they needed to.

After a little bit, the tyrar just scooped him up and carried him. She used a lift, which slowed them down, but perhaps not as much as him trying to climb tubes designed for seven foot tall furries.

The bridge was sensibly located. It was also little larger than the *Endeavour*'s bridge. He could even identify specific stations, despite the seating and consoles being made for a different physiology. Parallel evolution of engineering.

She set him down at the back of the bridge. And the stars rushed in. He was risking his life for them, but he couldn't tell them that, couldn't reveal the weakness within him. His muscles spasmed.

He was right at the edge of losing everything he was. He could feel it.

And he could feel the ship. Larger. Somehow more awake and aware. Like a voice in a language he did not know, a deep voice.

A tyrar voice.

Let me help you he tried in response, sure the ship would not and did not understand him.

But it was alive. He could tell that. Maybe the *Endeavour* was too, but it was a flatworm next to this.

He'd always thought giving ships a gender was objectification in English. Not so much in Spanish, where *everything* had gender. In English it felt like something that respected the object while disrespecting the woman. But this ship was relentlessly, certainly *he*.

And he could feel the problem now. Space was *torn*. As if by some great explosion.

Or as if by gravity.

"Black hole," he whispered. Perhaps the same wandering black hole that had doomed the Verrans. It could not be moving that fast relative to everything else, even as it all hurtled through space in its configuration, moving and still at the same time. But yes, he felt it, ripples and waves through both real space and hyperspace.

And then he reached out to the ship and pushed.

They tumbled into real space, and he was thrown into the air. Somehow, a tyrar body caught him.

That was his last awareness for a while. That and the stars whispering through him.

Just the stars, claiming his consciousness for their own.

He woke up in…the *Endeavour*'s medical bay. That alone told him how long he had been out.

He wriggled his toes. They still moved. He was restrained, but he felt somebody remove the restraints, not quite seeing them from this angle. He sat up.

"I told you not to…"

"If I hadn't, we'd probably still be in hyperspace."

The medic sighed. Obadiah was in the doorway. "Let me talk to him."

Obadiah came all the way in. "The tyrar pilot is recovering. The overload of the gravity wave made her faint, that was part of the problem."

"Uncharted black hole," José said, wryly.

"Oh, it was charted, by the tyrar at least. It moved."

José winced. "I bet it was the same one that dragged through the Verran system."

"I'm not taking that bet. Come on, let's get you some food."

"How long was I out?"

"Twelve hours. The tyrar came back, dropped us off, left again. Apparently they trust us *now*.

The tyrar also now knew that José had a problem. Hopefully they would not put it down to human frailty. He rather hoped somebody had told them it was a malfunction in him, not his entire species. Or maybe they would... "They'd better. I have a headache."

"Cure for that." Obadiah handed him a bottle of water.

He swigged it, almost instantly feeling better. Yeah, it ws that kind of headache. Dehydration and strain. And, now that Obadiah mentioned food, he was hungry too.

Obadiah didn't take him to the mess hall, but to the captain's table, a smaller room where the officers ate. He was glad. With his headache, he didn't want to deal with ten or fifteen people staring at him.

"Eat."

It was stew. He ate it rather mechanically, not really tasting it. Again, it was fuel. When was the last time he had truly savored a meal? "Ugh."

"You were warned."

"I don't think we'd have got out."

"We would eventually. Maybe. I don't know. What's the limit of time a ship can stay in hyperspace?"

"That one, probably quite a while." José let out a breath. "He's quite a ship."

"He?"

"Felt like a he." The *Endeavour* didn't feel like it had a gender. "I want to know what AI they have."

"One which couldn't get us out of that."

José nodded. "Maybe it's just size and age, but I'm pretty sure their ship is smarter than our ship."

"Wouldn't surprise me. But they might not have the AI hooked up to direct control of the drives. They might not trust them any more than we do." Obadiah's tone turned wry.

"They trust them enough to bring them along. Or maybe it was another hallucination. Maybe I *expected* their ship to be different."

"And bigger. Small wonder you passed out."

José shook his head. He could feel a faint vibration through the web. "No. Medical's right. I need to stop doing this."

He had half-expected to wake up paralyzed. This was the last warning, he could feel it. "What did the tyrar bring?"

"A half-finished ship."

José was, oddly, not surprised by that answer.

As José finished his food, Captain Chang walked in. Obadiah stood, and José shakily followed his lead.

"As you were. Especially you, Mr. Marin." A pause. "One of these days somebody's going to give you a ship."

José shook his head. "Without the shielding the tyrar have...and you can't shield the bridge."

"Maybe a space station then," she said, wryly. "You keep right on proving that we need you."

Maybe there was some way to fix the web, on Earth. José tried to recall what he knew about major repairs and upgrades. During the war, there hadn't been a way to upgrade.

But maybe somebody had come up with one since. He put that piece of hope in a back corner of his brain where it belonged. "You know I'm not officer material. If I was..."

"They'd have pinned it on you during the war. But they made a mistake. *You* were never meant to be army."

From her, he realized, that was an incredible compliment. The eternal inter-service rivalry had spread out into space with the development of the American and Chinese Space Forces and their fusion into Earthforce. Earthforce had swallowed the burgeoning space navies of other nations.

But they still didn't like gropos, any more than either aviators or wet navy types had in the past.

A compliment, but she might genuinely believe they had got his aptitude tests wrong. "I failed every single one of the Earthforce tests."

"No," Chang said. "You didn't."

She sounded as if she knew that rather than just saying it. That bothered him a little. Had she poked around? Had she found something?

Was she saying that tests had been fudged, in those days, when the war was something civilians knew nothing about but the brass thought inevitable? Because they needed infantry more? The suspicion he had started to have, blossoming outward. They had wanted his boots. He was right, painfully right.

Because they couldn't fight the war on Mars from space, not without destroying the very infrastructure they couldn't hold on to. Still, failing those tests was part of his identity. Sure, he was Earthforce *now*, in a bizarre way.

"I hate," she added, "to ask more of you. But the tyrar consider you a bit of a...hero is not quite the right word. I actually think the word they used is both complimentary and not at the same time."

People who lived in a herd might not be sure of people who stood out from it. "What do you want me to ask them for?"

"Well, for one thing, that shielding you were talking about. We're trying to find out how they do it so it can be built into future ships. Especially if there's a way to turn it on and off."

José nodded. "Because without it, induction webbed pilots...like the dolphin...are going to feel every jump even if they don't fly it."

"Exactly."

"There's something else. I think they have a central AI on their ship."

Chang nodded. "I asked for one. The brass refused. They said they were worried about a Hal situation."

José frowned. Early science fiction, haunting them again. "I can understand that, but what if you limit the AI's connections to the ship? Don't let it have full control."

If the AI had had control, it could have brought the ship out, damaged drives and unconscious pilot or no.

"Or," Chang mused, "you make very, very sure that the AI is your friend."

José considered that. "How?"

"You start by treating them as if they're human. You start by giving them the choice."

38

The real question on José's mind as he sat in the back of the shuttle - Lauxon was flying - was not how to talk the tyrar into handing over the secret of the shielding.

It was how to get them to understand what he wanted. They could pronounce English, which gave them what he felt was a somewhat unfair advantage.

They could converse without him even being able to hear them.

They saw him as a hero.

He didn't think of himself as one. He supposed he was, by at least some measures.

The web reminded him that he was also a villain.

The web reminded him how likely it was that he would die out here. If he did, would his consciousness spread amongst the stars?

Did he have a soul? He'd asked himself that question many times and ultimately come up with a negative answer. He went through the Christmas and Easter motions of Catholicism, but José did not believe in God, did not believe in souls or angels. Whatever he sensed was the result of chemicals and electromagnetic firings in his brain.

Lauxon didn't sense it the way he did. She just flew. She just controlled the ship, steering an inert lump of metal through the dangerous space that was hyperspace.

He flew *with* the ship. Did the dolphins? Maybe one day he'd get to ask one.

Maybe one day. Their shuttle found the tiny hatch on the side of the behemoth. Robots and suited tyrar were on the outside of the ship, repairing damage.

The second ship, if anything larger, hung in space.

A gift to the Verrans. Something they could put in orbit and live on while they finished it. A way off their planet. A way out of their system, in the end.

He hoped Chang had warned them about City Three.

He hoped her warning was enough. Landing on the deck. Stepping out into the slightly humid and faintly stable-smelling air of the tyrar ship.

What was his name? He realized he had never asked. Had never asked what the ship was called.

He was pretty sure that one of the three tyrar who greeted him was the one who had carried him to the bridge.

"Come," she said.

All the tyrar appeared to be she, he'd noted. Bad pronoun translation? A single sex ship?

"Can ask...personal?" he asked, stepping ahead of Lauxon.

"Yes?"

"Why all she?"

She laughed. "Not all she. Some he. Mostly she. More she than he."

He slowly parsed that into the concept that the tyrar had more female births than male. That might make women more...expendable. It would certainly affect relationships between the genders. "Same he as she." He indicated Lauxon.

"Ky'iin fewer she, but ky'iin have..."

"Three sexes." He thought he'd heard that.

"Yes."

He wondered about that. Three sexes seemed excessive. The Verrans had three too, but it was a different thing, a biological system that worked. "I heard the glyn don't have any?"

"All glyn lay eggs."

José nodded. So, everything was different. And she was friendlier.

She led him into...a huge room where a low-pitched sound thrummed through his bones.

He realized after a moment that he was feeling, rather than hearing, the sound of a tyrar cheer.

The welcome of a hero.

Once the crowd had settled down and some of them had got to touch him, she took him into a meeting room.

He recognized one of the tyrar present from the bridge. He was, in fact, pretty sure she was the captain of this vessel.

"José Marin?" she tried.

She pronounced his name like a gringo who had never learned Spanish. He managed not to laugh, correcting her.

She tried again, although she still struggled with the "José" part. This time she wasn't pronouncing it like a j, though.

He decided he'd take it.

She pointed at herself. "Tri Mrek."

"Tri Mrek," he tried. Both of the r's weren't quite r's, but it might be possible, he decided, to learn to pronounce it. With, of course, a frequency transposer.

"Close." Her expression shifted. "Thank you."

José bowed slightly. "Would have got out eventually?"

"Not without…more damage. We not use that, too…hard on pilots."

He didn't tell her it was an accident. But the small hope he had not realized he had that they might know how to fix or upgrade his web flew away.

"So, what do you want?"

"On our ship, feel every jump. Here."

"Aha. Yes, we can tell you how. Tell engineer?" She struggled slightly with engineer, the g closer to a j.

"Please." Could it be that easy? "Use…need for…" How did he explain about the dolphins and the fact that they didn't have hands?

"Your health," the tyrar said.

That wasn't what he had meant. He left it be for now, simply because of the language barrier. Somebody else could explain dolphins.

"Also. What ship…name?"

She laughed. "Myrrin," she said.

"Thank you."

"You name ships."

"We do, unlike the ky'iin." The glyn? He wasn't sure. But the ky'iin ships identified themselves only by numbers or the name of their captain.

"Good."

So, the tyrar felt that not naming ships was, what, weird? Disrespectful?

Then she leaned forward. "You know what we want from humans?"

She couldn't get human right either. Like José, it came out with something between a g and a j at the start.

"Planet fixing." Would the screw ups of the 21st century prove to be humanity's greatest trade good?

It would be ironic if so, an odd vindication for those who had refused to do anything about it until it was almost too late.

"Planet fixing. We want your ship to come to our world."

"I can't promise that. We need to go home. We have...survivors of another ship. Our resources."

"Then come once you have dealt with it."

Going back to Earth would help anyway. They didn't, José thought, have quite the *right* scientists on board. "We'll have to talk to the brass."

"Of course." Pause. "Brass?"

"Higher ups."

"Oh!" She growled a word which José tried to make a note of, given it was probably their slang for admirals. Their unflattering slang for admirals from the tone.

"Same in every species," Lauxon said from the door. "Admirals are always annoying."

At least that made the tyrar seem more human.

Or the humans seem more tyrar. At this point it didn't matter. Both were good.

The conversation, after that, turned to some mutual help...an exchange of vocabulary.

And José was properly introduced to Myrrin himself. The ship did indeed have an AI, but it couldn't control the hyperdrive.

There was no solid explanation as to why, but it seemed to be a combination of mistrust and the fact that hyperspace piloting required, as Lauxon put it, "A bit more creativity than you can manage if you're made out of computer code."

Myrrin, if he understood it, did not seem to be offended. But he also seemed to have some recognition of the way José had touched him during the jump.

It hadn't been entirely a hallucination. But brains and code alike were electromagnetic impulses. Machine telepathy was something which could be built into a web.

Which meant.

Put an AI on the ship and the pilot and AI could talk to each other directly. Which might... José set the possibility to one side. He didn't mention it in front of the tyrar.

What they wanted was ecological remediation.

"So, what happened to your world?" he voiced, eventually, taking a sip of the tea-like beverage the tyrar had provided.

She growled. "The ky'iin."

"You're allies now."

"Allies yes. Not friends." Her expression shifted, ears moving in what he was beginning to realize was a tyrar smile. "Maybe one day if they demonstrate that they learned."

"They tried to civilize you."

"Yes. And in some ways they succeeded."

"Humanity has a sordid history of doing that to ourselves," José explained. "We've not even changed that much. Are you sure you trust us?"

"No, but you are allies and, I suspect, friends before the ky'iin."

The other problem, José thought, was that the ky'iin, as apex predators, might well have issues with seeing the tyrar as prey. He didn't voice that, though. "We'll see, I suppose."

He liked the tyrar, but oddly, he found he liked the Verrans more. The tyrar were perhaps closer to humans in many ways.

Except that the Verrans were more like humans in their culture, except for their strange childrearing arrangements, and those were dictated by biology. The old nature versus nurture argument was going to show its face again. "So, what's the...I mean, what do you need to fix?"

"Clear cutting of forests, global warming. Fur mold." She made a face.

Some kind of skin condition caused by heat, he supposed. "Your ship is a little cold for me," José admitted.

Maybe their planet had been colder, just by a few degrees, before the ky'iin had come and industrialized. And maybe put stuff there because they didn't care about it as much as they did about their own planet. He could see that.

It was enough to make *him* not trust the ky'iin. To understand the difference between allies and friends.

The ky'iin were like white men, or had been. And maybe, like most white men, they had learned.

Or maybe not.

Mars proved how little humanity as a whole had learned from the errors of the past. It also proved that humanity could try different paths into the future.

"And, of course, there aren't a huge number of planets to colonize."

"No, there aren't," the tyrar mused. "But with what you have learned about fixing planets, maybe..."

Maybe the next step from remediation was terraforming. "We still don't have ours back to where it was. That's going to take centuries."

"But you walk down the road, one foot in front of the other."

It sounded like an attempt to translate a saying. Likely it was.

39

One foot in front of another, and José's path led him back to the *Endeavour*.

He wasn't sure he liked the tyrar better or even that he really understood them more.

All he knew for sure was that they were good people in their own way, but what did that make the ky'iin?

Predators. Predators who had tried to domesticate another species. Pretty much, in other words, human.

Doctor Lawrence cornered him as soon as he left the shuttle. "Wanted to snag you before the captain did. Did you learn anything?"

"A few vocabulary words, why they hate the ky'iin, and the fact that we might be going to their homeworld. Or somebody might."

Lawrence nodded, kind of steering him to the side. "So..."

"The ky'iin colonized them," José said, simply. "And it went as well as expected."

She frowned. "They're our allies."

"They both are. Maybe we can even mediate a little bit. A little bit." He wasn't sure how one handled that, not really. It would require a lot more knowledge of the various languages and cultures involved.

"I suppose..."

"We're more like the ky'iin. I don't even get the impression the tyrar knew how to fight a war until the ky'iin taught them," José said, softly. "At least the Verrans have a head start there."

Lawrence made a face. "And they're going to owe the tyrar a debt."

"I think the tyrar think they're more qualified to deal with them than we are, simply by virtue of the fact that they haven't colonized anyone yet." José made a face. "Any bets the ky'iin taught them how?"

"At least there's no question of ecological damage here."

And the tyrar had backed up José's theory and fear that nice, habitable planets were rare and generally already had occupants. Not in as many words, but he could tell from how they talked about it, the language and body language they used. The desire for terraforming. "The other issue is that it appears spare planets are rare."

"The Verrans may become entirely space-dwelling," Lawrence mused. "They're nocturnal and comfortable underground, so they might be well equipped to make that switch."

And what would they call themselves once Verr was gone? José shook his head. People. Humans. Their unpronounceable name for themselves. But it might change. Everything about them would change, because it would have to. "They may have no choice."

"Which might mean it's the ultimate fate of every species that doesn't destroy itself," she continued. "Sooner or later, your homeworld gets trashed and..."

"Let's not do any of the trashing," José said, wryly. "We did a good enough job on Earth."

"We pulled back from the brink. But the Verrans didn't ask for this."

He'd had that thought many times. "The tyrar may be giving them the best thing. They can reverse engineer it, copy it, start getting population off planet."

"We're giving them plans for the big Lagrange habitat. It might not be big *enough* for them, but..."

José nodded. "City Three's the worry. Any bets they'll try and steal the ship?"

"Not taking those bets."

He didn't blame her. But they didn't really have man-rated rockets. Man-rated. How would that language change? Would the definition of man simply expand?

José thought about that. He liked the idea of it expanding, beyond species, beyond gender. Just people.

He knew better than to think that would really happen.

Chang's debriefing was technical. Yes, they were offering the shielding, although it seemed unlikely that it could be retrofitted to the *Endeavour* without dry dock time.

"They want us to go to their homeworld."

"They didn't mention payment, but I have a feeling they intend to offer us something quite substantial," José said. "On top of the shielding."

"There are a lot of things we could negotiate for in return for the expertise they're asking for," Chang mused. "My suggestion to the brass is going to be for us to go back to Earth, pick up a professional diplomat and some ecology experts, then negotiate a proper agreement."

José felt odd to be this much in the loop. He was, after all, not an officer. As much as Chang thought he should be one. "I recorded the vocabulary words."

"Next time somebody goes over, they're getting a frequency transposer."

José would certainly be glad of one.

"So, once we have helped the Verrans with their new ship, we will be going back to Earth," Chang said. "Have you given thought to…"

"Unless we can retrofit with the shielding, ma'am, I can't. You're going to have to leave me."

He wanted to see the tyrar homeworld.

He wanted to feel the stars. He knew that none of it was possible.

He wanted to bond with the ship even more, and he knew that was a dangerous thought. Addiction.

"Which is clearly not what you want. We will have to…"

José shook his head. "First generation infantry webs like I and Lieutenant Smith have aren't upgradable or heavily reprogrammable. They didn't ever think that would be, well… needed."

Chang said something under her breath in Cantonese that he didn't like the sound of. "You're saying that we can't…"

"You can't give me something like whatever the dolphin is using, no." There was the possibility of external augmentation, José supposed, but that might not overcome the fact that the electromagnetic resonance was killing him. He finally had that thought bluntly. "I'll make it back to Earth. Maybe I can work in orbit."

Launchpad was gone, but would no doubt be rebuilt, better and more sophisticated. The ky'iin owed them that much. Maybe he could build ships and watch other people fly them.

It would be better than the cries of *araña, araña*. The cries of war criminal.

People there wouldn't even need to know what kind of web he had. He could say he was a beached pilot.

It could work.

"Maybe you could. The replacement for Launchpad will need

people, and there's talk of building a trade station."

That appealed to him too. He had picked up some tyrar, he wasn't a linguist, but if he put in the work he could manage with AI assistance.

Heck, that appealed more than Launchpad. For the first time, he realized that he had options that weren't going back to Puerto Rico to face those who had once been, if not friends, at least people like him.

Except to visit his father. "I have to admit, I'm looking forward to telling my old man what I'm allowed to tell him."

Chang laughed. "We'll make sure we're clear on what that is."

"He's used to not getting the full truth out of me, since the war," José said, wryly. "He'll understand."

But he could, he was sure, talk about the horse-smell of the tyrar, the chiming beauty of the glyn, the utter terror of the ky'iin.

The Verrans. What could he say about them?

"Captain Chang." The intercom. "To the bridge, please."

She nodded, stood and left. "Get some rest, Mr. Marin."

There was a part of him that wanted to say he'd rest when he was dead. Now that he had some hope, he was paradoxically more afraid that he was, after all, going to die.

That he might not be able to take another jump at all.

He took Chang at her word. His muscles felt oddly stiff, or rather a little lagged, as he made his way to his bunk.

He flopped on it, but he did not sleep or try to. Instead, he stared at the ceiling.

His web could not be upgraded, replaced, or removed.

And it was failing. The lag in his movements was the ultimate symptom of a failing web. It might not be repairable.

His excited thoughts about trade stations faded away. He would not be working on a trade station. Not the way his web was deteriorating, not without...he might end up in a powered chair. Maybe it could still work.

Maybe it wouldn't deteriorate further. Maybe all he would have to deal with was this stiffness, this slowness which had come on so suddenly. He knew he should go to medbay.

He knew there was nothing medbay could do. He would just manage until they got to Earth, not tell anyone. Hope he survived. He wanted to live even if he could never fly again. But he wanted to fly again. No, no point going to medbay.

They knew he might die. They didn't acknowledge it, so perhaps there was still hope. Chang saw him as having a long career.

Chang, he realized, was an optimist. Maybe he needed to take a leaf out of her book.

He redirected his thoughts. There was no sense thinking about it. He might as well direct his brainpower towards something more useful.

The Verrans had their ship. It might only hold a few thousand, but that was a few thousand. With gene banks, it might even be enough. They could do gene banks, that was easy technology.

Their species would survive. Change. Adapt. Become something new. As space dwelling humans might, eventually.

Become something new as they spread out. Or perhaps there was nowhere to spread out to. No place for them to go.

He pulled his thoughts back again. What could he think about that was productive?

The tyrar? The glyn? The issues they had talking to the ky'iin?

Now, there was a thought. If a web plus conditioning could make somebody more aggressive, maybe it could make them less. Maybe there was a good use, after all, for the technology that had turned him temporarily into a monster.

In some minds not temporarily.

Webbed diplomats who would have their urge to fight or flee dampened, perhaps not removed, but toned down so they could deal with it.

Children raised around ky'iin so that their instincts would be muted.

Domesticado.

He recoiled from that.

They tried to domesticate another sentient species.

Could they be trusted?

Was it possible to…he thought of sedated tigers in a zoo, sedated so people could pet them.

Domesticado.

Maybe it was not a concern. Maybe it was not a concern for the simple reason that humanity was already domesticated.

But the more he thought about it, the more the idea faintly nauseated him.

Or maybe that, too, was the failing web. It whispered through his bones, it reassured him it was still there.

But he was not sure for how much longer.

He was not sure how long he had.

40

The next day, things were worse. José was not sure exactly how much worse they were, just that he could feel the stiffness in his spine now.

He probably didn't have time to get back to Earth. He tried to get his mind into the mode where he could accept that.

There was no sense asking the aliens. The Verrans didn't have webs, and he did wonder how they were going to fly the ship.

They'd work it out. The tyrar would help them. But even asking those who did...human physiology was too different.

He was pretty sure the glyn, with their conductive exoskeletons, didn't use anything like it. How did you even do surgery on somebody with an exoskeleton in the first place?

He remembered the hospital. He remembered going under. He remembered the promises, the offers no sane man would refuse.

At least he hadn't been a prototype. He'd given informed consent. As much as you could give consent when it was a prerequisite to promotion, to extra money. No, he hadn't had the choice. He'd needed the money.

He'd needed the money when he walked into the enlistment office. Rich men waged war, poor men fought it. Always the way, perhaps less so now that military intelligence was less of an oxymoron than it had once been.

But it would always be the case that rich men made war and poor men...did all the dying.

Like an old man, he made his way to the mess hall for breakfast. There was no starsong in his veins now.

Obadiah caught him at the door. "José," he said.

The last person he wanted to see, the person avoiding would be

221

most suspicious. "I...join me?" he finally said. Making his way to the food counter.

He could feel his friend's eyes on him. Then Obadiah took his arm once he had his food, pulled him to a table.

"Stop trying to hide it, José."

José looked down. "There's nothing anyone can do."

"You don't know that."

"There isn't." He looked up at Obadiah.

"We could put you under."

It might work. Putting him into a coma until they were back on Earth. Or it could make things worse. "You know that could finish me off. I only have to last until we get back to Earth."

"And in what condition, José?" A dark hand was placed on his. "You want to be..."

"I don't want to be in a power chair, no. I'd deal, because I would have no choice" He couldn't quite keep his voice down, could only hope that the heads that turned caught only the fact that there was conflict, not the actual words. "But there's nothing we can do out here. We all knew the risks."

He had known the risk of not coming back. He hadn't expected it to take this form, but he knew. "Hostile aliens. Space weather. We're only lucky we've avoided somebody on the crew going berserk." He kept his tone even. "Obadiah. I'm not a man under your command."

"No, you're a man under Chang's."

That hurt. He respected the captain. "Who has enough to worry about without me."

"Another jump's going to kill you," Obadiah predicted.

"Whether I'm conscious or not. The only thing we can do is shield me somehow, and we don't have the materials." There was one other answer, maybe. But it would be a permanent exile. "The only thing we can do is leave me here."

Obadiah winced. "With the moles."

"The moles aren't so bad." José knew he'd regret that statement the moment it left his lips.

"City Three?" Obadiah pointed out.

He had nothing more to say to that.

The confrontation with Obadiah had not helped. Stress did not help.

But José knew he didn't want to be sedated in medbay for the rest of the time he had. He wanted to do something, achieve something, while he still could.

The web growled. That was the best way to describe it, the whispers having become broken, arcing. Maybe there were physical disconnections, he didn't know.

He'd survived the war. He'd survived all of this. Part of him insisted that he was a survivor, a survivor who could deal with this stuff. Part of him knew that it didn't matter how tough or skilled he was.

The stars whispered to him and the feeling that they were pulling him out of his body intensified for a moment. Hallucination, he knew. The *Endeavour* did not jump without warning.

He'd still felt the *Myrrin* jump even through the shielding. Even if they could put him in a box, he'd feel it. But he might survive.

A box. It wasn't a bad idea. He went to the workshop, worked on robot parts, putting the plan together in his head. There were no actual repairs to do, he was just fiddling. Killing time. Waiting for somebody to ask him to do something more important, more significant.

Fidgeting. That was honestly it, if he was willing to admit it. His hands felt heavy.

If the deterioration continued he wouldn't be able to do this job either. Obadiah was right. He should tell Chang. But what did he say to her?

He should tell Lauxon.

That thought floated up from the depths of his mind. She was webbed, and she knew Chang, they'd worked together before. She would know how to talk to Chang about this.

She was on duty on the bridge. He couldn't reach her right now, couldn't distract her with this. If she cared about him...

He wasn't sure. He thought she did.

A box. He sketched it out with awkward hands. But they didn't have the materials the tyrar used, the combination of plastics and ceramics. Easy enough to fabricate, if you had the basics. He could make such a box.

Or, given the state of his hands, instruct somebody else. It wouldn't have to be large.

He was a hero to the tyrar. Maybe they'd give him something.

Or maybe they'd already left. Below decks, he couldn't be sure what was going on outside the ship, or even outside the workshop.

Below decks. It was funny how they said that for places not the bridge, even though the *Endeavour* had no deck and the bridge was not elevated above it.

Would future spacefarers even know where it came from?

Below decks. Exiled from a place he had never belonged in the first place.

How did he tell Chang?

He gave up on all pretense of work. He designed the box. It might prove useful, if not for him than for somebody else. It was more productive than fidgeting.

It was useless, and he knew it. They didn't have the plastic they needed on board.

Maybe medical could try sedating him just for the jump, but he recoiled from the idea. There might not be time.

How many emergency jumps had they made?

"Mr. Marin to my ready room."

Chang.

He had about five minutes to work out how to tell her.

"Mr. Marin, I appreciate it when my people tell me the truth," Chang said from behind templed hands.

"You have enough..."

"You are my concern. So are forty-two other people. You didn't want to worry me."

"Not about something we can't fix." José sat back, feeling his spine creak. "We don't have the facilities to fix me, and it might not be possible. There's no way to sufficiently shield me from the next jump. You can't put me ashore here."

He thought about another solution to the problem, but he had never been the type.

"Don't tell me what we can and can't fix." Her dark eyes rested on him. "We all came out here for a reason. Some of us found a purpose."

She was talking as much about herself. "And at least I have that."

"I don't leave a man behind. That's part of my purpose."

When they had rescued Lauxon. She didn't leave a man behind. She'd risk the ship for him.

"I know that. But you..." He sighed. He couldn't lecture his commanding officer.

"I'm well aware that I can't save everyone. But that doesn't mean I am going to give up and not try."

He realized that this was exactly why his subconscious had feared to tell her. Obadiah had told her anyway.

He didn't know whether to punch him or thank him. Thanking him was probably safer. He doubted he could take on an unenhanced civilian right now.

"There really isn't anything you can do. If we can get me back to Earth, then an expert might be able to at least...do something." Keep him alive. Prevent further deterioration if he was lucky. He would never fly again, he might never walk again, but the web was not affecting his mind. He could still create beauty, still work, still add to society. He could...

...go back to school, he thought suddenly. Get a degree. Learn to do something with his brain not his hands. Before, he wouldn't have thought himself smart enough to, but he was beginning to realize he was smarter than he thought.

"Do something as in?"

"Keep me alive," José said. "The problem is that these older infantry webs are hard to repair and impossible to upgrade. Some of the first generation."

Chang shuddered. "Those infantry webs were a bad idea. And you know whose idea they were?"

"China's," he said, finally. "We're not stupid. We knew."

"We were preparing to try and hold on to Mars when we should have been negotiating our new relationship. But even more than America we couldn't let go."

"At least America should have known better."

It had been six weeks to Mars at the start of the war. It had been one by the end, but it had still been like Europe trying to keep the colonies.

"Humanity should have known better. If we form a colony out here, they will have to build a nation." Chang smiled.

She was right. "You came out here to help ensure that."

"I came out here because I have no desire to go back to China. When I retire I hope it will be...."

"Why not?" he found himself saying.

Maybe she talked because he kept secrets. Maybe because she knew in her heart he would soon not be able to talk.

"My family would not accept...certain life decisions I have made." She said it quite simply, but as if she was not sure she should admit to him. Perhaps she was afraid he would judge her, of losing his respect.

He could not imagine anything she could say that would do that. If anything, he had more for her now he knew she was, after all, human.

41

The observation bubble was "safe," but it was no longer a place people went when they didn't need to.

It made it a perfect place for José to hide. He had confidence in the patch, and he had been through enough that a mere explosion and leak was not exactly going to give him flashbacks.

He stood looking up at the stars. He could also see Lucifer, a dull orange globe, an ominous presence.

He tried to think of it by the Verran name.

You can't put me ashore here.

That was simple truth, but he would be willing to stay as a liaison to the Verrans. If it wasn't for the fact that he'd need medical attention they couldn't provide.

And could a man really live surrounded entirely by another species, could he really deal with that? He wasn't sure. It was a question that would need to be answered.

Around the arm of Lucifer he could see Verr. Ten years to the next conjunction, so they were not as close together as this perspective indicated. Verr would speed around the sun, catch up with the slower gas giant. And its fate was as inevitable as his own.

Except he probably didn't have ten years.

He saw sparks on the surface of Verr, frowned, and turned towards the lift. He knew the bridge would already know something was going on down there. He thought he could see the shape of the ship the tyrar had given the Verrans.

Was it being shot at?

He hated not knowing. He wanted to know everything, part of him wished he could know *everything* about these people before he died.

There wasn't time. He would, at best, leave never to return and soon.

He felt the *Endeavour* move, approaching the planet. Wished he was on the bridge. Wished Chang would say what was going on.

The ship was under attack.

City Three had made its move. The part of him that had fought a war had horrible thoughts about blown domes.

No.

There were children in that city, children's bodies thrown like rag dolls by the force of the explosion. Verran infants laid out for disposal, for returning to the earth.

Human children.

Rag dolls.

One of them had a gun, fallen away from his form. Not noncombatants.

Children fighting for their homes. Children fleeing to the shelters under the domes. Old people fleeing or making their stand. The girl in the storage compartment, something odd and frozen in her gaze.

They had been doomed to lose.

Would City Three, in the same situation, fight to the last mole?

He didn't know.

He didn't want to know. Knowing would mean it had happened.

They could not stop the Verrans from finishing Lucifer's job themselves.

Bitter, that. They could not. The tyrar might have given them what they needed but they had also given them an object.

They needed four ships, not just one. Or at least two. Give City Three their own, don't let the door hit them.

The ship lurched a little. Full sublight acceleration. Still not fast enough. Nothing was fast enough or it was too fast.

Sparks striking the ship. No explosion. It was, likely, too well built for that.

He went downstairs. He went to the shuttle bay. It was instinct that led him there, a gut feeling.

"Dammit, José, you shouldn't be here." Obadiah.

"You can use me. My reflexes aren't that shot yet."

"That's why you shouldn't be here. I'd have had an excuse if I couldn't find you. Get on Shuttle 3. Take a gun."

"What's happening?"

"Seems City Three had man-rated capsules after all. They just boarded and took the ship. They have hostages."

A ground fight. Stuttering, the web sprung into life, almost fully functional, at the thought.

He could do this.

And if he died it would solve every one of his problems.

He didn't try to fly the shuttle, with his reflexes the way they were. Obadiah took the controls himself. "We can't offer much help, but we can offer some."

Two shuttles, four people on each. Security personnel with some ground combat training. "You have the best tactical knowledge. Stay back and *use* it. Don't be a hero, José."

To the tyrar, he already was.

He didn't share his thoughts with Obadiah. Instead, memories flowed through him.

There would not be any children on the ship.

There would be civilians. "Do we have IFF on City Three?"

"Only the ethnic differences."

José swore. "That's not going to be enough when things go hot." He couldn't really tell the different Verrans apart.

"No, it isn't. Which is why we're using non-lethals."

José nodded. Non-lethals could still kill if you screwed up. But they were safer on a ship, and they reduced the chance of lethal friendly fire.

They did not eliminate it. So, no solid IFF, a layout they didn't know. He found himself excited by the idea. He had thought himself over that.

Worse, it was not just the stuttering web. It was him.

"And don't strain your web."

"Estoy haciendo esa respiración," José murmured. Obadiah either didn't understand or chose not to respond.

It was too late to say that. He had already done it. It was his own fault and it was circumstances and it was the initial malfunction.

And they were heading for exterior hatches. José pulled on a short duration suit...there were four on the shuttle. Obadiah already had his on.

The other two were copying José. They didn't need to be told. They didn't need to have it mentioned that they'd need them.

A clunk as the shuttle clasped on. These shuttles weren't designed for boarding action. They didn't have belly hatches.

"Somebody's going to have to go last and release everyone's tethers then free jump," José pointed out.

"No they aren't," Obadiah said. "The hatch has tether hooks. First to go hooks last to go."

"Phewf." José didn't want to free jump. Or to have anyone else do it.

"I'm going first," Obadiah added. "You're last, José, if anyone won't jump, push them."

The other two looked a little nervous.

José laughed. "Got it." Obadiah meant it, too, although this was a lot safer than skydiving, which is where *that* statement came from.

José had jumped out of more than one airplane. Part of training for using the drop pods. Teaching you not to be afraid, not to hesitate.

He was proud that he had never had to be pushed.

Obadiah jumped the short distance holding the end of José's tether. Hooked him to the ship as promised.

José didn't ask about leaving the shuttle unattended. The Verrans would have a problem stealing it, simply because none of them knew how to fly it.

The hatch was open, and they piled inside. The suit kept José from being aware of the temperature or atmosphere. Sensors on the outside told him it was acceptable. Breathable, within survival norms.

He still kept his helmet on. Gas was a concern.

At least the lights were on. Dim, but on. The Verrans had probably already adjusted the lighting to their preference.

Speaking of Verrans, one scurried out of a corridor. Held up their hands.

Obadiah growled through his helmet speaker. "Where are they?"

He didn't specify that he meant the intruders. The Verran concerned had a gun, but it was still attached to their belt. Presumably Obadiah figured that meant they weren't City Three.

José thought he was probably right. The mole pointed further inside, and then fell in behind them. No doubt they wanted to help, but didn't want to fight with only a handgun.

José decided they were a very sensible mole and kept moving.

José was in his element. And the web seemed to be working properly, as if a return to its original purpose had resulted in some temporary rejuvenation.

He took up rear guard, encouraging the mole ahead of him. They were nervous, but at least had pulled out their gun.

"Obadiah, I think we have our IFF!" he called.

"Sure do."

The mole would know who was on the initial skeleton crew and who wasn't, surely. Which meant they were a better IFF than any machine, any uniform or badge that might be misidentified.

"IFF?" they chittered.

"You tell us who the intruders are," José explained, checking each door as they passed so nobody could get behind them.

Hopefully the mole understood that. Of course they wouldn't, couldn't understand the jargon. But intruders should be guessable from context.

He hated this. The language barriers. The fact was they needed a universal translator or a protocol droid or both.

"Ahead!" the mole yelled.

Obadiah and the other two took care of the problem with non-lethals, two moles dropping in the corridor. They went past them.

'Their' mole stopped to pull a rifle and ammo from one of the unconscious forms, sticking the handgun back in their belt.

No, not a stupid mole at all. José took the other gun and slung it over his back after a moment. It probably didn't fire non-lethals.

It was not a good thing to leave lying around behind them.

Chittering came from the intercom.

"Intruders have bridge."

José felt something within him that was akin to...no. It was fear. Stark fear. They had the bridge.

This ship was not all the way finished.

It did have a working drive, or it wouldn't have been any use.

A working drive the tyrar would come back to teach the Verrans how to use, come back with different expertise.

You didn't need much knowledge to activate a hyperdrive. Just to do it *right*.

"Joy. We may have another black hole problem in this system, and it will be us!" Obadiah complained.

"Or they'll try to jump," José pointed out.

"Don't even go there."

"You mean you'd rather be taffied by a singularity?" said the female voice of one of the security people. She was a little Argentinian by the name of Maria Cabrera. He didn't know her full name. It didn't matter.

"Yes," Obadiah said. "I've already been stuck in hyper once this trip!"

The banter was how a squad felt better. How they worked together. It took him back, albeit to places he would rather not go.

"Most likely, they activate the drive and *that* taffies us into a singularity," José said. "We need to move. Where's the bridge?"

The mole shook their head. They pushed to the front next to Obadiah and then took off running. At least they weren't hard to keep up with like the tyrar.

José fell into the rhythm of running, checking the doors quickly. There was a tyrar sized tube upwards. It was going to be a horrible climb, but there was no way he was getting on a lift.

If he got to the bridge he wouldn't be shielded if they did jump.

This ship was new. It didn't feel like *Tyrrin*.

"Wait. Does this ship have an AI?"

"I don't even know," Obadiah called.

The mole, out of breath, had no answer.

42

Up the tube. The ladder, spaced for tyrar, a strain for humans and worse for Verrans.

Something for the retrofit list.

José's heart rate dropped. The web was stuttering again, as if it needed all of his adrenalin right now, and as things eased off it was worse. It made his arms and legs feel heavy, his hands were claws that could only hook onto rung after rung as they climbed.

Three decks, four, and then mercifully out into the corridor, out and running. It was like running wearing concrete overshoes, but as he sped up, it improved again. Maybe he had an answer there, a way to survive.

He tried not to think any more about it. A way to survive. He was not expecting to.

He did not care if he died on this alien ship.

He did.

He wanted to live. But he was going to die and better here doing something than in medbay waiting for it.

He ran to live, he let survival instincts take over, he set aside those thoughts which might cause him to, in Obadiah's terms, be a hero.

Turned to shoot a Verran. The mole didn't react, and the stranger had been turning towards their rear with a weapon. One shot, two, and they crumpled.

He hoped he hadn't killed them. Even if they were City Three, he didn't want to kill them, not a single member of what was, in many ways, an endangered species.

Why did they care who got the ship?

Genetic diversity.

That was why they cared. The ship needed to at least take seed from all four groups. Three was tolerable.

One?

One was bad.

So they cared. That and these people were allies, were starting to form a bond. On the human side.

What did a species that had no domesticated animals feel? Was it something alien to them, something new?

José did not know.

José did not know at all, so he ran. Ran right along the corridor. Obadiah shot another Verran. This one got a pot shot back. Hit Obadiah in the shoulder.

He grunted. "Not bad," he insisted.

Medbay could fix it later was what he meant. José wanted to move forward to apply first aid. Couldn't. The mole with them peered at the wound, perhaps fascinated with blood of a slightly different hue from their own, then handed Obadiah something from their belt.

A bandage. Obadiah slapped it onto the wound then started running again. Fix it later. That was how you acted during a mission. You fixed it later.

They were on level with the bridge, and then they ran into another room. If the layout of this ship was similar to the military version…in the military version this was ops. On this ship it was set up similarly.

There was nobody there.

Obadiah stopped, slumped a little. Maria moved to finish the job of bandaging the wound with deft hands. "He's right, it's not bad."

The mole, for their part, was peering at the navigation table. José looked at the bulkhead, the first of two bulkhead doors between them and the bridge.

It looked like it would hold, so he began a quick search of the room. The tyrar had given the Verrans a civilian model. It was designed to hold people. It was, designed to hold people for quite some time.

José laughed. "They gave the Verrans a starliner."

Obadiah looked up. "You think so?"

"It's designed to carry people for a while in reasonable comfort. Large common areas. It's probably something like a cruiseferry, to be honest."

A practical transport, between tyrar worlds and colonies. That gave hope that there could be colonies, if the tyrar hadn't already snagged all the good ones.

They'd been cagey about it. Maybe land was the biggest conflict.

José stepped back. Looked at the bulkhead. "Let's not shoot up the controls."

That was the last thing they needed. And could end with them being taffied into a singularity.

"Okay," Obadiah said. "Do we know how many?" He was turning to the Verran.

"I think so." They touched a couple of things on the ops board.

"Oh, nice," Obadiah said.

José turned. He could see five dots clustered in a room labeled "Ops" and eight on the bridge. Plus scattered other dots. It didn't seem able to distinguish humans from Verrans, but it didn't really need to.

"So, how many people should have been on the bridge?"

The Verran held up two fingers.

"Two people watching the bridge. Assuming they're still alive, six hostiles and two hostages."

"You did say they had hostages."

"That was mostly an assumption. That they wouldn't kill anyone they could use as a bargaining chip."

José rather thought you shouldn't make assumptions like that about aliens. However, it seemed likely. "And we don't want to shoot the hostages even with nonlethals if we can avoid it."

He frowned. "I'm the only one except maybe them," he jerked a finger at the Verran, "who's been on the bridge of this type of ship. Can they flood anything with gas?"

The Verran frowned. "Yes, but haven't yet."

Obadiah nodded. "Best case scenario, they don't know how. Wait. Can *we* flood the bridge with gas?"

He moved around the room, looking thoughtful.

"Not without knowing what effect that gas will have on Verrans," said Maria. "It might kill them."

"Good point."

The City Three Verrans might not care. José did care. Obadiah certainly did, from his tone.

"Looks like we get to do this the old-fashioned way."

"How are you holding up, José?"

"Fine for right now. A little sluggish." The web was definitely not responding as well as it might be, but his reflexes still seemed to be as good as the unwebbed humans. They would have to do.

It might unravel faster, but Obadiah needed him for this. Obadiah also knew what he would have said if not asked, jokes about not finding him aside.

"Okay. Position us," Obadiah said. "As you pointed out, you know the layout."

He did. He fiddled with the ops board until he had a blank screen. Sketched it out quickly. "First two people go in, go to the sides immediately. There's two back stations, those seats should provide cover."

He looked at the Verran. "You. Go up." He knew the Verrans could do that. He'd seen it. "Try to get the drop on them."

The Verran shouldered their rifle and he fancied he saw a grim expression on their snout.

"We stay back in the room between the bulkheads," he added, indicating the fourth member of the team. Charles Vicomte. The quietest man on the crew, so much so that some people suspected him of being a mute.

He was also a veteran, and José suspected him of being afraid to make friends. Some people had just lost so many friends they could not make new ones, not any more.

Vicomte nodded to him, not responding. He probably knew why José was holding him back - he was by far the largest of the team and would have even more difficulty than Obadiah hiding behind even a tyrar chair.

"If they come rushing out, we get them." He indicated either side of the door. "If not, we go in, but carefully."

If they were smart they'd have somebody watching the door.

"What's between the bulkheads?" Maria asked.

"If the layout is similar, it should be a crew conference room off set to one side, with a door to the captain's ready room on the right side. There should be a table and chairs, but not much else.

He was assuming the Verrans had had little time to make changes.

They would, no doubt, but that would come. They would make this ship theirs, one way or another.

He felt the faintest whisper of something along his veins. "Let's do this."

Obadiah nodded. José was flattered he'd let him call the play, but he also knew the reason had nothing to do with a compliment.

He and Maria moved forward to the first bulkhead. Pressed the button.

Nothing happened.

The mole moved. Fiddled with one of the consoles. "Got it!"

The door opened.

"Do the other one too," Obadiah said. Presumably they had tried to lock themselves in on the bridge.

Which told José they were going to do something. Or just had detected them ops and decided to lock the door in their faces.

As he had expected, the room beyond was indeed the crew meeting room. There was a dead Verran on the table, slumped, purplish blood dripping from it onto the floor. They had been dead a little while, for there was no more blood coming from the body.

This might mean seven hostiles, or it might not have been one of the bridge crew. José avoided looking at the Verran, who went past them and up. How did they grip like that?

Duh.

Retractable climbing claws. He hadn't noticed them before. Perhaps it was impolite to extend them around people, and it certainly seemed not done to use them as weapons.

The second door opened…

…and three armed Verrans came out before they could go through it. Their weapons spit fire into the empty center of the room, killing the poor dead mole a second time, but missing all of the living.

Their Verran swung by his arms, kicking two of the three, but missing the third. José fired for center of mass, watching the Verran fall backwards, but none of the three seemed to be dead. The one he shot was groaning. The two who had been kicked chittered angry insults and started firing up at the ceiling, but the mole was already through into the bridge.

José could not spare him any worry. He fired simultaneous with Maria and Charles. He wasn't sure which of the three of them hit the first one, who went down. The last got another shot off. It hit Charles and he went down, bleeding. José signaled to the others and dived for the wounded man. Could he stop the bleeding under fire?

He could immediately tell it was a waste of time. By luck or design, the Verran had managed a heart shot. Cursing, he half crouched to fire, wishing he wasn't armed with nonlethals.

He wanted *that* one dead. He aimed for the head.

Obadiah did not ask him what he was doing, either not noticing as he rushed the bridge or perhaps agreeing with José's decision.

There was not killing and then there was removing from the gene pool, and even if the gene pool was limited, it didn't really need *that* one, in José's mind.

He still didn't check to see if the Verran was dead before rushing the bridge.

Everything was in slow motion, the web fully operational, but he could feel ticks of pain along his limbs and in his chest which said he would pay a price for this.

There were four more Verrans. One was tied up in a corner. Two were moving to fire on him.

One was in the pilot's seat and one in the sensor seat. He hoped they were not pressing buttons at random.

The ship closed in around him as he rushed the bridge, as he got past the shielding. His web wanted it, but his web wanted the fight more. Or if he was honest, *he* wanted the fight at this point, for Charles Vicomte, for everyone else who had died in a stupid conflict in which a dying species battled over scraps and over who got to control their rebirth.

Control.

He moved towards the pilot's seat. "Don't touch *anything*!" he yelled, but either they didn't understand him, or they didn't care.

The web turned into blazing fire that flowed through every part of his body, a sensation neither quite agony nor quite pleasure.

The ship jumped.

43

The ship bucked like a crazy horse, twisting through hyperspace. Gasping, José slid to the ground, his awareness falling and leaping skyward at the same time. For a moment, he sensed that place where the universe is a point.

Became aware that it existed.

Became aware that no living thing could survive there.

Normal space. They had to find normal space, and fast. Fire enveloped his limbs, became the only thing he knew about his body. The only thing he could feel was the burning pain.

Normal space. It didn't matter that there were only a dozen people on the ship. Some were his friends.

Some were his enemies.

He couldn't leave a man behind.

Not even himself.

Starsong flowed through his veins, became something palpable he could hear and feel.

He thought he heard Obadiah's voice, from a long distance away or else from underwater, dolphin voice, but lower pitched.

"José!"

He focused on that voice. It was reality, it was his name, it was his self, and his self was in grave danger of being splattered across the universe, across space.

Even across time, and he knew why they could never reach that point, would never. Because it was all of the universe, from the Big Bang to the inevitable heat death.

He let the ship fold around him. The fire flared and faded, but he was the ship, for this moment. An alien ship, one which had no echoes of the past, no AI to talk to.

Lost. Tumbling in space, rocked by the final ripples of the forces which had set Lucifer and Verr onto their collision course.

There was no way out, no way back down. They were all going to die.

José accepted his own death. Embraced it. Then sought that way out, the way he could not see or find.

"José!"

"Shurrup," he slurred, the voice no longer a help but a distraction. His own words also sounding as from a great distance. He didn't know what Obadiah was seeing.

He didn't want to know. He could see, radiating out, all of the paths, and he wasn't sure some of them didn't lead into the unknown future or the forbidden past.

Would the universe let him go into the past?

He thought not, and he felt those paths as if they had thorns. Unsafe, the ship would not go that way.

The future? He could feel that a little more, brightly, and he didn't want to know what it brought.

The black hole. He felt that, rippling through hyperspace. It was a beacon.

It couldn't have moved that much. It sped through space, but so did they, so did space itself as it expanded and unfurled outwards into reality.

"O'diah," he managed. "Get me...the jump controls."

"José."

He heard something like despair. But he needed help. He couldn't move, and he couldn't see the bridge at all, only those stars, those points.

Those paths.

Fire flowed through him, fire that focused on the places Obadiah touched him.

"Thank..." was all he could manage, then the fire died again and with it his ability to feel anything but the ship, to hear anything but the starsong.

There was nothing else. Nothing but a shock through his hands. And he knew the ship was his. He didn't ask what happened to the Verran.

He would never know. The starsong through him, through the ship.

The stars burning. The black hole, there. A star there, a star there. He couldn't see the charts that he should have been using.

He no longer needed them. In that moment he saw all the landmarks he needed, burned into his brain. He saw the path, clear in front of him, and dived. Dived into the water.

Into the water off the beach on one of those days when it was safe to be out, but being in the water appealed more than anything else, when the ocean called his name, whispered it. Something was calling his name. *José.*

Space was the ocean, and it called to him, the natural place where he was supposed to live, not this space where humans could only ever be visitors.

The ship screamed as it dived, he felt strain on the hull, on the framework under it, but not so much that it was going to implode, no.

Through the barrier and into normal space, and there was nothing, no fire. Nothing.

Nothing but a darkness into which he tumbled. Fell like a stone.

Sank.

Sank below the surface of the water. His last thought was that there would be no awakening.

Only darkness.

44

There was, perhaps, the dimmest hint of light. "He's still breathing," came a voice. "Get him to medbay, now."

Or perhaps it was a dream. He floated. Halfway between surface and sea floor. Halfway between life and death.

Something, perhaps a touch, and then there was nothing again, deep in the depths. The sun threatened him if he came back out, a day when you stepped outside and felt your skin peeling even through the sunscreen.

A memory of fire.

He fled the fire, deeper into himself, deeper into the cool waters. Time ceased to have any kind of flow to it.

The point where time and space became one. As forbidden as the square root of zero, as unreachable as the heart of a star.

Sometimes, though, he thought he was there, or there were no sometimes.

Then there was nothing at all, then...

Light.

He blinked. The light was still there, dim, but slowly coming into focus as the ceiling of a room. The air smelled wrong, off.

He wasn't on the *Endeavour*. Smell told him that first off, more than sight could have. The air did not have the slightly metallic scent of the controlled environment of the ship.

It smelled faintly of...green. Of life.

He was on Earth.

Somehow, he was on Earth. And he could see. He could hear. Faint sounds in the distance.

He could feel. Straps across his chest and arms. He was secured to a hospital bed. He didn't panic. He'd been in this situation before.

Instead, he tried to wriggle his fingers. Odd shocks went through his arms. He tried again.

He thought he felt something. Real? A phantom, a memory?

He tried to speak, but it caught in his dry throat. He tried to tilt his head upwards. There appeared to be an IV in one of his arms, one of the broad ones used for nutrition and fluids.

He'd been here a while.

Footsteps. A voice. "Are you awake?"

He tried to speak again. Croaked out a yes.

Whoever it was tilted the bed upwards. He could see where he was. A hospital room, which would have been dreary except that somebody, or several somebodies, had put large numbers of flowers on a table at the end of his bed.

He couldn't read any labels on them, but he had a bet at least one of the bouquets came from Obadiah, if he was alive. "Where am I?" he croaked out.

"New Walter Reed," came the voice.

Military hospital. He turned his head and saw the woman the voice was attached to. Her brown hair was caught in a neat bun at the back of her head. "I'm alive," he said, hesitantly.

"You didn't call me an angel. I'm almost disappointed."

A weak laugh.

"Here." She had a sippy cup, put it to his lips. Water. It made his mouth feel better. "I'll get the doctor in here to talk to you."

He could see his body now. He tried his fingers again. They were following the instructions of his brain, but something still wasn't quite right.

He knew he'd get nothing out of the nurse, though. You never did. "Okay," he said.

She smiled. "Hang on in there."

Then she left, presumably to get the doctor rather than using an impersonal intercom. But there was something in her body language.

Relief? Satisfaction? He wasn't sure.

The nurse returned in a couple of minutes with an older, dark-skinned man.

"Let's see here. Scans look good. How are you feeling?"

"My hands seem to work," José said wryly. "I feel...a little... desplezada."

That was the best way to put it, the closest he could find. His hands worked. His toes worked. But they weren't the same.

"You'll probably get over that when we get you into physical therapy." The doctor scanned him once more, then nodded to the nurse.

He felt a brief pain as she withdrew the IV and put a bandage where it had been. Pain was good. Bodies were supposed to feel pain.

The doctor pressed a button and the straps retracted. "Can you sit up?"

José tried. "Looks like I can."

"Don't try to stand just yet. You've been in a coma for a month. There's going to be some muscle atrophy."

José knew the doctor meant it. "You...fixed it?" he asked, finally.

He'd felt the fire. And then the numbness. His web had burned out even as he brought the ship back. Saving a dozen people and...who knew how much money and resources.

The people mattered. He wanted to know what was happening on Verr.

The doctor pulled up a chair. "It's a little more complicated than that."

"What did you do to me?" An odd hope and disappointment mingled. Had they successfully removed the web? "Did you...manage to...take it out?"

The man paused. "Yes and no. As you know, once you adapt to a web, parts of your natural nervous system atrophy. We haven't yet found a way to cause them to regenerate, even with stem cells."

José nodded. That was all from his briefing. The knowledge that this was all a one-way trip.

"When you came in, you barely had autonomic functions. In fact, you'll probably be in the market for a new heart...in twenty years or so."

José thought that was medical humor. A way of saying how much stress he had put on himself.

"And your web was almost completely burned out. We might have been able to get you a couple of years...on full life support. You weren't in a position to consent to anything, but...we talked to your father. He said you wouldn't want that. So...we tried something that has been iffy in its results."

The feeling of smooth energy through his limbs. The slightly different response. "You *replaced* it?"

"Yes. You are a very lucky man. You're the first full success we've had."

A new web. He was still a spider, but he was at least a fully functional one. And his father had been right.

The doctor added, "In terms of restoring full function, anyway. You're going to be in physical therapy for a while. What you had in there was an early generation infantry web. High strength, moderate reflexes...and it was never quite put in right. This is a different model."

"Which is a good thing. If it had been...I'd be dead," José said. That was all he was going to mention, not knowing what this military doctor was cleared for.

"You aren't going to be needing infantry capabilities where you're going. Well, assuming you don't head back to civvie street."

Where he was going? Not infantry?

"Where I'm...Chang wants me back on the ship." No wonder he felt as if his brain was a step behind his hands. "This is a *pilot* web."

"Yes. With a couple of tweaks." The doctor smiled.

His entire body, repurposed to something else, to that place where he had so briefly belonged. He should have been angry.

Instead, he felt tears, and they weren't sad or angry tears. "I..."

"Are you up to some visitors before I throw you over to the tender mercies of physical therapy?"

José wanted to say no. He found himself saying yes.

The doctor and nurse slipped out, leaving him to realize he didn't have their names.

They were replaced by two figures. The first...was Captain Chang. Right behind her was a taller Chinese woman, a woman he did not recognize. Something in their body language, though, hinted towards all he needed to know.

"I'm glad to see you awake, Ensign Marin."

The puta had promoted him while he was asleep and couldn't argue! He found himself laughing slightly.

"This is for you." He knew what was in the small box. "I know you might not have wanted it, but we did think you were going to die. Also, I'd like you to meet Li-Min. My wife."

José lay back. He didn't even know what to say to that, except that 'why she left China' had fallen into place. Her family must have had traditional views on marriage. "And the primary construction director for rebuilding Launchpad."

Li-Min was saying something, but a third person had come into the room.

José had been told not to try to stand. He completely forgot that... and the presence of his captain and her lady...and rushed to hug his father.

Epilogue

The bridge had been cleaned and tidied up while the *Endeavour* was dry docked.

José sat in the pilot's chair. He felt like himself again. Perhaps he would always feel as if his body was slightly alien, but it was slowly fading. Perhaps the body was only hardware and one day they would all change bodies, becoming aliens or ships or something which could reach that point.

The point where, if there was a God, They dwelt. If there was a God. José still was not sure what he thought.

Except that he thought there was something. Something in that space beyond space, that time beyond time. Something which had guided him home. Or perhaps that something was a part of him. Perhaps he was part of the universe being aware of itself, and so was everyone else, every human, every alien, even every cat.

He looked at the controls. At his hands, seeing the silver glint at his wrists, brighter than it had been.

Chang strode onto the bridge. "Activate the PA."

Comms did so. She almost looked a little older, perhaps from the strain. Jane Kirk was at weapons.

It was a flashback moment.

"Ladies and gentlemen. You know the drill. We're going to go check on our Verran friends. Then we're going to the tyrar homeworld to see what we can do to help them."

They"d already gone over the briefing. Chang liked to remind people. Liked to keep them all on the same page.

"Mr. Marin. Take us out."

And he did, sliding the ship away from dry dock, away from Earth as it spun below. He'd walked to beaches. He'd dived in the ocean.

He'd reminded himself of the tastes of home - and brought some spices for the cook to use. He'd thought about everything.

And he knew his place, now, was here. On this ship, he was not a spider. He was a man.

The *Endeavour* glided through space. The nascent AI written into its computer core would learn on the job, as they all had to do. The tyrar were right on that front.

The ky'iin barely used AIs, not anywhere near as much as humans did. Every race different. Every one valuable. First, back to Verr, find out how they were doing in their quest to flee their dying planet. See the first hints of what they would become.

Then help the tyrar.

Then find worlds for humanity to settle, so that they would one day need the big transports themselves, spread out.

Learn from themselves, from each other, from their new allies.

Grow.

"Shall we?"

He put his hands on the jump controls. Like a racehorse from a stall, the *Endeavour* leapt into hyperspace.

There was no stuttering fire. There was no sense of being one with everything, of reaching for that point.

There was only starsong and the true, pure joy of flight.

Author's Note

Some years ago a call was put out for a Robert A. Heinlein homage anthology. I wrote and submitted a story called "The Veteran." Which was meant to be in conversation, in many ways, with *Starship Troopers*.

The world building of that story expanded, grew out of control, and became the background for *Transpecial*.

In the mean time, I made a number of attempts to shop "The Veteran" with no success, likely because it isn't very good. But when coming back to it, I realized I had the core of a good story here.

Araña doesn't much resemble its roots. It's been years and I've grown and matured as a writer in the interim. I like to think this book is much better than *Transpecial* because I've had more practice.

But it does still exist, to a certain degree, in conversation with *Starship Troopers*. The hint of libertarianism of a similar type on Mars that is explored more in *Transpecial* and the military tendencies. And the ethnicity of the main character. José was originally Mexican, but while getting drunk in Barfly Central at RavenCon it hit me that he was meant to be Puerto Rican. This decision ended up with a lot of research and the need to talk to people from that wonderful island. *Araña* is not and is not meant to be a "Puerto Rican story" – I leave that to those more qualified. But it is a story about a Puerto Rican and I can only hope I do José Marin justice.

More than that, though, this is a story about the people I know who have come back from war but been unable to fully return. I don't have the personal experience that Tolkein had that led to the Scouring of the Shire. But I know these people, and I honor them. Most especially the veterans of Vietnam, a war which we lost and both Gulf Wars, where we managed to win the war and then thoroughly lose the peace.

It is also in conversation with *Star Trek*. This is very conscious (Obadiah, an important secondary character is a Trekkie and José is familiar with the show). *Araña* engages with the concept of the Prime Directive and comes out on the opposite side to Gene Roddenberry. That we can and *should* intervene, but at the same time we need to bear in mind our own colonialism, our own past...especially as white people. That it is wrong to leave people to die even if it means we impact and change their culture; but that it is equally wrong to impact and change a culture that is doing just fine without us in ways which are exploitative.

If we ever move out into the stars, we are going to need to address this and we are going to need to have these conversations. I hope that people will read this book and disagree with it, because that is *how* we have these conversations.

It's also a space adventure, and I hope you enjoy(ed) it as such.

Acknowledgments

As usual, full acknowledgements to my husband, Gregory. To my editor, Jennifer Melzer (everything that is good is her responsibility, all remaining mistakes are mine) and my cover artist Starla Huchton.

To everyone who helped as a consultant or reader on this book. And to Frank the puppy, because it's his fault this book is coming out slightly later than previously intended.

Other Books

Other Books by Jennifer R. Povey

Transpecial
The Silent Years (Mother, Crone, Maiden)

The Lost Guardians Series:
Falling Dusk
Fallen Dark
Rising Dawn
Risen Day

Daughter of Fire

The Lay of Lady Percival

www.ingramcontent.com/pod-product-compliance
Lightning Source LLC
Chambersburg PA
CBHW031026260626
47153CB00017B/2256